A Nest of the Gentry

A Nest of the Gentry

Ivan Turgenev

Translated by Michael Pursglove

ALMA CLASSICS

ALMA CLASSICS LTD
3 Castle Yard
Richmond
Surrey TW10 6TF
United Kingdom
www.almaclassics.com

A Nest of the Gentry first published in Russian in 1859
This translation first published by Alma Classics Ltd in 2016

Cover image: Sergei Prokudin-Gorsky / Library of Congress

Printed and bound by CPI Group (UK) Ltd, Croydon, CR0 4YY

ISBN: 978-1-84749-590-7

Contents

Ivan Turgenev (1818–83)

Pauline Viardot

Louis Viardot

"Paulinette",
Turgenev's daughter

Marya Savina as Verochka in
A Month in the Country

Bougival, France, where Turgenev spent the end of his life

Turgenev's funeral procession in Petersburg in 1883

Drawing of Ivan Turgenev
by Adolph Menzel

Introduction

Between 1856 and 1877, Ivan Turgenev published six novels; *A Nest of the Gentry* was the second of these. Begun in France in 1856, completed in Russia, on Turgenev's estate – his "home nest" – at Spasskoye-Lutovinovo in 1858, it was published in the January 1859 number of the *Sovremennik* (*Contemporary*). After some hesitation, he set it in 1842, the year before he met Pauline Viardot. His lifelong relationship with her was going through an unhappy period when he wrote *A Nest of the Gentry* and has clear echoes in this novel, which is, like all Turgenev's novels, at its heart a love story. Although *A Nest of the Gentry* is significantly longer than its predecessor, *Rudin*, which is no longer than the average novella, it is not always described as a novel. For instance, a modern critic, David Lowe, describes the work as an "overgrown novella". This echoes Turgenev's own words in a letter to Countess Lambert of January 1858, in which he speaks of working on a "'large story' (*bolshaya povest'*), the main character of which is a girl – a religious being". This pithy characterization of the novel is interesting in other ways too: it was written before the addition of Chapter 35, which supplies Liza's biography and is clearly intended to explain her piety. This additional chapter was included by Turgenev at the instigation of the same Countess Yelizaveta Yegorovna Lambert (1821–83), the recipient of over a hundred letters from Turgenev and a devout Christian. The feature of the novel which is probably best remembered is the denouement. Given Turgenev's avowed scepticism towards organized religion, this resolution of the plot may well come as something of a surprise to most readers and was largely due to the influence of Countess Lambert. The book contains a good many religious, ecclesiastical and liturgical references, and in the descriptions of worship (Chapters 31, 32 and 44) the sharply satirical note which characterizes the church scene in Chapter 8 of *Virgin Soil*, though occasionally present, is considerably muted. There is even a religious significance to some of the names: Lavretsky's surname, for instance, derives from one of his two estates, Lavriki, the name of which suggests a small monastery (*lavra*), while his given name, Fyodor, is the Russian equivalent of Theodore (i.e. "gift of God").

In sharp contrast to the critical furore created by Turgenev's final three novels (*Fathers and Children*, *Smoke* and *Virgin Soil*), the reception of *A Nest of Gentry*, by critics of every political persuasion, was, with the exception of minor reservations, very favourable. At least thirteen review articles were devoted to the novel in 1859 and 1860. Pavel Annenkov, who himself wrote a long piece in praise of the novel, records in his memoirs that "satisfied with all the reviews of the work and even more so by various critiques which all tinged with sympathy and praise, Turgenev could not fail to see that his reputation as a social writer, a psychologist and a painter of social mores was firmly established by this novel". Indeed, Turgenev did not fail to see this. In 1880, he wrote: "*A Nest of the Gentry* enjoyed the greatest success which had ever fallen to my lot. From the moment the novel appeared I began to be regarded as a writer who merited the attention of the public." The radical critic Dmitry Pisarev rated the novel on a par with the classics *Eugene Onegin*, *A Hero of our Time*, *Dead Souls* and *Oblomov*. The *St Petersburg News* found the novel to be "pure, lofty poetry" and, in a letter to Annenkov written shortly after the publication of the novel, the satirist Saltykov-Shchedrin said, "it's a long time since I was so shaken", and speaks of the "lucid poetry suffused through every sound of the novel".

This favourable critical response was, of course, due mainly to the excellence of Turgenev's writing, but there were two other, secondary, factors to account for this critical unanimity. Firstly, unlike Turgenev's later novels, *A Nest of the Gentry* appeared before the

Emancipation of the Serfs in 1861, at a time when the whole of Russia was expecting reform. Opposition figures, liberal and radical, Westernizing and Slavophile, overcame their many differences in the hope that the Tsar, Alexander II, would effect the changes Russia so badly needed. Some of the more liberal Slavophiles, for instance, attempted to align their views with those of the socialist Alexander Herzen. In the event, the Emancipation decree proved a disappointment, particularly for those on the radical left, and their differences with gradualist liberals such as Turgenev became more acute. Secondly, *A Nest of the Gentry* was published before the major split in the editorial board of the *Sovremennik* between the plebeian radicals Nikolai Dobrolyubov and Nikolai Chernyshevsky, supported by the editor, Nikolai Nekrasov, on the one hand, and the aristocratic Turgenev, Dmitry Grigorovich and Leo Tolstoy on the other. The split had been simmering since 1856, but only came to a head in early 1860, when Turgenev, Grigorovich and Tolstoy left the journal and ceased to publish their works in it.

There is one curious exception to the widespread acclaim with which the novel was received. The author Ivan Goncharov, whose *Oblomov* began to appear in January 1859, the same month in which *A Nest of the Gentry* was published, claimed that elements of his next novel *The Precipice* (eventually published in 1869) had been discussed with Turgenev in 1855 and then plagiarized by him for *A Nest of the Gentry*. The argument rumbled on between 1858 and 1860 and led to the convening of a panel of experts to adjudicate on the matter. Their verdict was bland and non-committal, and relations between Turgenev and Goncharov were patched up. However, in 1875 and 1876 Goncharov committed an account of the affair to paper, in a piece which was published 1924 under the title *An Unusual Story*. In it he claims that *The Precipice* was the unacknowledged source not only of *A Nest of the Gentry* but of all Turgenev's subsequent four novels.

The novel had considerable influence on Turgenev's contemporaries. Dostoevsky, in his famous "Pushkin speech" of 1880, placed Liza Kalitina on a par with Pushkin's Tatyana (from *Eugene Onegin*) and Tolstoy's Natasha Rostova (from *War and Peace*) as an archetypal portrait of Russian womanhood. The influence of the novel has also been detected, with varying degrees of plausibility, in works by Chekhov, Saltykov-Shchedrin, Lev Tolstoy, Henry James, Joseph Conrad, George Moore, John Galsworthy and the Danish author Herman Bang.

Liza is indeed far removed from the stereotypical females who inhabited Russian literature before 1820 and takes her place alongside the strong-minded women who feature in every one of Turgenev's six novels, culminating in Marianna, the "new woman" heroine of *Virgin Soil*. However, although *A Nest of the Gentry* is perhaps the most autobiographical of Turgenev's novels, the character of Liza, like most of Turgenev's characters, is not based on any one person but is an amalgam of a number of real-life prototypes. However, the celebrated playwright Alexander Ostrovsky dissented from the prevailing view of Liza, declaring that "...for me Liza is insufferable: the girl seems to be suffering from internalized mumps".

Liza is everything that Varvara Pavlovna is not: chaste, demure, sincere, self-sacrificing, self-denying, patient and pious. Above all however, she is Russian, so much so that, for Lavretsky, she becomes, in effect, a symbol of Russia. Varvara Pavlovna is, of course, also Russian, but she belongs to that class of Frenchified, French-speaking Russians whom Turgenev lambasts in *Smoke*. It is this quality of Russianness which sometimes gives rise, somewhat misleadingly, to the novel's being sometimes classified as "Slavophile"; Richard Freeborns's reference to "diluted Slavophilism" is nearer the mark.

Broadly speaking, Fyodor Lavretsky, the landowning son of a peasant girl and a landowner father, belongs to a type which stretches back to the 1820s in Russian literature, and beyond that in French literature, and to which Turgenev gave a name in 1850 with his short story 'Diary of a Superfluous Man'. However, he is a new variant of the type. Unlike Rudin and Nezhdanov (from *Virgin Soil*), he does not die but, like Litvinov (from *Smoke*), opts to settle on his country estate – his family "nest", his *gnezdo*, and, to quote a phrase from the closing lines of *A Nest of the Gentry*: "to do what has to be done" (literally: "to do the deed"). The same phrase occurs in *Rudin*, together with the quintessential "superfluous man" question: "What is to be done?" Lavretsky has an answer to this, which occurs in his reply to Panshin in Chapter 33 and, more fully, in the Epilogue:

> Lavretsky had the right to be satisfied: he had become a really good landowner, had really learnt how to plough the earth and had not toiled for himself alone. As far as he was able, he had safeguarded and secured the welfare of his peasants.

The fact that the "deed" involves a gradualist rather than a radical approach makes the landowner Lavretsky, in Turgenev's terms, a "Hamlet" rather than a "Don Quixote". His sensitivity to Nature is a major theme in the novel, a precursor of the engineer Solomin (from *Virgin Soil*); the gradualist views expressed by both Lavretsky and Solomin largely reflect those of Turgenev himself.

Although she is, of course, essential for the development of the plot, Varvara Pavlovna – like Panshin, Gedeonovsky, Lemm, Mikhalevich, Marya Dmitriyevna, Marfa Timofeyevna, Agafya, Anton and Nastasya Karpovna, as well as the characters in the "flashback" chapters (8–16) – is a secondary character. Nevertheless, none of these characters are mere ciphers, and, unlike the secondary characters in *Rudin*, are fleshed out and fully motivated.

Francophone and Anglophone readers of the novel were, from the very outset, fortunate in having excellent translations available, both of them approved by Turgenev himself. The first – into French – by Turgenev's aristocratic fellow writer Count Vladimir Sollogub and the editor of the *Revue des Deux Mondes*, Alphonse de Calonne, appeared in 1861; interestingly it was given the title

Nichée de gentilhommes (*A Brood of Gentry*) rather than the more obvious *Nid de gentilhommes*, the name used by subsequent translators into French. Turgenev apparently gave his approval to Sollogub's version, just as he did to the English title of W.R.S. Ralston's 1869 translation: *Liza*. Turgenev even claimed that he preferred Ralson's title, and that the title *Nest of the Gentry* was suggested by Nikolai Nekrasov. Ralston was light years ahead of his time as a translator, checking difficulties with the author and taking none of the casual liberties with the text so characteristic of many Victorian translators. He had a good knowledge of Russian and was also an assiduous promoter of Russian literature in translation, whose efforts were largely responsible for the high standing enjoyed by Turgenev in the English-speaking world. No subsequent translator followed Ralston's lead as far as the title is concerned, and the novel has been known by at least eight other titles. The title of the present translation makes a ninth attempt to render the deceptively simple Russian title: *Dvoryanskoye gnezdo*. Ralston also pays tribute to the 1862 German translation (*Das adelige Nest*) by Paul Fuchs, which he describes as "wonderfully literal". The Russian title has passed into the language as a general term for a rundown aristocratic estate and was used as such, for instance, by Vladimir Gilyarovsky in his famous *Moscow and the Muscovites*, published in 1935.

All translators build to some extent on the efforts of previous translators. Ralston's version, which is still in print, has been frequently consulted in the preparation of the present version. So too have the works of two distinguished Turgenev scholars, Patrick Waddington and Richard Freeborn. Waddington's edition of the Russian text, on which the current translation is based, elucidates a large number of factual and linguistic difficulties. His study of the novel, in the same volume, running to more than fifty pages, remains an invaluable seminal study, while Freeborn's 1970 translation (*Home of the Gentry*) has hitherto been the standard modern translation.

The novel was the most popular of Turgenev's novels during his lifetime and retained much of its popularity after his death and into the twentieth and twenty-first centuries. A park, laid out in 1903 in Turgenev's native town of Oryol, is named after the novel and is now adorned with a bust of the author. There have been numerous stage versions of the novel, and a celebrated film version was made by Andrei Konchalovsky in 1969.

Russian colleagues from the universities of Oryol, Nizhny Novgorod and Ryazan respectively, Felix Abramovich Litvin, Olga Vladimirovna Petrova, Yelena Sergeyevna Ustinova and Yakov Moiseyevich Kolker, helped and encouraged me to write about Turgenev and translate his novels. Christian Müller, as always, combined courtesy, accuracy and speed in editing the text.

– Michael Pursglove

A Nest of the Gentry

1

THE BRIGHT SPRING DAY was declining into evening; there were little pink clouds high in a clear sky which seemed not to be passing over but rather to be retreating into the very depths of the azure.

Before the open window of a fine house, in a street on the outskirts of the provincial town of O—* (this was in 1842), sat two women – one of about fifty, the other of seventy.

The first woman was called Marya Dmitriyevna Kalitina. Her husband, a former provincial public prosecutor, a well-known businessman in his time, a confident, decisive, dyspeptic, stubborn man, had died some ten years previously. He had received an excellent upbringing, had studied at Moscow University, but, born into impoverishment, had soon learnt the necessity of making his own way in the world and of piling up the cash. Marya Dmitriyevna married him for love: he was not bad-looking, was clever and, when he wanted to be, affectionate. Marya Dmitriyevna, whose maiden name was Pestova, had lost her parents while still a child. She spent several years at boarding school in Moscow; when she returned, she lived nine miles from O— in her ancestral village Pokrovskoye, together with her aunt and elder brother. This brother soon moved to Petersburg to enter government service and kept his sister and aunt on a very tight rein until his sudden death curtailed his career. Marya Dmitriyevna inherited Pokrovskoye, but did not live there long; in the second year of her marriage to Kalitin, who had succeeded in winning her heart in a matter of days, Pokrovskoye was exchanged for another estate, which was more profitable, but was not beautiful and lacked a manor house. At the same time Kalitin acquired a house in O—, where he settled permanently with his wife. The house had a large garden which, on one side, adjoined open fields outside the town. "So," decided Kalitin, who was not at all fond of rural tranquillity, "there's no point in dragging ourselves off to the country." In her heart of hearts, Marya Dmitriyevna missed her pretty Pokrovskoye, with its cheerful little river, broad meadows and green copses; but she did not gainsay her husband on anything and revered his intellect and worldly knowledge. When, after fifteen years of marriage, he died, leaving a son and two daughters, Marya Dmitriyevna had already grown so used to her home and to urban life that she had no desire to leave O—.

In her youth Marya Dmitriyevna had enjoyed a reputation as a pretty blonde; even at fifty her features were not displeasing, although a little more fleshy and filled out. She was more sensitive than kind and retained her boarding-school quirks into her maturity; she pampered herself, was easily irritated and even wept when her routine was disrupted. On the other hand she was kind and agreeable when her wishes were carried out and no one gainsaid her. Her house was one of the most pleasant in the town. Her finances were extremely sound: they were not so much inherited as legally acquired from her husband. Both her daughters lived with her; her son was being educated at one of the best public educational establishments in Petersburg.

The old woman sitting with Marya Dmitriyevna beneath the window was the same aunt, her father's sister, with whom she had once spent several solitary years in Pokrovskoye. Her name was Marfa Timofeyevna Pestova. She was considered an eccentric, was independent-minded, spoke the truth bluntly to everyone and, although of extremely modest means, behaved as if she had thousands. She had not been able to stand the late Kalitin and, as soon as her niece married him, had withdrawn to her own village, where she lived for a whole ten years in a peasant's smoky hut. Marya Dmitriyevna was afraid of her. Raven-haired, sharp-eyed even in her old age, small and with a pointed nose, Marfa Timofeyevna walked briskly, held herself erect and spoke quickly and clearly in a refined and sonorous voice. She invariably wore a white mob cap and a white blouse.

"Why are you doing that?" she suddenly asked Marya Dmitriyevna. "Why are you sighing, my dear?"

"I just am," replied the latter. "What wonderful clouds."

"Are you sorry for them, then?"

Marya Dmitriyevna did not reply.

"Why doesn't Gedeonovsky come?" said Marfa Timofeyevna, rapidly plying her knitting needles (she was making a large woollen scarf). "He could have sighed with you – or else told you some tall story."

"How hard on him you always are! Sergei Petrovich is much respected."

"Respected!" the old woman echoed reproachfully.

"And how devoted he was to my late husband!" said Marya Dmitriyevna. "To this day he cannot be indifferent to his memory."

"So I should think. Your husband dragged him out of the mud by his ears," said Marfa Timofeyevna grumpily and began to wield her knitting needles even faster.

"He looks such a harmless type," she began again. "Completely grey-haired, but when he opens his mouth it's either to lie or spread scandal. And what's more, he's a State Councillor.* Which only goes to show he's the son of a priest!"

"Who is without sin, Auntie? He does have that weakness, of course. Sergei Petrovich didn't get an education, of course; he doesn't speak French. But, begging your leave, he's a nice man."

"Yes, he's always licking your hand. He doesn't speak French – how tragic! I myself am not very good at the French lingo. It would be better if he didn't speak anything at all: he wouldn't tell lies then. Incidentally, talk of the devil – here he is," Marfa Timofeyevna added, glancing at the street. "Striding along he is, your nice man. What a lanky fellow he is – just like a stork."

Marya Dmitriyevna adjusted her hair. Marfa Timofeyevna gave her a sarcastic look.

"What's this? You haven't found a grey hair, have you, my dear? Give that Palashka of yours a telling-off. What's she got eyes for?"

"Auntie, you're always..." muttered Marya Dmitriyevna in exasperation, drumming her fingers on the arm of her chair.

"Sergei Petrovich Gedeonovsky!" piped a red-cheeked pageboy, leaping out from behind the door.

2

IN CAME A TALL MAN, wearing a smart frock coat, short trousers, grey chamois gloves and two cravats – a black one on top and a white one underneath. Everything about him exuded propriety and seemliness, from his fine-featured face and smoothly combed temples to his boots, which had neither heels nor shanks. He bowed first to the lady of the house, then to Marfa Timofeyevna, and, slowly drawing off his gloves, took Marya Dmitriyevna's hand. Kissing it respectfully twice in succession, he sat down unhurriedly in an armchair and, wiping the very ends of his fingers, said with a smile:

"Is Yelizaveta Mikhailovna well?"

"Yes," replied Marya Dmitriyevna, "she's in the garden."

"And Yelena Mikhailovna?"

"Lenochka* is in the garden too. Have you any news for us?"

"There's always something, ma'am, there's always something," returned the guest, blinking slowly and pursing his lips. "Hmm! How about this for news, and very surprising news at that: Lavretsky, Fyodor Ivanovich Lavretsky, has come."

"Fedya,"* exclaimed Marfa Timofeyevna. "I don't believe you. You're not making this up, are you?"

"Not at all, ma'am. I saw him with my own eyes."

"Well, that's still no proof."

"He's in rude health," Gedeonovsky continued, affecting not to have heard Marfa Timofeyevna's remark. "His shoulders are broader and he has colour in his cheeks."

"In rude health," said Marya Dmitriyevna deliberately. "I wonder what the reason for that is."

"Yes, ma'am," returned Gedeonovsky, "anyone else in his position would have been ashamed even to show his face in society."

"Why's that?" interrupted Marfa Timofeyevna. "What rubbish is this? A man has returned home – where else would you want him to go? It's not as if he was guilty of anything."

"I make so bold as to say, ma'am, that the husband is always to blame when a wife behaves badly."

"You say that, sir, because you haven't been married."

Gedeonovsky gave a forced smile.

"Allow me to indulge my curiosity and enquire," he said, after a short silence, "for whom this delightful scarf is destined."

Marfa Timofeyevna shot a quick glance at him.

"It is destined for anyone who doesn't gossip, does not use low cunning and doesn't tell tall stories, if such there be in the world. I know Fedya well: the only thing he did wrong was to spoil his wife. Well, that, and the fact that he married for love, and nothing sensible ever comes from these love matches," the old woman added, giving a sideways glance to Marya Dmitriyevna and rising to her feet. "Now, sir, you can stick your knife into anyone you like, even me – I'm going and I won't stop you."

And Marfa Timofeyevna retired.

"She's always like that," said Marya Dmitriyevna, following her aunt with her eyes. "Always!"

"It's her age! What can you do, ma'am?" Gedeonovsky observed. "Mark you, she was kind enough to refer to 'anyone who does not use low cunning'. Who isn't deceitful nowadays? It's the times we live in! A friend of mine, a much respected man and, I may say, a man whose rank is not of the lowest, was saying that nowadays even a hen will use low cunning to approach seed – will use any device to approach it from the side. But when I look at you, dear lady, I see you have a truly angelic temperament. Permit me to kiss your snow-white hand."

Marya Dmitriyevna smiled wanly and extended her chubby hand to Gedeonovsky with her little finger raised. He touched it with his lips; she moved her chair towards him and, leaning forward slightly, asked in an undertone:

"So you've seen him? Is he really – all right, well, happy?"

"He's happy, he's all right," replied Gedeonovsky in a whisper.

"And have you heard where his wife is now?"

"She was recently in Paris; I hear she's moved to one of the Italian states now."

"Fedya's situation is really awful – I don't know how he stands it. True, everyone has their misfortunes, but his, one might say, have been broadcast throughout the whole of Europe."

Gedeonovsky sighed.

"Yes, indeed. They say she's friends with actors, pianists and with what they like to call 'lions', and with other wild beasts. She's lost her sense of shame completely..."

"I'm very, very sorry," said Marya Dmitriyevna. "I speak as a relative: he is, after all, as you must know, Sergei Petrovich, my great-nephew."*

"Of course, of course. How could I fail to know everything that concerns your family? Good gracious."

"Do you think he'll come and see us?"

"One would suppose so. However, I hear he intends to go to his place in the country."

Marya Dmitriyevna lifted her eyes heavenwards.

"Ah, Sergei Petrovich! Sergei Petrovich! It's my opinion that we women must be careful how we behave."

"There are women and women, Marya Dmitriyevna. Unfortunately, there are those – of unstable temperament... and, well, of a certain age: then there are those in whom the rules have not been inculcated from an early age." Sergei Petrovich took a blue checked handkerchief from his pocket and began to unfold it. "Such women, of course, do exist." Sergei Petrovich raised a corner of the handkerchief to each eye in turn. "But, talking in general terms, if one considers... There's an unusual amount of dust in town," he concluded.

"*Maman, maman*," cried a pretty little girl of some eleven years, running into the room. "Vladimir Nikolayevich is coming on horseback."

Marya Dmitriyevna stood up; Sergei Petrovich also stood up and bowed. "My warmest regards to Yelena Mikhailovna," he said, withdrawing into a corner out of a sense of propriety and beginning to blow his long, straight nose.

"What a wonderful horse he's got," the girl went on. "He was by the gate just now and told Liza and me that he'd ride up to the front door."

A clatter of hooves was heard, and an elegant rider on a handsome bay appeared in the street and halted in front of the open window.

3

"HOW DO YOU DO, MARYA DMITRIYEVNA!" the rider called out in a resonant, pleasant voice. "How do you like my new purchase?"

Marya Dmitriyevna went up to the window.

"How do you do, Woldemar!* Oh, what a splendid horse! Who did you buy it from?"

"From a remount officer... He charged a lot, the bandit."

"What's she called?"

"Orlando... But that's a stupid name; I want to change it... *Eh bien, eh bien, mon garçon...** How mettlesome he is!"

The horse snorted, pawed the ground and tossed its foam-flecked muzzle.

"Lenochka, stroke him. Don't be afraid."

The little girl put her hand out of the window, but Orlando suddenly reared and made a sudden sideways movement. The rider did not panic, sat tight, laid the whip across his neck and, despite the horse's resistance, again placed him before the window.

"*Prenez garde, prenez garde*,"* Marya Dmitriyevna said, repeating her warning.

"Lenochka, give him a pat," the rider persisted. "I won't let him be headstrong."

The little girl again put out her hand and timidly touched the twitching nostrils of Orlando, who kept shaking himself and champing at the bit.

"Bravo!" exclaimed Marya Dmitriyevna. "Now dismount and come in."

The rider made a tight turn, gave the horse a touch of the spur, rode down the street at a smart gallop and entered the yard. A minute later he burst through the door from the entrance hall to the drawing room, waving his riding crop; at the same time there appeared on the threshold of the opposite door a tall, graceful, raven-haired girl of about nineteen – Marya Dmitriyevna's eldest daughter, Liza.

4

THE YOUNG MAN to whom we have just introduced the reader was called Vladimir Nikolayevich Panshin. He worked in the Ministry of Internal Affairs in Petersburg and was responsible for special assignments. He had come to O— on temporary government business and was attached to the governor, General Sonnenberg, to whom he was distantly related. Panshin's father, a retired cavalry captain, second class, a celebrated gambler, a man with ingratiating eyes, crumpled features and a nervous tic around the lips, had spent his whole life hobnobbing with the aristocracy, visited the English Clubs of both capitals* and had a reputation for being a clever, not very reliable but pleasant and affable fellow. In spite of all his cleverness he was almost permanently on the brink of penury, and he bequeathed his only son meagre and chaotic finances. On the other hand he did, in his own way, concern himself with his son's education: Vladimir Nikolayevich spoke excellent French, good English and bad German. However, it is possible to let slip a German witticism in certain, mostly comical, situations, *c'est même très chic*,* as the Petersburg Parisians say. From the age of fifteen, Vladimir Nikolayevich could enter any drawing room without embarrassment, circulate there and withdraw at the appropriate moment. Panshin's father passed many of his contacts on to his son; as he shuffled the cards between two rubbers or after a successful grand slam, he missed no opportunity to put in a word for his "Volodka"* with some important personage and enthusiastic gambler. For his part, during his time at university, which he left with a very poor degree, Vladimir Nikolayevich got to know several young aristocrats and gained acceptance in the best houses. He was welcome everywhere; he was very good-looking, always fit and ready; where necessary he was respectful; where possible he was bold, a first-rate companion, *un charmant garçon*.* A promised land opened up before him. Panshin soon realized the secret of the way of the world; he was able to imbue himself with real respect for its code, was able with semi-ironic importance to concern himself with trivia and to give the appearance that he considered everything important to be trivial; he was an excellent dancer and dressed English-style. In short order he acquired a reputation as one of the most congenial and bright young people in Petersburg. Panshin really was very bright – every bit the equal of his father – but he was also very talented. He could do anything: he sang nicely, drew with great facility, wrote verse and was not at all a bad actor. He was only just turned twenty-seven, was already a *kammerjunker** and held an exceptionally high rank. Panshin was a firm believer in himself, in his intellect and in his perspicacity; he was making upward progress boldly, cheerfully and at full speed; his life was running smoothly. He was used to being liked by everyone, old and young alike, and imagined that he had a knowledge of people, especially women: he had a great knowledge of their everyday foibles. As a man with a penchant for art, he felt within himself passion, a certain enthusiasm and exaltation, as a result of which he allowed himself some latitude where rules were concerned: he caroused, made friends with people outside polite society and in general acted in a free-and-easy manner. Inwardly, however, he was cold and calculating, and during the most riotous revels his intelligent brown eyes were always watching, always vigilant; this bold, freewheeling youth could never forget himself or get completely carried away. To his credit, it must be said that he never boasted about his conquests. He turned up at Marya Dmitriyevna's house immediately upon his arrival in O— and quickly made himself completely at home. Marya Dmitriyevna thought the world of him.

Panshin bowed cordially to everyone in the room, shook hands with Marya Dmitriyevna and Lizaveta Mikhailovna, clapped

Gedeonovsky lightly on the shoulder and, turning on his heels, took hold of Lenochka's head and kissed her on the forehead.

"Aren't you afraid to ride such a difficult horse?" Marya Dmitriyevna asked him.

"Begging your pardon, but he's very docile; but I'll tell you what I am afraid of: I'm afraid of playing preference with Sergei Petrovich; yesterday, at the Belenitsyn's, he cleaned me out."

Gedeonovsky gave a thin, servile laugh; he fawned on the brilliant young official from Petersburg, a favourite of the governor. In his conversations with Marya Dmitriyevna he often mentioned Panshin's remarkable capabilities. After all, he reasoned, how could one not praise him? In the highest spheres of life, too, the young man was successful; his work was exemplary and he was not in the slightest bit proud. Moreover, he was considered an efficient official even in Petersburg: he had a constant stream of work on his hands; he joked about this, as befitted a man of the world who did not ascribe any particular significance to his labours, but he was a "doer". The authorities like such subordinates; he himself never doubted that, if he wanted to, he would be a minister in due course.

"You took it upon yourself to say that I cleaned you out," said Gedeonovsky, "but who won twenty roubles off me last week? What's more—"

"You villain, you," Panshin interrupted with affable, but almost disdainful casualness, and, paying no further attention to Gedeonovsky, he turned to Liza.

"I couldn't find the overture to *Oberon** here," he began. "Madame Belenitsyna was merely boasting when she said that she had every piece of classical music. In reality, apart from polkas and waltzes, she hasn't got anything. However, I've already written to Moscow, and a week from now you'll have the overture. By the way," he went on, "yesterday I wrote a new romance. The words are mine too. Would you like me to sing it to you? I don't know how it's turned out; Madame Belenitsyna found it very nice, but her words don't mean anything. I want to know your opinion. However, I think it may be better later."

"Why later?" put in Marya Dmitriyevna. "Why not now?"

"Yours to command," said Panshin with a kind of bright and sugary smile which appeared then suddenly vanished. He moved a chair up with his knee, sat down at the piano and, having played a few chords, began to sing the following romance, carefully delineating the words:

"Above the earth the moon floats by
And pale clouds stream;
And, wave-like, now comes from on high
A magic beam.

"My tidal soul will ebb and flow
With thou its moon.
It moves alike in joy and woe
Through thee alone.

"The pangs of shattered dreams, the pangs of love
My soul o'errun;
My spirits sink but thine will rise above,
As does that moon."

Panshin sang the second verse with particular power and expressiveness: the surging waves could be heard in the stormy accompaniment. After the words "My spirits sink", Panshin gave a gentle sigh, dropped his eyes and lowered his voice – *morendo*. When he had finished, Liza praised the motif, Marya Dmitriyevna said, "Charming," and Gedeonovsky even cried: "Delightful! Both the poetry and the harmony are equally delightful!..." Lenochka contemplated the singer with childish reverence. In a word, the young dilettante's composition pleased everyone present, but behind the door of the drawing room, in the entrance hall, stood a new arrival, a man, already old, to whom, to judge by the expression on his downcast face and the shrug of his shoulders, Panshin's romance, though very nice, afforded no pleasure. Pausing awhile and brushing the dust off his boots with a thick handkerchief, the man suddenly screwed up his eyes, gloomily pursed his lips, hunched his already bent back and slowly went in to the drawing room.

"Ah! Khristofor Fyodorovich, how do you do!" Panshin exclaimed before anyone else, quickly leaping from his chair. "I had no idea you were here. I wouldn't have gone ahead and sung my romance in your presence for anything. I know you're not keen on light music."

"I vos not listening," said the new arrival in bad Russian and, bowing to everyone, remained standing awkwardly in the middle of the room.

"Monsieur Lemm," said Marya Dmitriyevna, "have you come to give a music lesson to Liza?"

"No, not to Lissaveta Mikhailovna but to Ellen Mikhailovna."

"Ah, well that's fine. Lenochka, go upstairs with Mr Lemm."

The old man was about to follow the little girl when Panshin stopped him.

"Don't go away after the lesson, Khristofor Fyodorovich," he said. "Lizaveta Mikhailovna and I will play a Beethoven sonata for four hands."

The old man muttered something under his breath, but Panshin went on in badly pronounced German:

"Lizaveta Mikhailovna showed me the religious cantata which you brought her – a splendid piece! Please don't imagine that I am not able to appreciate serious music – on the contrary: it's sometimes boring, but, on the other hand, it's very beneficial."

The old man blushed to the roots of his hair, threw a sidelong glance at Liza and hastily left the room.

Marya Dmitriyevna asked Panshin to sing his romance again, but he declared that he did not want to offend the ears of the learned German and suggested to Liza that she should tackle the Beethoven sonata. Then Marya Dmitriyevna gave a sigh and, for her part, suggested that Gedeonovsky should go for a walk in the garden with her. "I would like," she said, "to have a talk with you and get your advice about our poor Fedya." Gedeonovsky grinned, bowed and with two fingers picked up his hat and the gloves which had been carefully laid on one of its brims; he then withdrew with Marya Dmitriyevna. In the room there remained Panshin and Liza; she got out the sonata and opened it; they both sat down silently at the piano. From upstairs came the faint sounds of chords played by Lenochka's uncertain fingers.

5

CHRISTOPH-THEODOR-GOTTLIEB LEMM was born in 1786 in the town of Chemnitz in the kingdom of Saxony, the son of indigent musicians. His father played the French horn, his mother the harp; he himself was practising on three different instruments before he was five. He was orphaned at the age of eight, and from the age of ten he began to earn his crust through his musical skill. For a long time he led a nomadic life, performing everywhere – in taverns, at fairs, at peasant weddings and at balls. Finally he joined an orchestra and, moving ever higher through its ranks, attained the post of conductor. He was a fairly poor performer, but had a thorough grounding in music. In his twenty-eighth year he moved to Russia. He was hired by a grand seigneur, who could not stand music himself but maintained an orchestra out of vanity. Lemm spent some seven years with him as kapellmeister and left his employ empty-handed; the noble lord was ruined and offered to give him a promissory note in his own name, but subsequently refused him even that – in short, he didn't pay him a single copeck. Lemm was advised to leave Russia, but he did not want to return home from that country penniless, from the great country of Russia, that goldmine for artistes. He decided to stay and try his luck. For twenty years the poor German tried his luck. He worked for various noblemen, lived both in Moscow and in provincial towns, put up with a great deal, bore it patiently, experienced poverty, thrashed about like a landed fish, but the thought of returning to his native land never left him amidst all the disasters which befell him: it alone sustained him. Fate, however, did not see fit to grant him this first and last consolation: fifty years old, sick and prematurely aged, he ended up for good in the town of O—, having abandoned all hope of leaving a Russia which he hated, somehow supporting his meagre existence by giving lessons. Lemm's appearance did not work in his favour. He was small in stature, stooped, with shoulder blades which protruded at an angle, a concave stomach, large, flat feet, pale-blue nails on the stiff, inflexible fingers of his sinewy red hands. He had a lined face, hollow cheeks and compressed lips, which he constantly moved and chewed. Taken with his habitual taciturnity, this produced an almost sinister impression. His grey hair straggled over his low brow; his tiny, motionless eyes glowed like newly doused coals; his gait was ponderous and his cumbersome body swayed at every step. Some of his movements were reminiscent of the clumsy preening of an owl in a cage, when it feels it is being watched but can scarcely see anything with its huge, yellow, timorously and drowsily blinking eyes. Longstanding, implacable grief had made an indelible mark on the poor music-maker and had distorted and disfigured his already unsightly appearance. But anyone who did not stop at first impressions could discern something good, something honourable, something unusual in this semi-wreck of a man. A devotee of Bach and Handel, a master of his craft, endowed with a lively imagination and that boldness of thought to which only the German race can aspire, Lemm would, with time – who knows? – have joined the ranks of the great German composers if life had treated him differently. But he was not born under a lucky star! He had written a great deal in his time, but had not succeeded in seeing a single one of his works published; he had no idea how to set about things in the right way, how to bow at the appropriate moment or pick the right time to busy himself. Once, a long time ago, a friend and admirer of Lemm's and, like him, a poor German, had published two of his sonatas at his own expense, but they had remained untouched in the basements of music shops and then sunk quietly and without trace, as if someone had thrown them in the river at night. Eventually, Lemm gave up; the years had taken their toll: he had become crusty and as inflexible as his fingers. He lived alone in O— with his old cook, whom he had rescued from the poorhouse (he had never married), in a little house not far from the Kalitins. He took frequent walks, read the Bible, a collection of Protestant metrical psalms and Shakespeare in Schlegel's translation.* He had not composed anything for a long time, but clearly Liza, his best pupil, knew how to stir him. He wrote the cantata for her which Panshin had mentioned. The words of the cantata were borrowed from a collection of metrical psalms; he had added some verses of his own to them. It was sung by two choirs – a choir of the Blessed and a choir of the Afflicted; by the end both were reconciled and sang together: "O merciful Lord, pardon us sinners, put away from us all wicked thoughts and worldly hopes." Written meticulously, drawn even, on the title page stood the words: "Only the Righteous are justified. A Spiritual Cantata. Composed for and dedicated to Miss Yelizaveta* Kalinina, my dear pupil, by her teacher Kh.T.G. Lemm." The words "Only the Righteous are Justified" and "Yelizaveta Kalinina" were encircled by beams of light. Below had been added the words: "For you alone – *für Sie allein*". That was why Lemm had both blushed and thrown a sidelong glance at Liza; he was very pained that Panshin had spoken about his cantata in his presence.

6

PANSHIN PLAYED THE FIRST CHORDS of the sonata loudly and firmly (he was playing the bass part), but Liza did not begin her part. He stopped and looked at her. Liza's eyes were fixed on him and expressed displeasure: there was no smile on her lips and her whole face was stern and almost sorrowful.

"What's the matter?" he asked.

"Why did you not keep your word?" she said. "I showed you Khristofor Fyodorovich's cantata on condition that you would not mention it to him."

"I'm sorry, Lizaveta Mikhailovna. It just came out."

"You've upset him – and me too. Now he won't trust even me any more."

"How could I help it? Ever since I was so high I haven't been able to see a German without wanting to tease him."

"What are you saying, Vladimir Nikolayevich! That German is a poor, lonely, devastated soul – and you're not sorry for him?"

Panshin became flustered.

"You're right, Lizaveta Mikhailovna," he said. "My eternal thoughtlessness is to blame for everything. No, don't gainsay me: I know my own failings very well. My thoughtlessness has done me great harm. Thanks to it I've gained a reputation as an egoist."

Panshin fell silent. However he began a conversation, he usually finished it by talking about himself, and did so somehow in a pleasant, mild, heartfelt way, as if he were doing so involuntarily.

"Even in your house," he went on, "your mother, of course, thinks well of me – she's so kind – but I don't know what you think of me; your aunt, on the other hand, simply can't stand me.

I must have upset her too, must have offended her with a stupid, thoughtless word. She doesn't like me, does she?"

"Yes," said Liza after a slight hesitation, "she's not fond of you."

Panshin quickly ran his fingers over the keys; a barely perceptible smirk slid across his lips.

"Well, and what about you?" he said. "Do I seem an egoist to you too?"

"I don't know you well as yet," Liza returned, "but I don't consider you an egoist. On the contrary, I should be grateful to you—"

"I know what you're going to say," Panshin interrupted, and again ran his fingers over the keyboard, "for the scores and the books which I bring you, for the bad drawings with which I adorn your album and so on and so forth. I can do all that – and still be an egoist. I make so bold as to think that you're not bored in my company and that you don't consider me a bad man, but all the same you suppose – how does the saying go? – that I'd spare neither father nor friend for the sake of a witticism."

"You're abstracted and forgetful, like everyone who moves in society circles," said Liza. "That's all there is to it."

Panshin gave a slight frown.

"Listen," he said, "let's not talk about me any more. Let's play our sonata. One thing only I ask of you," he added, smoothing the sheets of music on the stand. "Think what you like of me, even call me an egoist – so be it! – but don't call me 'someone who moves in society circles' – I find that description intolerable... *Anch'io sono pittore*. I too am an artist, albeit a poor one, and it's precisely that – that I'm a poor artist – that I'm going to prove to you in practice. Let's begin."

"Certainly, let's begin," said Liza.

The first adagio went quite well, although Panshin made several mistakes. He played his own compositions and music he'd learnt quite nicely, but his sight-reading was poor. As a result, the second part of the sonata – a fairly brisk allegro – went completely haywire: in the twentieth bar, Panshin, who was two bars behind, could stand it no more and laughingly pushed his stool back.

"No!" he exclaimed. "I can't play today; it's a good job Lemm didn't hear us: he would have had a fit."

Liza stood up, closed the piano and turned to Panshin.

"What shall we do now?" she asked.

"How like you that question is! You can't bear to sit still and do nothing. All right, let's do some drawing if you like, while it's still light. Perhaps another Muse – the Muse of Drawing – what's her name, I've forgotten – will be more kindly disposed towards me. Where's your album? As I recall, the landscape I did in it isn't finished."

Liza went into another room to get the album, while Panshin, left alone, took a cambric handkerchief from his pocket, rubbed his nails with it and cast a kind of sideways look at his hands. His hands were very beautiful and white; on his left thumb he wore a spiral gold ring. Liza returned; Panshin took a seat by the window and opened the album.

"Aha!" he exclaimed. "I see you've begun to copy my landscape – and done so splendidly. Very good! But here – let me have the pencil – the shadows aren't done strongly enough. Look."

With a flourish, Panshin drew several long strokes. He invariably drew one and the same landscape: in the foreground, large, dishevelled trees, in the distance, a clearing, and on the horizon, jagged mountain peaks. Liza looked over his shoulder at his efforts.

"In drawing, as in life in general," said Panshin, inclining his head first to the right, then to the left, "lightness and boldness are the most important things."

At that moment Lemm came into the room and, bowing stiffly, attempted to withdraw, but Panshin threw the album and pencil to one side and barred his way.

"Where are you going, my dear Khristofor Fyodorovich? Won't you stay and take tea with us?"

"I'm going home," said Lemm in a gloomy voice. "I have a headache."

"Well, what does that matter? Do stay. You and I can discuss Shakespeare."

"I have a headache," the old man repeated.

"In your absence we made a start on the Beethoven sonata," Panshin went on, amiably taking him by the waist and smiling brightly, "but it didn't go at all well. Just imagine, I couldn't play two notes in succession correctly."

"You vould hef been besser to sing your romance again," retorted Lemm, removing Panshin's hands and leaving the room.

Liza ran after him. She caught him up on the porch.

"Khristofor Fyodorovich, listen to me," she said in German, as she escorted him to the gate over the short green grass of the yard. "I owe you an apology. Please forgive me."

Lemm made no reply.

"I showed your cantata to Vladimir Nikolayevich. I was sure he'd appreciate it – and indeed, he did like it very much."

Lemm halted.

"It doesn't matter," he said in Russian, then, in his native tongue, added, "but he cannot understand anything. How come you don't see that? He's a dilettante – no more, no less."

"You're being unfair to him," Liza protested. "He understands everything and can do almost anything himself."

"Yes, anything second-rate, lightweight, rushed. People like that, and they like him, and he's pleased with that. Well, good luck to him. But I'm not angry; the cantata and I are both old fools; I'm a little ashamed, but it doesn't matter."

"Please forgive me, Khristofor Fyodorovich," Liza repeated.

"It doesn't matter, it doesn't matter," he repeated, again in Russian. "You're a good girl... But here's someone coming to see you. Goodbye. You're a very good girl."

And Lemm hurried off towards the gate, through which had come a gentleman he did not know, wearing a grey greatcoat and a broad-brimmed straw hat. Bowing politely to him (he bowed to every new person he met in the town of O—, but he had made it a rule to turn his back on those he knew and met in the street), Lemm walked past and disappeared beyond the fence. The stranger stared after him in surprise and, with a glance at Liza, went straight up to her.

7

"YOU DON'T RECOGNIZE ME," he said, removing his hat, "but I recognized you, even though eight years have passed since I last saw you. You were a child then. I am Lavretsky. Is your mother at home? May I see her?"

"Mother will be very pleased," Liza replied. "She'd heard about your arrival."

"I think you're Yelizaveta, aren't you?" said Lavretsky as he mounted the steps of the porch.

"Yes."

"I remember you well: you've got the sort of face one doesn't forget. In those days I used to bring you sweets."

Liza blushed and thought what a strange man he was. Lavretsky paused for a moment in the entrance hall. Liza went into the drawing room, where Panshin's voice and laughter could be heard: he was relaying some town gossip to Marya Dmitriyevna and Gedeonovsky, who had already come back in from the garden, and was himself laughing loudly at what he was saying. At the name of Lavretsky, Marya Dmitriyevna became totally flustered, turned pale and went to meet him.

"How do you do, how do you do, my dearest *cousin*," she exclaimed in a drawling, almost tearful voice. "How pleased I am to see you!"

"How do you do, dear cousin?" replied Lavretsky, affectionately shaking her outstretched hand. "How's life treating you?"

"Take a seat, take a seat, my dear Fyodor Ivanovich. Oh, how pleased I am! First, let me introduce my daughter Liza—"

"I've already made the acquaintance of Lizaveta Mikhailovna," Lavretsky interposed.

"Monsieur Panshin... Sergei Petrovich Gedeonovsky... But do take a seat! When I look at you I can scarcely believe my eyes. How are you keeping?"

"As you can see, I'm flourishing. And you, cousin, if I'm not tempting fate, have not lost weight in these eight years."

"To think we haven't seen each other for so long," said Marya Dmitriyevna reflectively. "Where have you come from? Where have you left... That is, I meant to say," she hastily corrected herself, "I meant to say, will you be staying with us long?"

"I've just come from Berlin," Lavretsky replied, "and tomorrow I'm going away to the country – probably for a long time."

"You're going to live in Lavriki, I suppose."

"No, not Lavriki. I own a little estate about twenty miles from here, so I'll go there."

"Is that the estate you inherited from Glafira Petrovna?"

"It is."

"Forgive my saying so, Fyodor Ivanovich, but you have such a magnificent house in Lavriki."

Lavretsky gave a slight frown.

"Yes... but the other estate has a lodge; I don't need anything else at present. That'll do me for now."

Marya Dmitriyevna was again so flummoxed that she sat bolt upright in her chair and spread her hands helplessly. Panshin came to her aid and engaged Lavretsky in conversation. Marya Dmitriyevna calmed down, leant back in her chair and only put in the occasional word. But for all this, she looked so pityingly at her guest, sighed so meaningfully and shook her head so despondently that finally he could stand it no longer and enquired rather sharply whether she felt all right.

"Yes, thank Heavens," Marya Dmitriyevna replied. "Why do you ask?"

"It seemed to me you weren't yourself."

Marya Dmitriyevna assumed a dignified and rather injured look. "If that's the case," she thought, "it's a matter of complete indifference to me; to you, my dear sir, it's just like water off a duck's back. Any other man would have wasted away with grief, but you're even thriving on it." Inwardly Marya Dmitriyevna did not mince words; outwardly she expressed herself more delicately.

Lavretsky really did not look like a victim of fate. His rubicund, wholly Russian face, with its high, white forehead, rather thick nose and broad, regular lips exuded the healthiness of the steppes, strength and durability. He was very well built and had the fair, curly hair of an adolescent. Only his eyes, blue, protuberant and somewhat motionless, betrayed something between thoughtfulness and weariness and his voice sounded somehow too bland.

Panshin meanwhile continued to keep up the conversation. He broached the topic of sugar-refining and its advantages, about which he had read recently in a couple of French pamphlets, the gist of which he began to outline, calmly and modestly, without, however, saying a word about them.

"It really is Fedya!" The voice of Marfa Timofeyevna was heard suddenly coming through the half-open door from the next room. "Fedya, and no mistake!" And the old woman hurried into the drawing room. Lavretsky did not have time to rise from his chair before she embraced him. "Let me have a look at you. Let me look," she said, drawing back from his face. "Oh, how well you look. A bit older, but not a bit less handsome. But why are you kissing my hands? Kiss me, if my wrinkled cheeks don't repel you. I don't suppose you asked whether your old aunt was alive or not. I had you as a babe in arms, you scallywag! Well, what's all that to you? What cause did you have to remember me! But good for you for coming back. Well, Mother," she added, turning to Marya Dmitriyevna, "have you given our guest anything?"

"I don't need anything," said Lavretsky hastily.

"Well, at least have some tea, my dear. Good grief! The man arrives from God knows where and they don't give him a cup of tea. Liza, go and see to it. Chop, chop! I remember that when he was little he was a real trencherman and he must still like eating."

"My respects to you, Marfa Timofeyevna," said Panshin, approaching the discomfited old lady from the side and bowing low.

"Forgive me, sir, in my excitement I didn't notice you. You've grown very like your dear mother," she continued, turning to Lavretsky, "but you always had your father's nose, and still have. Well – will you be with us long?"

"I'm leaving tomorrow, Auntie."

"Where are you going?"

"To my own place, Vasilyevskoye."

"Tomorrow?"

"Yes, tomorrow."

"Well, if you say tomorrow, tomorrow it is. Good luck to you – you know best. Only mind you come and say goodbye." The old lady patted him on the cheek. "I didn't think I'd live to see you again – not that I intended to die. No, I'm good for another ten years perhaps. We Pestovs are a long-lived lot. Your late grandfather used to say we lived twice over. Lord alone knows how much longer you were going to knock around abroad. Anyway, you're a fine figure of a man, you really are. I expect you can lift a twenty-five-stone weight with one hand, like you used to. Your late father who, if you'll forgive my saying so, was a prize clot, nevertheless did the right thing in hiring that Swiss. Do you remember having fist fights with him? Is that what they call 'gymnastics'? However, why have I been prattling on like this for? I've only stopped Mr Pan*shin* (she always pronounced the name wrongly, stressing the second syllable) from having his say. Besides, we'd do better to have some tea. Let's go onto the terrace and drink it there, my dear. We have wonderful cream here, not like the stuff you get in your Paris or your London. Let's go, let's go, and you, my dear Fedya, give me your arm. Oh, what a stout arm you have! There's no danger of falling over with you."

Everyone stood up and repaired to the terrace, with the exception of Gedeonovsky, who surreptitiously withdrew. Throughout the course of the conversation between Lavretsky, the lady of the house, Panshin and Marfa Timofeyevna, he had sat in the corner, blinking attentively and pursing his lips with childlike curiosity; now he hurried off to spread news of the new guest throughout the town.

That same day, at eleven o'clock in the evening, this is what happened in the house of Madame Kalitina. Downstairs, on the threshold of the drawing room, seizing an opportune moment, Vladimir Nikolayevich was taking his leave of Liza and saying, as he held her hand: "You know who it is that attracts me here; you know why I am always coming to your house; what use are words when everything is clear without them." Liza did not answer him and unsmilingly contemplated the floor, blushing and slightly raising her eyebrows; however, she did not take her hand away. Meanwhile, upstairs in Marfa Timofeyevna's room, by the light of the lamp which hung before some ancient and faded icons, Lavretsky sat in an armchair, his elbows on his knees; the old lady stood before him and occasionally stroked his hair in silence. He had spent more than an hour with her after taking his leave of the lady of the house. He had said almost nothing to his kind old friend, and she had not asked him anything... What was the point of talking? What was the point of asking questions? She understood everything anyway and sympathized with everything that exercised his heart.

8

FYODOR IVANOVICH LAVRETSKY (we must ask the reader's permission to break the thread of our story temporarily) was a scion of an ancient noble family. The founder of the line came from Prussia during the reign of Vasily II* and was granted three hundred acres in the Bezhetsk Upland.* Many of his descendants served in various posts, including remote provincial governorships under princes and other potentates, but none of them rose to the top or acquired significant property. The richest and most eminent of all the Lavretskys was Fyodor Ivanovich's great-grandfather Andrei, a cruel, bold, intelligent and cunning man. To this day there persists talk of his arbitrary justice, his wild temperament, senseless prodigality and insatiable greed. He was tall and very stout, with a swarthy, beardless face, pronounced his Rs French-style and appeared somnolent, but the quieter he spoke, the more everyone around him trembled. He found himself a wife to match. With protuberant eyes, an aquiline nose and a round, yellow face, she was a gypsy by birth, fiery and vindictive, who never gave in to her husband in any way, even though he well-nigh killed her, and who did not outlive him, even though she had fought with him tooth and nail for ever. Pyotr, Andrei's son and Fyodor's grandfather, did not take after his father: he was an uncomplicated landowner of the steppes, rather peculiar, loud-mouthed, sluggardly and coarse. However, he was not malicious, was hospitable and liked hunting with dogs. He was in his thirties when he inherited from his father two thousand souls in prime condition, but he soon dispersed them, sold off part of the estate and indulged his household serfs. The hoi polloi, known to him and unknown, infiltrated his warm, spacious, untidy chambers; they stuffed themselves silly with whatever came to hand, drank themselves stupid, made off with anything they could, praising their kind host and honouring his name; their host, for his part, when he was out of sorts, honoured his guests with the name of layabouts and scoundrels, but was bored without them. Pyotr's wife was a meek creature; he had taken her from a neighbouring family by choice and order of his father. Her name was Anna Pavlovna. She never interfered in anything, received guests affably, paid visits willingly, although, to quote her own words, powdering her hair was death to her. In old age she would relate how they used to put a felt band on her head, backcomb all her hair, smear it with animal fat, sprinkle it with flour and stick iron pins into it – you couldn't wash it out afterwards. But you couldn't pay visits without powder – people took offence and it was sheer torture!* She loved to go out driving behind trotters, was ready to play cards from dawn to dusk and always put her hand over the note of her trivial winnings whenever her husband came near the card table. However, she handed over to him without question all her dowry, all her money. She had two children with him: a son, Ivan, Fyodor's father, and a daughter, Glafira. Ivan was brought up, not at home but with a rich old aunt, Princess Kubenskaya; she had nominated him as her heir (but for this his father would not have let him go); she dressed him up like a doll, hired a variety of teachers for him and placed him in the care of a governor, a certain M. Courtin de Vaucelles, a Frenchman, former abbé and disciple of Jean-Jacques Rousseau.* He was an adroit and subtle intriguer – the very, as she put it, *fine fleur** of emigration. She ended up, at the age of nearly seventy, by marrying this *fine fleur*; she transferred all her assets to him and, shortly afterwards, berouged, perfumed with ambergris *à la Richelieu*,* surrounded by blackamoors, thin-legged dogs and screeching parrots, she expired on a crooked silken Louis XV divan, clutching an enamelled snuffbox by Petitot* – and expired abandoned by her husband: the obsequious Monsieur Courtin had preferred to take himself off to Paris, together with her money. Ivan was not yet twenty when this unexpected blow (we speak of the princess's marriage, not her death) struck him. He had no desire to remain in his aunt's house, where, from being a rich heir, he had suddenly become a poor relation. In Petersburg the society in which he'd grown up closed its doors to him. He had an aversion to the obscure drudgery involved in working his way up from the lower ranks (all this happened at the very beginning of the reign of Alexander I).* Reluctantly he had to go back to his father's estate in the country. His family nest seemed dirty, impoverished and shabby. The remote and suffocating nature of life on the steppes offended him at every turn; boredom gnawed at him, and at the same time everyone in the household, except his mother, viewed him with hostility. His father didn't like his metropolitan habits, his dress coats, his jabot, books or flute, nor his studied neatness in which he thought he detected contempt and loathing. From time to time he carped resentfully at his son. "Nothing here is to his liking," he would say. "At table he picks at his food or doesn't eat; he can't stand a stuffy room or the smell of people; the sight of drunks upsets him; you daren't resort to fisticuffs in his presence; he doesn't want to enter government service – his health is delicate, wouldn't you know. What a softie he is! And all because his head is full of that Voltaire." The old man was particularly scathing about Voltaire and "that extremist" Diderot,* although he hadn't read a single line of their works. Reading was not his thing. Pyotr Andreyevich was not wrong: his son's head was indeed full of Diderot and Voltaire, and not just them – his head was full of Rousseau, Raynal, Helvétius* and many other writers like them. But it wasn't only his head. Ivan Petrovich's former tutor, the retired abbé and encyclopedist, had taken pleasure in the wholesale inculcation of the entire store of eighteenth-century wisdom into his pupil, who was, as a result, brimful of it. It lodged within him without mixing with his blood, penetrating his soul or expressing itself in firm convictions... And could one expect firm convictions from a young man fifty years ago when we're not mature enough to have them even today? Ivan Petrovich also embarrassed visitors to his father's house; he avoided them like the plague and they were afraid of him; and he didn't get on at all with his sister Glafira, who was twelve years older than him. This Glafira was a strange creature: plain, hunchbacked, skinny, with severe staring eyes and a tight, thin mouth, she took after a gypsy grandmother, Andrei's wife, in her face, in her voice and in her quick angular movements. Unyielding and power-loving, she would not hear of marriage. She took a dim view of Ivan Petrovich's return; while he was in the care of Princess Kubenskaya she had hoped to get at least a half of her father's estate: she took after her grandmother too in miserliness. Furthermore, she envied her brother: he was so educated, spoke French so well and with a Parisian accent, while she could scarcely say "*Bonjour*" and "*Comment vous portez-vous*?"* True, her parents didn't know a word of French, but this was no consolation to her. Ivan Petrovich was beside himself with frustration and boredom. He'd spent just short of a year in the country, but it seemed like ten. Only with his mother could he open his heart, and he would sit with her for hours in her low-ceilinged rooms, listening to the inconsequential chatter of the good woman and eating a surfeit of jam. It so happened that among the maidservants of Anna Pavlovna was a very pretty girl with gentle, clear eyes and fine features. Her name was Malanya; she was both clever and modest. And from the very start she was drawn to Ivan Petrovich with all her heart; he fell in love with her: he loved her shy allure, her bashful answers, her quiet voice, her quiet smile. With each passing day she seemed more and more desirable. She formed a deep attachment to Ivan Petrovich, as only Russian girls know how to – and gave herself to him. In a country manor house no secret can be kept for long: soon everyone knew about the young master's liaison with Malanya; news of it finally reached Pyotr Andreyevich himself. At another time he would probably not have paid any attention to such a trivial matter, but he'd long taken against his son and was delighted with the chance of shaming a Petersburg dandy and know-all. A tremendous hoo-ha ensued: Malanya was locked in the pantry and Ivan Petrovich was summoned to his parent. Anna Pavlovna also came running when she heard the noise and tried to calm her husband down, but Pyotr Andreyevich was not in a mood to take heed of anything. He swooped on his son like a hawk, accusing him of immorality, godlessness and hypocrisy; while he was about it, he vented on him all his accumulated resentment against Princess Kubenskaya, heaping imprecations on him. At first Ivan Petrovich said nothing and took all this stoically, but when his father took it into his head to threaten him with condign punishment, he could stand it no longer. "That extremist Diderot is in play again," he thought, "so I'll put him into practice, just you see. I'll surprise the lot of you." Whereupon, in a calm, level voice, although shaking inwardly in every limb, Ivan Petrovich declared that it was no use his father accusing him of immorality; that, although he did not intend to justify his guilt, he was ready to make amends for it, the more so because he felt himself to be above all prejudices, by marrying Malanya. By uttering these words Ivan Petrovich undoubtedly achieved his object: he so shocked Pyotr Andreyevich that his eyes stood on stalks and he was momentarily struck dumb. However, he immediately collected himself and, just as he was, in squirrel-fur jacket and with his bare feet thrust into shoes, he hurled himself, fists flailing, at Ivan Petrovich, who had deliberately adopted an *à la Titus* hairstyle* that day and donned a new blue English dress coat, boots with tassels and modishly tight elk-skin trousers. Anna Pavlovna gave a mighty yell and covered her face with her hands, while her son ran right through the house, leapt into the yard, from there dashed into the kitchen garden and the flower garden, and flew out onto the road. He kept running without a backward glance until at last he could no longer hear either the clatter of paternal footsteps behind him or his intermittently loud shouts... "Stand still, you villain!"

shrieked his father. "Stand still! Curse you!" Ivan Petrovich took refuge with a neighbouring smallholder; Pyotr Andreyevich returned home, worn out and sweaty, and, scarcely drawing breath, announced that he was depriving his son of his blessing and his inheritance. He gave orders for all these "idiot books" to be burnt and for the "wench" Malanya to be sent off to a distant village. Kind people were found who sought out Ivan Petrovich and told him the whole story. Humiliated and infuriated, he swore revenge on his father, and that very night he ambushed the peasant cart in which Malanya was being taken away, abducted her by force, galloped with her to the nearest town and married her. He was supplied with money by a neighbour, a permanently drunk and extremely affable former sailor, who was hugely fond of any "noble story", as he put it. The next day Ivan Petrovich wrote a bitingly cold and polite letter to Pyotr Andreyevich and set off for the village where his second cousin Dmitry Pestov lived with his sister, Marfa Timofeyevna, who is already familiar to the reader. He told them everything, declared that he intended to go to Petersburg to find a job and begged them to shelter his wife, at least for a time. At the word "wife" he shed bitter tears and, notwithstanding his metropolitan education and philosophy, humbled himself and bowed low to his relatives' feet, like any peasant supplicant, even striking the ground with his forehead. The Pestovs, kind and compassionate people, readily acceded to his request; he spent some three weeks living with them, secretly hoping for a reply from his father; but no reply came – nor could it have come. On learning of his son's marriage, Pyotr Andreyevich took to his bed and forbade mention of the name of Ivan Petrovich in his presence. His mother, however, unbeknown to her husband, borrowed five hundred paper roubles* from the rural dean and sent them, together with a small icon, to Malanya. She was afraid to write, but ordered her wiry peasant messenger, a man who could cover forty miles in twenty-four hours, to tell Ivan Petrovich that he shouldn't be too downcast; that, with God's help, everything would be sorted out and that his father would exchange wrath for mercy; that she would have preferred another daughter-in-law, but that it was clear that God's will had been done, and that she was sending Malanya Sergeyevna her parental blessing. The wiry peasant messenger, given a rouble for his trouble, requested and received permission to see the new mistress, to whom he was godfather, kissed her hand and ran back home.

Meanwhile, Ivan Petrovich set off for Petersburg with a light heart. An uncertain future awaited him; poverty might possibly threaten him, but he had broken away from the hated rural life and, most importantly, he had not betrayed his mentors: he really had "put into practice" and vindicated by deed Rousseau, Diderot and *La Déclaration des droits de l'homme*.* A sense of duty done, of triumph and pride, filled his heart; even separation from his wife did not unduly frighten him; he would have been more disconcerted by any necessity of living permanently with her. That matter was dealt with; he had to tackle other business. In Petersburg, rather contrary to his expectations, luck was on his side: Princess Kubenskaya, whom Monsieur Courtin had already succeeded in ditching but who had not yet succeeded in dying, in order somehow to make amends to her nephew, introduced him to all her friends and gave him five thousand roubles – almost the last of her money – and a Lépine watch* inscribed with his monogram in a garland of cupids. Three months had not passed before he was appointed to a post in the Russian mission in London and left for overseas by the first outward-bound English sailing ship (there were no steamships in those days). A few months later he received a letter from Pestov. The kind-hearted landowner congratulated Ivan Petrovich on the birth of a son, who had made his appearance on 20th August 1807 in the village of Pokrovskoye and had been named Fyodor in honour of the saint and martyr Theodore Stratelates.* On account of her very weak condition, Malanya Sergeyevna only added a few lines, but even these few lines amazed him: he had not known that Marfa Timofeyevna had taught his wife to read and write.

However, Ivan Petrovich did not indulge himself in the sweet thrill of parental feelings for long: he was courting one of the celebrated Phrynes or Laises of the day (classical names were still popular at the time). The Treaty of Tilsit* had just been concluded, and there was a general haste to enjoy oneself; everything was one mad whirl: a pert black-eyed beauty had set Ivan's head spinning too. He had very little money but he had luck at cards, cultivated acquaintances, participated in every sort of entertainment – in a word, he had the wind behind him.

9

For a long time, old man Lavretsky could not forgive his son for his marriage; if, after half a year, Ivan Petrovich had come to him contritely and fallen at his feet, he might well have pardoned him after first roundly berating him and giving him a few blows with his walking stick to frighten him. But Ivan Petrovich lived abroad and couldn't have cared less. "Be silent! Don't you dare!" Pyotr Andreyevich would repeat to his wife every time she tried to incline him towards compassion. "That puppy ought to remember me in his prayers for ever, because I didn't lay a curse on him. My late father would have killed that no-good with his own hands, and he'd have done right." On hearing such terrible words Anna Pavlovna merely crossed herself surreptitiously. As far as Ivan Petrovich's wife was concerned, at first Pyotr Andreyevich did not want to hear of her and even, in reply to a letter from Pestov in which he referred to Pyotr's daughter-in-law, ordered him to be told that he had no knowledge of any so-called daughter-in-law, that it was against the law to harbour runaway serf girls and that he considered it his duty to warn him of this. But then, on learning of the birth of a grandson, he softened and gave orders that he should be made privy to any news about the mother's health. He also sent her a little money, anonymously. Fedya was not yet a year old when Anna Pavlovna fell terminally ill. A few days before her death, already unable to rise from her bed, with timid tears welling up in her dying eyes, she announced to her husband, in the presence of her confessor, that she wanted to see her daughter-in-law, say goodbye to her and bestow her blessing on her grandson. The grief-stricken old man soothed her and immediately sent his own carriage to fetch his daughter-in-law, calling her Malanya

Sergeyevna for the first time. She arrived with her son and Marfa Timofeyevna, who absolutely refused to let her go alone and was determined to stick up for her. Half-dead with terror, Malanya Sergeyevna entered Pyotr Andreyevich's study. She was followed by a nanny carrying Fedya. Pyotr Andreyevich regarded her in silence; she went up to him to kiss his hand. Her trembling lips scarcely formed themselves into a soundless kiss.

"Well, you greenhorn noblewoman," he said finally, "how do you do? Let's go and see the mistress."

He stood up and bent over Fedya; the child smiled and stretched out his pale little hands towards him. The old man was bowled over.

"Oh," he said, "my little orphan child! You've pleaded your father's case and I won't abandon you, my chick."

When Malanya Sergeyevna entered Anna Pavlovna's bedroom, she fell to her knees by the door. Anna Pavlovna beckoned her to approach her bed, embraced her and blessed her son. Then, turning towards her husband a face eaten away by a cruel disease, she made as if to speak.

"I know, I know what you want to ask," said Pyotr Andreyevich. "Don't worry: she'll stay with us, and for her sake I'll forgive Vanka."*

With an effort, Anna Pavlovna caught her husband's hand and pressed it to her lips. That same evening she was no more.

Pyotr Andreyevich kept his word. He informed his son that, to honour his wife's dying wish and for the sake of baby Fedya, he was restoring his blessing and letting Malanya remain in his house. She was allotted two rooms on the mezzanine floor and introduced her to Pyotr Andreyevich's two most honoured guests, the one-eyed brigadier Skurekhin and his wife; he gave her two maids and a boy to run errands for her. Marfa Timofeyevna took her leave of her; she hated Glafira and had quarrelled with her three times in the course of a single day.

Things were hard and awkward for the poor woman at first but then she learned to put up with things and got used to her father-in-law. He got used to her too and even grew to like her, although he almost never said anything to her and although in his very endearments a certain involuntary contempt could be detected. Malanya suffered most at the hands of her sister-in-law. During her mother's lifetime Glafira had already managed, little by little, to take over the whole house. Everyone, beginning with her father, deferred to her; no lump of sugar was given out without her permission. She would have chosen to die rather than share power with another mistress – especially not this mistress! Her brother's marriage upset her even more than it did Pyotr Andreyevich: she set about teaching the upstart a lesson and, from day one, Malanya Sergeyevna became her slave. And what chance did she, a meek, permanently put-upon, fearful creature in poor health, have in any battle with the autocratic and arrogant Glafira? Not a day passed but that Glafira reminded her of her previous situation or praised her for not forgetting herself. Malanya would have willingly reconciled herself to these reminders and praises, however bitter... but Fedya was taken away from her. That is what grieved her. On the pretext that she was in no condition to bring him up, she was almost barred from seeing him. Glafira took on the task: the child became her sole responsibility. In her grief, Malanya began to implore Ivan Petrovich in her letters to come home as soon as possible; Pyotr Andreyevich himself wanted to see his son. He, however, merely sent back a formal reply, thanking his father for looking after his wife and for sending money, and promising to come home soon. But he didn't come. Finally 1812 called him back from foreign parts. Meeting for the first time after a six-year separation, father and son embraced and said not a word about their former quarrels. That was not the time for it: the whole of Russia was up in arms against the enemy and both men felt that Russian blood was flowing in their veins. Pyotr Andreyevich equipped a whole militia regiment at his own expense. But the war ended and the danger passed. Ivan Petrovich again became bored and yearned for distant places, for a world of which he was a part and where he felt at home.

Malanya Sergeyevna could not detain him: she meant too little to him. Even her hopes had been dashed: her husband also decided that it was much more appropriate to entrust Fedya's upbringing to Glafira. Ivan Petrovich's poor wife found this blow, this second separation, too much. In a few days, without complaint, she began to fade away. Throughout her whole life she had never been able to withstand anything, and she did not even fight her illness. She was already unable to speak; already the shadow of the grave lay upon her face, but as ever her features expressed patient bewilderment and constant meekness and resignation. She looked at Glafira with the same mute submissiveness and, just as Anna Pavlovna had on her deathbed kissed Pyotr Andreyevich's hand, so she kissed Glafira's hand and handed her only son over to her. Thus a quiet and kind creature, wrenched, God knows why, from her native soil and discarded, roots towards the sun, like a grubbed-up tree, ended her earthly journey. This creature withered and vanished without trace, and no one mourned it. Her maidservants and even Pyotr Andreyevich regretted her passing. The old man missed her silent presence. "Forgive me. Farewell, my lamb!" he whispered, bowing to her one last time in church. He wept as he threw a handful of earth into her grave.

He did not survive her long, not more than five years. In the winter of 1819 he died peacefully in Moscow, where he'd moved to with Glafira and his grandson. In his will he asked to be buried next to his wife and "Malasha".* At the time Ivan Petrovich was in Paris, enjoying himself, having retired shortly after 1815. On learning of his father's death, he decided to return to Russia. He needed to think about the management of his estate; furthermore Fedya, according to a letter from Glafira, was over twelve, and the time had come to think seriously about his education.

10

IVAN PETROVICH RETURNED to Russia full of Anglomania. His hair cut short, his jabot starched, a long pea-green frock coat with a multitude of collars, a sour expression on his face, something cutting and at the same time careless in his manner, enunciation through his teeth, sudden hollow laughter, a non-existent smile, exclusively political and politico-economic talk, a passion for rarely done roast beef and port wine – everything about him exuded Great Britain. He seemed imbued through and through with its spirit. But – wonderful to relate – having embraced Anglomania, Ivan Petrovich became a patriot at the same time, or at least he called himself a patriot, even though he did not know Russia at all well, did not adhere to any Russian custom and expressed himself oddly in Russian. In ordinary conversation his speech, leaden and turgid, was plastered with Gallicisms. But as soon as the conversation turned to important subjects, Ivan Petrovich began to use expressions such as "display new proofs of individual zeal", "the above does not accord with the essential nature of the circumstance" and so on. Ivan Petrovich brought with him several handwritten plans for the ordering and betterment of the state; he was very displeased with everything he saw – the lack of any system especially aroused his bile. When he met his sister, the first thing he said was that he intended to introduce radical changes on his own estate and that henceforth everything would be run according to a new system. Glafira Petrovna did not reply, but merely clenched her teeth and thought: "Where do I come into all this?" However, when she arrived at the estate with her brother and nephew, her mind was soon set at rest. A few changes had indeed taken place in the house: poor relations and various layabouts were immediately given their marching orders; among these victims were two old women, one blind, the other paralysed, as well as an infirm and frail old major from the time of Ochakov* who, on account of his truly remarkable greediness, had been fed nothing but black bread and lentils. An order also went out that former guests were not to be received: they were all replaced by a distant neighbour, some fair-haired scrofulous baron, a very well-educated and very stupid man. New furniture from Moscow appeared; spittoons, bell pulls, washstands were brought in; lunch began to be served in a different manner; foreign wines ousted vodka and cordials; the servants got new liveries and to the family crest were added the words: "*In recto virtus…*"* In essence Glafira's power was in no way diminished: all outgoings and purchases depended on her, as before; the foreign butler brought in from Alsace, who tried to compete with her, lost his job, despite the fact that Ivan Petrovich protected him. As far as running the household and the estates was concerned (Glafira Petrovna was involved here too), in spite of Ivan Petrovich's frequently expressed intention to "breathe new life into this chaos", everything stayed just as it was, except that rent in lieu went up, corvée labour became more onerous and the peasants were forbidden to appeal directly to Ivan Petrovich. The patriot was very contemptuous of his fellow citizens. His system was fully applied only to Fedya: his education really did undergo a "radical change" – his father took sole charge of it.

11

As we have already said, before the return of Ivan Petrovich from abroad, Fedya had been in the care of Glafira Petrovna. He was not yet eight when his mother died; although he had not seen her every day he had loved her passionately. The memory of her, of her quiet, pale face, her sad gaze and shy caresses had imprinted itself on his heart for ever. But he had vaguely understood her position in the house and sensed that between him and her there existed a barrier which she dared not and could not break down. He was wary of his father, and Ivan Petrovich himself never showed him any kindness. His grandfather occasionally stroked his head and allowed him to kiss his hand, but called him a bogey man and regarded him as a fool. After the death of Malanya Sergeyevna, his aunt took full charge of him. Fedya was afraid of her, was afraid of her bright, piercing eyes and her strident voice. She did not want to hear a peep out of him in her presence; sometimes he only had to start fidgeting in his chair for her to hiss: "Where are you going? Sit still." On Sundays, after church, he was allowed to play, that is to say he was given a mysterious thick book, the work of one Maximovich-Ambodik, entitled *Symbols and Emblems*.* This book was a medley of about a thousand extremely enigmatic drawings and an equal number of equally enigmatic interpretations in five languages. A chubby, naked Cupid played a large role in these drawings. To one of them, entitled "The Saffron Flower and the Rainbow", was appended the interpretation "This hath the greater effect". Opposite another, which depicted a "Heron Flying with a Violet in its Mouth", stood the caption "To thee are they all known". "Cupid and the Bear Licking its Cub" denoted "little by little." Fedya examined all these drawings, knew them all, down to the smallest detail. Some of them, always the same ones, made him think and stimulated his imagination; he knew no other forms of amusement. When the time came to teach him languages and music, Glafira hired an old spinster for a pittance: she was a hare-eyed Swede, who spoke French and German equally badly, played the piano after a fashion and, in addition, was brilliant at pickling cucumbers. Fedya spent four whole years in the company of this preceptress, his aunt and an old maidservant, Vasilyevna. He used to sit in a corner with his *Emblems*, sit there for hours. The low-ceilinged room smelt of geraniums; a single tallow candle burned dimly, a cricket chirruped monotonously, as if bored; a small wall clock ticked rapidly; a mouse scratched and gnawed furtively behind the wallpaper and the three old spinsters, like the Parcae,* plied their knitting needles speedily and silently. The shadows cast by their hands first flitted by, then quivered strangely in the semi-darkness, and the child's head teemed with strange, similarly semi-dark thoughts. No one would have called Fedya an interesting child: he was rather pale, but fat, ungainly and clumsy – a real peasant, as Glafira Petrovna put it. The pallor would soon have disappeared from his face if he had been allowed out more often. He did his lessons well enough, although he was often lazy; he never cried, yet at times he was visited by a savage obstinacy, when no one could cope with him. Fedya did not like any of the people around him... Woe to the heart which has not loved when young!

This is how Ivan Petrovich found him and, losing no time, he set about applying his system to him. "I want to make a man of him before anything else, *un homme*," he said to Glafira Petrovna. "Not only a man, but a Spartan." Ivan Petrovich began to implement his intention by dressing his son Scottish-style: the twelve-year-old began to walk about with bare calves and a cockerel feather in his bonnet. The Swedish woman was replaced by a young Swiss who was an expert at gymnastics. Music, as an occupation unworthy of a man, was banished for ever. The natural sciences, international law, mathematics, carpentry, as recommended by Jean-Jacques Rousseau, and heraldry, for the maintenance of chivalric sentiments – these are what a future "man" had to study. He would be woken up at four o'clock in the morning, immediately splashed with cold water and made to run round a tall column on the end of a string. For food he had one dish once a day; he rode on horseback and shot from a crossbow. He practised firmness of will at every suitable opportunity, following the example of his parent, and every evening he wrote an account of the day and his impressions of it in a special book. For his part Ivan Petrovich wrote homilies for him in French, in which he called him "*mon fils*" and "*vous*". When speaking Russian, Fedya used the familiar form to address his father, but did not dare to sit down in his presence. "The system" scrambled the boy's mind, inserted a jumble of ideas into his head, put him under pressure; on the other hand, the new way of life had a beneficial effect on his health: at first he caught a fever, but he soon recovered and became a fit young man. His father was proud of him and, in his strange parlance, called him a "son of nature, my product". When Fedya reached the age of sixteen, Ivan Petrovich considered it his duty to instil in him a precocious contempt for the female sex, and the young Spartan, timid of soul, with the first down on his lips, full of vital juices, strength and blood, tried to appear indifferent, cold and coarse.

Meanwhile time marched on. Ivan Petrovich spent most of the year in Lavriki (such was the name of his main ancestral estate), but in winter he would arrive in Moscow alone, put up in a tavern, visit his club assiduously, hold forth in drawing rooms and expound his plans – and, more than ever before, behave like a crotchety elder statesman and *anglomane*. But then came 1825 and with it a great deal of grief.* Friends and close acquaintances of Ivan Petrovich were subjected to painful trials. Ivan Petrovich hastened to take himself off to the country and shut himself away in his house. Another year passed and Ivan Petrovich suddenly began to wilt; he grew weak and went into a decline; his health let him down. The freethinker began to go to church and to order private prayer to be said for him; the European began to steam himself in the bathhouse, to dine at two, go to bed at nine and drop off to the sound of the old butler's chatter. The statesman burned all his plans and correspondence, trembled before the provincial governor and fidgeted uneasily before the chief constable. The man with the iron will whimpered and complained when he got a boil or when he was served a bowl of cold soup. Glafira Petrovna again took charge of everything in the house; once again stewards, bailiffs and ordinary peasants began to come in through the back door to see the "old battleaxe" – her nickname among the household serfs. The change in Ivan Petrovich deeply shocked his son; he was already in his nineteenth year, was beginning to think for himself and free himself from the hand which oppressed him. Even before this he had noticed the disconnect between the words and deeds of his father, between his broad, liberal theories and harsh, petty despotism; but he had not expected such an abrupt change. The chronic egoist suddenly revealed himself in his entirety. Young Lavretsky was about to go to Moscow to prepare for the university when a new, unexpected disaster broke over the head of Ivan Petrovich: he went blind, incurably blind, in the course of a single day.

Distrusting the skill of Russian doctors, he began to solicit permission to go abroad. It was refused. Then he took his son and for three whole years wandered round Russia from one doctor to another, ceaselessly travelling from town to town and driving the doctors, his son and his servants to despair by his pusillanimity and impatience. He returned to Lavriki a completely broken man, a self-pitying, capricious child. Bitter days ensued; everyone suffered mightily at his hands. Ivan Petrovich calmed down only during dinner: never had he eaten so greedily and so much. The rest of the time he gave no peace either to himself or to anyone else. He prayed, grumbled about fate, cursed himself, cursed politics, cursed his system, cursed everything about which he had boasted and on which he had prided himself, everything which he had held up as an example to his son. He kept repeating that he believed in nothing and started praying again: he could not bear to be alone for a moment and demanded of his servants that they should sit by his armchair day and night and regale him with stories, which he kept interrupting with exclamations: "You're forever lying – what a load of rubbish!"

Glafira Petrovna was especially on the receiving end: he absolutely could not do without her – and to the end she tried to satisfy all the invalid's whims, although on occasions she decided not to answer him straight away so as not to betray by her voice the anger which was choking her. He lingered on thus for another two years and died in early May, having been carried out onto the balcony into the sun. "Glasha! Glashka!* Some broth, some broth, you old halfw…" his stiffening tongue mumbled, which then, without completing the last word, fell silent for ever. Glafira Petrovna, who had just snatched a bowl of broth from the hands of the butler, halted, looked her brother in the face, slowly made a broad sign of the cross and withdrew without speaking; his son, who was there too, also said nothing, but leant on the balcony rail and for a long time gazed into the garden. It was all fragrance and greenery, all gleaming in the rays of the golden spring sunlight. He was twenty-three; how terribly quickly, how imperceptibly quickly those twenty-three years had passed!… Life was opening up before him.

12

AFTER BURYING HIS FATHER and handing over to the immutable Glafira Petrovna the running of the estate and supervision of the stewards, young Lavretsky set off for Moscow, drawn there by an obscure but powerful feeling. He was conscious of the shortcomings in his education and resolved to repair the neglect as far as possible. In the last five years he had read a great deal and seen a thing or two; many thoughts were fermenting in his head; any professor would have envied him some of the things he knew; but at the same time he was ignorant of much of what every schoolboy had known for a long time. Lavretsky was conscious that he wasn't free; he secretly felt himself to be weird. The Anglomania of his father had played an unkind trick on the son; a capricious upbringing had brought forth its fruit. For many long years he had instinctively humbled himself before his father; when, finally, he got wise to him, the deed was already done and habits had become ingrained. He was not able to mix with people; twenty-three years old, with an unquenchable thirst for love in his timorous heart, he still did not dare to look any woman in the eye. Given his mind, so lucid and healthy but somewhat ponderous, given his tendency to stubbornness, introspection and indolence, he should have been cast into the whirlpool of life at an early age, but he had been kept in artificial isolation… Now the enchanted circle had been broken, but he continued to stand in the same place, locked in, turned in on himself. At his age it was comical to don a student uniform, but he was not afraid of mockery. His Spartan upbringing had benefitted him at least to the extent of developing an indifference to other people's opinions – and he donned a student uniform with no sense of embarrassment. He entered the Faculty of Physics and Mathematics. Fit, rosy-cheeked, taciturn and already with a bushy beard, he left a strange impression on his fellow students: they did not suspect that in this stern adult, who arrived punctually at lectures in a wide, rustic sledge drawn by a pair of horses, there lurked a near-child. To them he seemed some sort of quirky pedant; they did not need him and sought nothing from him, and he avoided them. During his first two years at university he made friends with only one student, from whom he took Latin lessons. This student, Mikhalevich by name, was an enthusiast and a poet; he sincerely liked Lavretsky and, quite by chance, was responsible for an important change in his life.

Once, in the theatre (Mochalov* was then at the height of his fame and Lavretsky did not miss a single one of his performances), he caught sight of a girl in a box in the dress circle, and although no woman could go past his gloomy figure without making his heart flutter, never had it begun beating as violently as it did now. Leaning her elbows on the velvet edge of the box, the girl did not stir; youthful, sensitive vivacity played in every feature of her dark, round, attractive face; a refined mind was evident from her lovely eyes, which gazed out from beneath fine eyebrows, in the fleeting smile on her expressive lips, in the very carriage of her head, arms and neck. She was dressed charmingly. Beside her sat a sallow, wrinkled woman of about forty-five, in a low-cut dress and a black bonnet; she had a toothless smile on her tense, worried, vacant face. In the depths of the box could be seen an elderly man wearing a wide dress coat and a high cravat; his small eyes had an expression of obtuse grandeur and a certain ingratiating suspiciousness; his moustache and side whiskers were dyed and he had a massive but unimpressive forehead and furrowed cheeks. Everything pointed to a retired general. Lavretsky could not take his eyes off the girl who had so arrested his attention; suddenly the door opened and in walked Mikhalevich. The appearance of the man who was almost his only acquaintance in the whole of Moscow, his appearance in the company of the only girl who had absorbed all his attention, seemed ominous and strange to Lavretsky; even Mochalov, although that evening in "top form", did not make his usual impression on him. In one very pathos-filled scene Lavretsky involuntarily looked at his beauty: she was leaning right forward, her cheeks glowing. Under the influence of his relentless gaze, her eyes, which had been fixed on the stage, slowly turned and settled on him... He dreamt about those eyes all night. At last the artificially erected dam burst; he was both shivering and feverish, and the next day he went to see Mikhalevich. From him he learnt that the beauty was called Varvara Petrovna Korobina, that the elderly man and woman sitting with her in the box were her father and mother and that he himself, Mikhalevich, had got to know them a year ago, during his spell as a temporary tutor at the estate of Count N. near Moscow. The enthusiast spoke of Varvara Pavlovna in the most glowing terms. "Brother, this is, this girl is," he exclaimed in his characteristically tremulous sing-song, "is an amazing being, a genius, an artist in the true sense of the word, and extremely kind with it." Noticing from Lavretsky's questioning what an impression Varvara Pavlovna had made on him, Mikhalevich suggested that he should introduce him to her, adding that he was like one of the family, that the general was not a proud man, but that the mother was so stupid she wouldn't say boo to a goose. Lavretsky blushed, muttered something inaudible and hurried off. For five whole days he wrestled with his timidity; on the sixth day the young Spartan donned a new uniform and put himself at Mikhalevich's disposal; he, being his own man, restricted himself to combing his hair – and the two set off for the Korobins.

13

Varvara Pavlovna's father, Pavel Petrovich Korobin, a retired major general, had spent his whole career in Petersburg; in his youth he was reputed to be nimble both in the ballroom and on the parade ground, but, through lack of funds, he found himself an adjutant to two or three nondescript generals and married the daughter of one of them, acquiring a dowry of some twenty-five thousand roubles. He had got training and inspections to a fine art and slogged away till finally, after some twenty years, he reached the rank of general and was given a regiment. At that point he ought to have relaxed and consolidated his fortune unhurriedly; he was indeed counting on that, but he set about things a bit carelessly; he had dreamt up a new method of putting public money into circulation: it turned out to be an excellent method, but he lacked largesse at the crucial moment. Someone informed against him and the result was a scandal which was more than unpleasant – it was sordid. The general somehow wriggled out of the scandal, but his career was over and he was advised to retire. For another couple of years he hung around Petersburg in the hope that a cushy civilian post would come his way. It didn't; his daughter left the Institute,* his expenses mounted with every passing day… Reluctantly, he decided to move to Moscow, where things were cheaper; he rented a tiny low-roofed house on Old Stables Street,* which had a coat of arms seven feet high on the roof. Here he settled as a retired Moscow general, spending 2,750 roubles a year. Moscow is a hospitable city, happy to receive all and sundry, especially generals. The ponderous shape of Pavel Petrovich, which was not, however, devoid of military bearing, began to appear in the best Moscow drawing rooms. The back of his head, bald but for tufts of dyed hair, and a greasy ribbon of St Anne,* which he wore over a raven-black cravat, became familiar to all the pale, listless youths who mooched morosely round the gaming tables during the dances. Pavel Petrovich knew how to make the best of himself in society: he spoke little and, as had long been customary, through his nose – but not, of course, with members of the top ranks. He played a cautious game of cards, ate at home in moderation but, in other people's houses, enough for six. There is almost nothing to say about his wife: she was called Kalliopa Karlovna, and a tear was permanently welling up in her left eye, by virtue of which (incidentally she was of German origin) Kalliopa Karlovna considered herself a woman of sentiment. She was perpetually afraid of something, had a half-starved expression and wore narrow velvet dresses, a toque and matt, tubular bangles. The only daughter of Pavel Petrovich and Kalliopa Karlovna, Varvara Pavlovna, was just seventeen when she left the Institute, where she was regarded as, if not the top beauty, then certainly the top brain and the best musician, and where she received the Empress's cipher.* She was not yet nineteen when Lavretsky saw her for the first time.

14

THE SPARTAN'S LEGS WERE GIVING WAY under him when Mikhalevich led him into the Korobins' somewhat poorly appointed drawing room and introduced him. But the feeling of timidity which engulfed him soon disappeared: in the general the innate kind-heartedness common to all Russians was augmented by a particular kind of affability characteristic of a somewhat tarnished repute. The general's wife was somehow soon out of the picture; as for Varvara Pavlovna, she was so calm, collected and gracious that in her presence everyone felt at home. Moreover, everything about her – her whole captivating body, her smiling eyes, her innocently sloping shoulders, her pale pink arms, her nonchalant and at the same time languorous gait, the very sound of her voice, slow and sweet, exuded an elusive, insidious charm, like a subtle fragrance, a soft and as yet shy voluptuousness, something which it is difficult to convey in words but which touched and aroused. Already it was not timidity that was aroused. Lavretsky turned the conversation to the theatre, to the previous day's performance; she at once began speaking of Mochalov and did not confine herself to mere exclamations and sighs, but made some accurate observations, full of womanly insight, about his performance. Mikhalevich mentioned music; she, without further ado, sat down at the piano and gave a clear rendition of several Chopin mazurkas, which were then only just coming into fashion. Dinner time arrived; Lavretsky tried to leave but was restrained from doing so. Over dinner the general regaled him with a good Lafite, which the general's servant was sent by cab to Desprez's* to fetch. Late that night Lavretsky returned home and sat for a long time without undressing, covering his face with his hands, in a stupor of delight. It seemed to him that only now had he understood what it meant to live; all his assumptions and intentions, all that stuff and nonsense, had disappeared in an instant; his whole soul coalesced into one feeling, one desire, the desire for happiness, possession and love, the sweet love of a woman. From that day onward he began to make frequent visits to the Korobins. Six months later he declared himself to Varvara Pavlovna and offered her his hand. His proposal was accepted. For a long time, almost since Lavretsky's first visit, the general had been asking Mikhalevich how many serfs Lavretsky had; moreover, Varvara Pavlovna herself, who – throughout the young man's courtship and even at the very moment when he confessed his love – had maintained her usual composure and lucidity – even she knew that her betrothed was rich. Kalliopa Karlovna thought: "*Meine Tochter macht eine schöne Partie*,"* and bought herself a new toque.

15

SO HIS PROPOSAL WAS ACCEPTED, but on certain conditions. First, Lavretsky had to leave the university forthwith – who marries a student? What a strange thought – a rich landowner taking lessons like a schoolboy at twenty-six. Secondly, Varvara Pavlovna took on the task of ordering and buying her trousseau, and even chose the presents her betrothed was to give her. She had a great deal of practical common sense, a great deal of taste, a very great deal of fondness for comfort and a great deal of skill in acquiring that comfort for herself. This skill especially amazed Lavretsky when, immediately after the wedding, he and his wife set off for Lavriki in the comfortable carriage she had bought. How well everything that surrounded him had been thought out, anticipated and provided for by Varvara Pavlovna! What charming travelling requisites, such as delightful vanity cases and coffee pots, appeared in various cosy nooks, and how nicely Varvara Pavlovna made coffee in the mornings! However, Lavretsky was not, at that time, interested in observing: he was in clover, revelling in happiness, abandoning himself to it like a child... This young Alcides* was also as innocent as a child. Not for nothing did the whole being of his young wife radiate charm; not for nothing did she promise the senses new and mysterious, voluptuous pleasures. She withheld more than she promised. Arriving at Lavriki in high summer, she found the house dirty and dark, the servants comical and superannuated, but she did not consider it necessary to intimate as much to her husband. If she had intended to settle at Lavriki, she would have revamped everything, beginning, naturally, with the house; but the idea of remaining in this steppe backwater never entered her head for a moment; she, as it were, camped out in it, meekly tolerating all the inconveniences and making amusing fun of them. Marfa Timofeyevna came to see her former charge; Varvara Pavlovna very much took to her, but she did not take to Varvara Pavlovna. The new mistress also did not get on well with Glafira Petrovna; she would have left her in peace, but old man Korobin insisted on meddling in his son-in-law's affairs: it was no shame, he said, even for a general to manage the estate of such a close relative. It must be supposed that Pavel Petrovich would not have disdained to take on the estate of a complete outsider. Varvara Pavlovna conducted her attack extremely skilfully: giving nothing away and apparently completely immersed in the joys of the honeymoon months, in the tranquillity of rural life, in music and reading, she gradually brought Glafira to the point where, one morning, she dashed into Lavretsky's study like a thing possessed and, hurling her bunch of keys onto the table, announced that she was no longer up to managing the household and did not want to remain in Lavriki. Prepared in advance for this, Lavretsky at once agreed to her departure. Glafira Petrovna had not expected this. "Very well," she said, her look becoming sombre, "I can see I'm not wanted here. I know who's driving me out, from my native nest. Mark my words, nephew: you'll never make yourself a nest anywhere. You'll be a wanderer all your life. That's my legacy to you." That very day she retired to her own little estate, and a week later General Korobin arrived and, with a pleasant melancholy in his looks and his movements, took on the management of the whole estate.

In September, Varvara Pavlovna took her husband off to Petersburg. They spent two winters in Petersburg (transferring to Tsarskoye Selo* for the summer) in a splendid, light, exquisitely furnished apartment; they made many acquaintances in the middle and even the upper circles of society, they entertained and themselves went out a great deal, and hosted the most delightful musical and dance soirées. Guests were attracted to Varvara Pavlovna like moths to a flame. Fyodor Ivanovich did not particularly like such a life of distraction. His wife advised him to enter government service, but he, either in deference to his father's memory or from personal conviction, did not wish to – but, to please his wife, he remained in Petersburg. However, it soon occurred to him that no one was preventing him from seeking isolation, that it was not for nothing he had the most quiet and comfortable study in the whole of Petersburg and that his solicitous wife was ready to help him find isolation; from that moment everything went swimmingly. Once again he sought to further his own, as he saw it, incomplete education, again began to read and even embarked on the study of English. It was strange to see his powerful, broad-shouldered figure forever hunched over his desk, his generous, hairy, ruddy face half-covered by the pages of a dictionary or exercise book. He would spend every morning on work, have an excellent dinner (Varvara Pavlovna was an accomplished housekeeper) and in the evenings he would enter a luminous, magic, fragrant world, entirely inhabited by bright young things – and the focus of this world was that same assiduous hostess, his wife. She delighted him with the birth of a son, but the poor child did not live long: he died in the spring, and that summer, on the advice of doctors, Lavretsky took his wife abroad to take the waters. It was essential for her to be distracted after such a misfortune, and moreover her health required a warm climate. They spent the summer and autumn in Germany and Switzerland, but, as might be expected, went to Paris for the winter. In Paris Varvara Pavlovna bloomed like a rose and was able to make herself a nest just as quickly and adeptly as she had in Petersburg. She found the most charming little apartment on one of the quiet but fashionable Parisian streets; she made a dressing gown for her husband the like of which he had never worn before; she hired an elegant maid, a superb cook and an energetic footman; she acquired a splendid little carriage and a very nice piano. A week had not passed before she was crossing the street wearing a shawl, opening an umbrella and putting on gloves like a pure-blooded Parisian lady. And she quickly made acquaintances.

At first only Russians visited her, then Frenchmen began to appear, extremely agreeable, polite, unmarried, with beautiful manners and fine-sounding surnames; they all spoke quickly and volubly, bowing with easy familiarity and narrowing their eyes in pleasing fashion. In all of them white teeth gleamed behind rosy lips. And how they could smile! They all brought along their friends and *la belle Madame de Lavretzki* soon become known from the Chausée d'Antin to the Rue de Lille. In those days (this was 1836) the tribe of sketch writers and columnists, which today is so rife everywhere, like ants in a disturbed anthill, had not yet begun to multiply. But then a certain Monsieur Jules began to appear in Varvara Pavlovna's salon, a gentleman of unprepossessing appearance, with a scandalous reputation, base and brazen, like all duellists and men who have been slapped in the face. Varvara Pavlovna found this Monsieur Jules repellent, but she received him because he wrote for various newspapers and invariably mentioned her, calling her Mme de L...tzki one minute and *Mme de —, cette grande dame russe si distinguée, qui demeure rue de P...** He told the whole world – that is to say a few hundred subscribers who had no interest at all in Mme de L...tzki – how nice and pleasant was this lady, whose wit and intelligence marked her out as a true French woman (*une vraie Française par l'esprit*) – the French have no higher praise – what an exceptional musician she was and how astonishingly well she waltzed (Varvara Pavlovna did indeed waltz in such a way as to snare all hearts in the folds of her light, wispy dress). In a word, he spread her worldly renown – which, whatever one might say, is pleasant. Mademoiselle Mars had already retired from the stage and Mademoiselle Rachel had not yet appeared;* nevertheless Varvara Pavlovna visited the theatre assiduously. She raved about Italian music and laughed at Odry in *Les Ruines*,* yawned decorously at the Comédie Française and was moved to tears by Mme Dorval's acting* in some ultraromantic melodrama. Most importantly Liszt* twice played at her house and was so nice, so unassuming. Delightful! Amid such pleasant sensations the winter passed; by the end of it Varvara Pavlovna had even been presented at court. For his part Fyodor Ivanovich was not bored, although life sometimes seemed heavy upon his shoulders – heavy because it was empty. He read newspapers, attended lectures at the Sorbonne and the Collège de France, followed the debates in the Assemblée Nationale and embarked on a translation on a well-known academic work on irrigation. "I'm not wasting time," he thought. "This is all useful. But by next winter it is imperative I return to Russia and do something definite." It is difficult to say whether he had a clear idea what this "something" actually consisted of, and Lord knows whether he would have succeeded in returning to Russia by winter. Meanwhile he travelled with his wife to Baden-Baden*… An unexpected event destroyed all his plans.

16

ONCE, WHEN VARVARA PAVLOVNA was away, Lavretsky went into her room and saw on the floor a small, carefully folded piece of paper. He picked it up automatically, automatically unfolded it and read the following, written in French:

*My dear angel Betsy (I can't bring myself to call you Barbe or Varvara). I waited for you in vain on the corner of the boulevard; come to our apartment at half-past one tomorrow. Your nice fatty of a husband (*ton gros bonhomme de mari*) is usually buried in his books about that time; we'll again sing that song of your poet Puskin* (*de votre poète Pouskine*) which you taught me: "Aged husband, baleful husband!"* I kiss your hands and feet a thousand times. I'm waiting for you.*

Ernest

Lavretsky did not immediately understand what he had read; he read it a second time – and his head began to spin and the floor to move beneath his feet like the deck of ship in a swell. He shouted, sighed and wept all at the same time.

His reason failed him. He had trusted his wife so blindly; the possibility of deceit, of betrayal, had never entered his mind. This Ernest, his wife's lover, was a fair-haired, good-looking youth of about twenty-three, with a turned-up nose and thin moustache, almost the biggest nonentity among all her acquaintances. Several minutes passed; half an hour passed; Lavretsky remained standing where he was, his hand clenched round the note, his gaze fixed uncomprehendingly on the floor. He fancied he saw pale faces through some dark whirlwind; his heart froze agonizingly within him; it seemed to him that he was falling, falling, falling endlessly. The familiar rustle of a silk dress roused him from his stupor: Varvara Pavlovna, in hat and shawl, was returning hastily from a walk. Lavretsky's whole body shuddered and he rushed out; he felt that at that moment he could have torn her apart, beaten her half to death, peasant-fashion, or throttled her with his own hands. The astounded Varvara Pavlovna tried to stop him from leaving; he could only whisper "Betsy" and run out of the house.

Lavretsky took a cab and ordered to be taken out of town. All the rest of that day and all night long he wandered about, constantly stopping and wringing his hands: one moment he was out of his mind, the next he felt a kind of absurd euphoria. In the morning, chilled to the marrow, he went into a miserable tavern on the edge of town, asked for a room and sat down on a chair in front of the window. He yawned convulsively. He was out on his feet, his body was exhausted, but he did not feel tired; however, tiredness soon got the better of him. He sat and gazed, understanding nothing – not what had happened to him, not why he found himself alone in a strange, empty room, with stiff limbs, a bitter taste in his mouth and a weight on his chest. He did not understand what had made her, Varya,* give herself to this Frenchman, or how she was able, knowing herself to be unfaithful, to remain as composed as ever, as affectionate and trusting towards him as ever. "I don't understand anything!" his parched lips whispered. "Who will guarantee me now that in Petersburg…" He left the question unfinished and again yawned, his whole body trembling and tensing. Memories both light and dark tormented him equally; he suddenly remembered that a few days previously, when both he and Ernest were present, she had sat down at the piano and sung: "Aged husband, baleful husband!" He recalled the expression on her face, the strange gleam in her eyes and the colour in her cheeks; he rose from his chair, wanting to go and say to them: "It was a mistake to make fun of me: my great-grandfather hanged peasants by the ribs and my grandfather was a peasant himself" – and then to kill them both. Then he suddenly felt that everything that was happening to him was a dream, or not even a dream but some sort of mirage; all he would have to do was shake himself, look round... He did look round and, like a hawk sinking its talons into a bird it has caught, so anguish cut ever deeper into his heart. To cap everything, Lavretsky hoped to become a father in a few months... The past, the future, his whole life had been poisoned. Finally he returned to Paris, put up in a hotel and sent Varvara Pavlovna Monsieur Ernest's note, together with the following letter:

> *The attached will explain everything. Incidentally I should say that I found it most unlike you: that you, who are always so careful, should drop such important papers.*

(Poor Lavretsky had prepared and honed this phrase over the course of several hours.)

> *I cannot see you any more; I assume that you too have no desire to see me. I will assign you 15,000 francs a year: I'm unable to give you any more. Send your address to the estate office. Do what you will; live as you will. I wish you happiness. No reply is needed.*

Lavretsky wrote to his wife that he did not need a reply... but he waited for, yearned for, an explanation of this incomprehensible, inexplicable matter. That same day Varvara Pavlovna sent him a long letter in French. It was the final blow; his last doubts vanished and he was ashamed that he still had doubts. Varvara Pavlovna did not seek to justify herself: she merely wished to see him, entreating him not to condemn her irrevocably. The letter was cold and strained, although here and there traces of tears could be seen. Lavretsky smiled bitterly and ordered the messenger to say that everything was fine. Three days later he left Paris and went, not to Russia, but to Italy. He did not know himself why exactly he had chosen Italy; essentially it was all the same to him where he went, as long as it wasn't home. He sent word to his bailiff about his wife's allowance, ordering him at the same time to take immediate control of the estate from General Korobin, without waiting for the accounts to be drawn up, and to make arrangements for the immediate departure of His Excellency from Lavriki; he pictured vividly to himself the confusion and futile pomposity of the ousted general and, despite all his grief, felt a certain malicious pleasure. Then, in a letter to Glafira Petrovna, he asked her to return to Lavriki and sent a power of attorney in her name. Glafira Petrovna did not return to Lavriki and quite unnecessarily had a statement concerning the annulment of the power of attorney printed in the newspapers. Holed up in a little Italian town, Lavretsky was unable for a long time to prevent himself from keeping tabs on his wife. He learnt from the newspapers that she had left Paris, as intended, for Baden-Baden; her name soon appeared in a piece signed by the same Monsieur Jules. In this article a certain friendly sympathy showed through the usual frivolous tone; reading this article made Fyodor Ivanovich sick at heart. Then he learnt that he had a daughter; some two months later he was informed by his bailiff that Varvara Pavlovna had asked for the first third of her allowance. Then ever worse rumours began to circulate; finally a tragicomic scandal broke in all the newspapers, in which his wife played an unenviable role. Everything was over: Varvara Pavlovna had become a "celebrity".

Lavretsky stopped keeping tabs on her, but he paid for it for a long time. Sometimes he missed his wife so badly that he felt he would give anything – would even, perhaps... forgive her – if he could only hear her sweet voice again and again feel her hand in his. He was not a born martyr; his robust health came into its own. Much became clear to him: the blow itself, which had floored him, did not seem unforeseen any longer; he began to understand his wife – you only fully understand those near to you when you part from them. Once again he was able to do things and work, although with far less than his former zeal: scepticism, born of life experience and education, had infiltrated his soul. He became very indifferent to everything. Some four years passed and he felt able to return to his homeland and meet his own people. Without stopping in either Petersburg or Moscow, he arrived in O—– where we took our leave of him and to where we ask the gentle reader to return with us.

17

Some time before ten o'clock on the morning after the day we have described, Lavretsky was going up the steps to the Kalitins' house. Liza, wearing a hat and gloves, came out to meet him.

"Where are you going?" he asked her.

"To Mass. It's Sunday today."

"Do you really go to Mass?"

Liza looked at him in silent astonishment.

"Forgive me, please," said Lavretsky. "I… I didn't mean to say that. I've come to say goodbye – in an hour I'm off to my estate."

"Isn't that quite near here?" Liza asked.

"About fifteen miles."

Lenochka appeared on the threshold, accompanied by a maid.

"Mind you don't forget us," said Liza, coming down the steps.

"Nor you me. Listen," he added, "you're going to church – say a prayer for me too while you're about it."

Liza halted and turned to him.

"Certainly," she said, looking him straight in the eyes, "I'll pray for you too. Let's go, Lenochka."

In the drawing room Lavretsky found Marya Dmitriyevna alone. She smelt of eau de Cologne and mint tea. She claimed that she had a headache and had had a disturbed night. She received him with her usual languid affability and by degrees became more talkative.

"Is it not true that Vladimir Nikolayevich is such a pleasant young man?"

"Which Vladimir Nikolayevich is that?"

"Why, Panshin, who was here yesterday. He was awfully taken with you. I'll tell you in confidence, *mon cher cousin*, he's simply mad about Liza. What of it? He's from a good family, holds an excellent post, is clever, and he's a *kammerjunker* and, if God wills it… I, for my part, as a mother, will be extremely glad. Of course, it's a big responsibility; of course, children's happiness depends on their parents, and it should be said too that, for better or for worse, I did everything on my own: I brought the children up, I taught them – that was all me – and now I've hired a French governess from Madame Bolus*…

Marya Dmitriyevna launched into a description of her worries, her endeavours and her maternal feelings. Lavretsky listened to her in silence, twisting his hat round in his hands. His cold, grave look checked the lady's volubility.

"And what do you think of Liza?" she asked.

"Lizaveta Mikhailovna is a very fine girl," replied Lavretsky, before standing up, bowing and making his way to Marfa Timofeyevna's room. Marya Dmitriyevna watched him go with a sense of displeasure and thought: "What a clumsy oaf! A peasant! Well, now I understand why his wife couldn't stay faithful."

Marfa Timofeyevna was sitting in her room, surrounded by her usual circle. It consisted of five beings, all almost equally close to her heart: a fat-cropped tame bullfinch, to which she had taken a fancy because it had stopped whistling and carrying water, a timid and docile little dog called Roska, an angry cat called Matros,* a dark-complexioned, hyperactive little girl of about nine, with huge eyes and a pointed nose, who was called Shurochka, and an elderly woman of about fifty-five, wearing a white mob cap and a brown *katsaveika* jacket over a dark dress – her name was Nastasya Karpovna Ogarkova. Shurochka was the orphan daughter of a tradesman. Marfa Timofeyevna had taken her in out of pity, as she had Roska. She had found both dog and girl on the street: both were thin and hungry, both were being soaked by autumn rain. No one claimed Roska, and Shurochka was given up willingly to Marfa Timofeyevna by her uncle, a drunken shoemaker who himself did not get enough to eat and who did not feed his niece but beat her over the head with his last. Marfa Timofeyevna had got to know Nastasya Karpovna in a monastery while on a pilgrimage; she had approached her herself in church, having taken a liking to her because, as she put it, she prayed very tastefully. Marfa Timofeyevna had struck up a conversation with her and invited her home for a cup of tea. From that day onward they were inseparable. Nastasya Karpovna was a woman of cheerful and mild temperament, a childless widow of impoverished noble stock. She had a round head, grey hair, soft white hands, a soft face with strong, kind features and a somewhat comical turned-up nose. She revered Marfa Timofeyevna, who in turn loved her, although she made fun of her tender heart. Nastasya Karpovna had a weakness for all young people and blushed involuntarily, like a young girl, at the most innocent joke. Her entire capital consisted of twelve hundred paper roubles; she lived at Marfa Timofeyevna's expense, but on an equal footing with her – Marfa Timofeyevna would not have tolerated servility.

"Ah, Fedya," she began as soon as she saw him. "Yesterday you didn't see my family: take a good look at them. We've all gathered to have tea – it's our second tea, for a special occasion. You can give them all a hug – but Shurochka won't let you and the cat will scratch. Are you off today?"

"Yes." Lavretsky sat down on a low chair. "I've already said goodbye to Marya Dmitriyevna. I saw Lizaveta Mikhailovna too."

"Call her Liza, old chap. Why should she be Mikhailovna to you? And sit still or you'll break Shurochka's chair."

"She was going to Mass," Lavretsky continued. "Is she religious?"

"Yes, Fedya, very. More than you or me, Fedya."

"But aren't you religious?" said Nastasya Karpovna in a hushed tone. "You didn't go to the early Mass today, but you'll go to the late one."

"Oh no I won't – you'll go on your own: I feel idle, my dear," rejoined Marfa Timofeyevna. "I'm overindulging myself with tea." She used the familiar form of address with Nastasya Karpovna, although they lived together on an equal footing. Not for nothing was she a Pestov: three Pestovs are recorded in Ivan the Terrible's Book of Remembrance.* Marfa Timofeyevna was aware of this.

"Tell me, please," Lavretsky began again. "Marya Dmitriyevna was just taking to me about that – what's his name? – Panshin. What's this gentleman like?"

"Good Lord, what a chatterbox she is!" muttered Marfa Timofeyevna. "I expect she told you – in confidence – that he's in the offing as a suitor. She should stick to whispering with that son of a priest of hers, but obviously that's not enough for her. But nothing's happened yet, thank Heavens! But she's already chattering."

"Why 'thank Heavens'?" asked Lavretsky.

"Because I don't like the young fellow – anyway, why make a song and dance about it?"

"You don't like him?"

"No, I don't. He can't charm everyone. It's enough for him that Nastasya Karpovna here is in love with him."

The poor widow was completely unnerved.

"How can you, Marfa Timofeyevna? You no longer fear God!" she exclaimed, and in an instant a deep blush spread over her face and neck.

"And, you know, the crafty rogue knows how to flatter her," interrupted Marfa Timofeyevna. "He's given her a snuffbox. Fedya, ask her to give you a pinch of snuff: you'll see what a splendid snuffbox it is: on the lid there's a picture of a hussar on horseback. You'd best not try and justify yourself, my dear."

Nastasya Karpovna merely waved this away.

"And Liza," Lavretsky asked, "is she far from indifferent to him?"

"She seems to like him, but Lord alone knows! Another's heart is like a dark forest, you know, and a young girl's even more so. Take Shurochka's – try and make that out! Why's she been hiding, but not going away, since you got here?"

Shurochka gave a snort of suppressed laughter and fled from the room; Lavretsky rose from his place.

"Yes," he said deliberately, "you can't make out a young girl's heart."

He began to take his leave.

"Well then, will we see you soon?" asked Marfa Timofeyevna.

"As needs be, Auntie: it's not far away after all."

"Yes – after all you're going to Vasilyevskoye. You don't want to live in Lavriki – well, that's your affair. But drop by there, pay your respects to your mother's grave, and your grandmother's too. You picked up all sorts of learning over there, abroad – and, who knows, perhaps, even in their graves, they'll sense that you've come to them. And don't forget, Fedya, to have a requiem mass said for Glafira Petrovna too. Here's a rouble. Go on, take it – it's me who wants a requiem said for her. I didn't like her in life, but it can't be denied she was a spirited wench. She was clever – and, well, she did you no harm. Now go, with my blessing, or I'll bore you silly."

And Marfa Timofeyevna embraced her nephew.

"And Liza won't marry Panshin, don't worry – she deserves a better husband than that."

"I won't worry at all," replied Lavretsky, and withdrew.

18

SOME FOUR HOURS LATER he was on his way home. His tarantass rolled briskly along the untended byway. There had been a drought for about a fortnight; there was a milky fogginess in the air, which wreathed the distant woods and gave off a smell of burning. Banks of darkish clouds with ill-defined edges crept across a pale-blue sky. Dry gusts of wind blew steadily and unceasingly across, without dissipating the heat. His head on a pillow and his arms crossed on his chest, Lavretsky surveyed the field strips as they unfolded like a fan, the glimpsed willows, the stupid crows and rooks which cast suspicious sideways glances at the passing carriage, at the long boundary strips, overgrown with mugwort, wormwood and rowans. This he surveyed… and the fresh, lush remoteness and bareness of the steppe, this verdure, these long hills, these ravines with their stunted oaks, these grey hamlets, these scattered birches – this whole Russian picture, which he had not seen for a long time, evoked in him feelings both sweet and, at the same time, almost sorrowful, and weighed down on him with an almost pleasant weight. His thoughts slowly wandered; their outline was as blurred as the high, seemingly wandering clouds. He recalled his childhood, his mother, remembered how she lay dying, how he was taken to her and how she, pressing his head to her breast, began to intone softly a lament for the dead over him and how she had then looked at Glafira Petrovna – and fallen silent. He remembered his father, at first robust, discontented, strident, then blind, maudlin and with an unkempt grey beard; he remembered how his father had once drunk a glass too much wine at table, spilt sauce over his napkin, had suddenly burst out laughing and, blushing and blinking his sightless eyes, had begun to tell of his conquests. He remembered Varvara Pavlovna – and winced involuntarily, as a man winces from momentary internal pain, and shook his head. Then his thoughts settled on Liza.

"Here," he thought, "is a new being, just at the start of life. A splendid girl. What will become of her? She's good-looking. A pale, fresh face, such serious eyes and lips and an honest, innocent way of looking. It's a pity that she seems somewhat intense. A fine figure and a sweet voice, and she treads so lightly. I particularly like it when she stops suddenly, listens attentively, unsmilingly, then becomes pensive and tosses back her hair. It's a fact – I see it myself – that Panshin is unworthy of her. But what's bad about him? And why am I daydreaming like this? She'll run off down the same path that everybody runs down. I'd better get some sleep." And Lavretsky closed his eyes.

He could not sleep, but fell into the drowsy numbness of the weary traveller. As before, images of the past slowly rose to the surface of his mind, inextricably mingling with other tableaux. Lavretsky – Lord knows why – began thinking of Robert Peel,* of French history, of how he would have won a battle had he been a general. He imagined shots and cries... His head slipped to one side and he opened his eyes. The same fields, the same view of the steppe; the worn-down shoes of the trace horses flashed intermittently through the swirling dust; the driver's shirt, yellow with red gussets, billowed out in the wind... "A fine state to come home in" – the words flashed through Lavretsky's mind. He shouted: "Move!", wrapped himself in his greatcoat and pressed his head more firmly into his pillow. The tarantass jolted; Lavretsky straightened up and opened his eyes wide. Before him, on a little rise, stretched a small hamlet; a little to the right could be seen a decrepit manor house with closed shutters and a crooked little entrance porch; nettles, green and thick as flax, covered the broad courtyard, right from the gate. In the courtyard stood a sturdy little oak storehouse. This was Vasilyevskoye.

The driver turned towards the gate and halted the horses; Lavretsky's servant stood up on the box and, as if readying himself to jump down, called out: "Hello!" A hoarse, muffled barking was heard, but even the dog did not show himself; the servant again readied himself to jump down and again called: "Hello!" The feeble barking was repeated and, a moment later, from somewhere or other, a man in a nankeen kaftan, with hair as white as snow, ran out into the yard; shielding his eyes from the sun, he took a look at the tarantass, suddenly slapped his thighs with both hands, dithered a little, then hastened to open the gate. The tarantass entered the yard, its wheels swishing over the nettles, and stopped in front of the entrance porch. The white-haired man, obviously an extremely nimble fellow, was already standing, bow legs wide apart, on the bottom step. He unfastened the front cover of the tarantass, tugging the leather convulsively up, helped his master down and kissed his hand.

"Greetings, old fellow, greetings," said Lavretsky. "You're Anton, I think. Still going strong then?"

The old man said nothing, but bowed and ran to get the keys. While he did that, the coachman sat slouched and motionless, gazing at the locked door; meanwhile, Lavretsky's servant had jumped down and held a picturesque pose, with one arm flung over the box. The old man brought the keys and, writhing unnecessarily like a snake, raised his elbows up high and unlocked the door; then he stood aside and bowed from the waist.

"Here I am back home," thought Lavretsky as he entered the tiny entrance hall; meanwhile, the shutters were being opened one by one, with many a rattle and squeak, and the light of day penetrated the deserted rooms.

19

THE SMALL HOUSE TO WHICH Lavretsky had come, and where, two years before, Glafira Petrovna had died, had been built in the previous century from stout pine. It had a decrepit appearance, but looked as if might well last another fifty years or more. Lavretsky went round all the rooms and, to the great consternation of the torpid, half-dead flies sitting motionless under the lintels, their backs covered in white dust, he ordered all the windows to be opened – no one had opened them since the death of Glafira Petrovna. Everything in the house had remained untouched. The spindly-legged white sofas in the drawing room, threadbare and sagging, upholstered with shiny grey material, were mementos of Catherine the Great's time. In the drawing room also stood the mistress's favourite armchair, with its high straight back, against which she had never leant, even in old age. On the main wall hung an ancient portrait of Fyodor's great-grandfather, Andrei Lavretsky: the dark, splenetic face was scarcely distinguishable from the warped and blackened background; the small, malign eyes gazed morosely from underneath drooping, seemingly swollen lids; black, unpowdered hair stood in bristles above a heavy, furrowed brow. On the corner of the portrait hung a dusty wreath of immortelles. "Glafira Petrovna herself was pleased to make it," Anton announced. In the bedroom stood a high, narrow bed under a tester made from antique, but high-quality striped material; a pile of faded pillows and a thin quilted counterpane lay on the bed, at the head of which hung an icon of *The Presentation of the Blessed Virgin Mary in the Temple* – the very same icon to which the old spinster, dying alone and forgotten by everyone, had pressed lips already growing cold. By the window stood a little inlaid dressing table, with brass escutcheons and a crooked mirror in a tarnished gilt frame. Next to the bedroom was the icon room, a small room with bare walls and a heavy icon case in the corner; on the floor lay a threadbare, wax-spattered bit of carpet on which Glafira Petrovna would pray, falling to her knees and bowing her head to the ground. Anton went off with Lavretsky's servant to open the stable and the barn; in his place appeared an old woman, his near-contemporary, her head swathed in a kerchief down to her eyebrows. Her head shook; her eyes were weak, but simultaneously expressed devotion, an ingrained habit of unquestioning service and a kind of respectful commiseration. She kissed Lavretsky's hand and halted by the door, awaiting her instructions. He could not for the life of him remember what she was called, could not remember even whether he had ever seen her. It turned out she was called Apraxeya; some forty years previously, Glafira Petrovna had banished her from the house and ordered her to look after the chickens. She said little, however, as if suffering from dementia, and wore a servile look. Apart from the two old people and three pot-bellied children in long shirts, Anton's great-grandchildren, the manor house was home to a one-armed, tax-exempt peasant: he chuntered like a black grouse and was incapable of doing anything. Almost equally useless was the decrepit dog which had greeted Lavretsky's return with its barking. For some ten years it had sat on the end of a heavy chain, bought on the instructions of Glafira Petrovna, and was scarcely in any condition to move and drag that burden. Having inspected the house, Lavretsky went out into the garden and was pleased with what he saw. It was all overgrown with high grass, burdock, gooseberry bushes and raspberry bushes, but in it there was much shade and many old lime trees, notable for their huge size and the strange pattern of their branches; they had been planted too close to each other and at some point – a hundred years ago or thereabouts – pruned. The garden ended in a small, clear pond, fringed with red-brown rushes. Traces of human life soon disappear: Glafira Petrovna's estate had not yet reverted to nature, but already seemed plunged into that peaceful slumber slept by everything on earth when uninfected by restless humanity. Fyodor Ivanovich also took a walk through the village; cheeks resting in hands, women gazed at him from the doorsteps of their houses; men bowed from a distance; children ran away and dogs barked indifferently. Finally he grew hungry, but he was not expecting his servants or cook until evening; a convoy of provisions from Lavriki had not yet arrived, so he was compelled to turn to Anton. Anton at once took action: he caught, slaughtered and plucked an old hen; he spent a long time rubbing and washing it, as if he were laundering it, before placing it in a saucepan. When, at last, it was cooked, Anton cleared and laid a table, placing before Fyodor's place a blackened, three-legged plated salt cellar and a cut-glass decanter with a round glass stopper and a narrow neck. Then he announced to Lavretsky in a sing-song voice that dinner was served. He himself took up his position behind Fyodor's chair, wrapping his right fist in a napkin and giving off a strong age-old smell, like that of cypress wood. Lavretsky drained the soup, exposing the chicken: its skin was completely covered in large pimples; a thick tendon ran up each leg and the meat tasted of wood and lye. Having had dinner, Lavretsky said that he would like a cup of tea if— "Coming right up, sir. I'll get it," the old man interrupted – and he was as good as his word. A pinch of tea, wrapped in a scrap of red paper, was found; a small but highly temperamental and noisy samovar was found; sugar, in small lumps which appeared to have thawed, was found. Lavretsky drank some tea from a large cup; he had childhood memories of this cup: it had playing cards depicted on it and only guests drank from it – and he was drinking from it like a guest. Towards evening his servants arrived; Lavretsky did not want to sleep in his aunt's bed and ordered a bed to be made up for him in the dining room. After extinguishing the candle he spent a long time looking round and thinking unhappy thoughts; he experienced a sensation familiar to anyone who has had to spend a night for the first time in a long-deserted place. It seemed to him that the darkness which had enveloped him on all sides could not become inured to the new inhabitant, that the very walls of the house were puzzled by him. Finally, he sighed, pulled the blanket over him and fell asleep. Anton remained on his feet longer than anyone else; for a long time he whispered with Apraxeya, groaned under his breath and crossed himself a couple of times. Neither of them had expected that the master would settle with them in Vasilyevskoye when he had available such a splendid estate with a very well-ordered manor house and grounds; they did not suspect that it was precisely this manor house that Lavretsky found repellent, evoking, as it did, painful memories. Having had enough of whispering, Anton took a stick and beat the long-silent board which hung by the barn and at once dropped off to sleep in the yard, leaving his white head uncovered. The May night was quiet and soothing, and the old man slept soundly.

20

THE NEXT DAY LAVRETSKY ROSE fairly early, spoke to his bailiff, visited the threshing floor and ordered the yard dog to be unchained; it merely barked a little, but did not even leave its kennel. On returning home, Lavretsky fell into a kind of peaceful torpor, from which he did not emerge all day. "Now at last I've reached the very bottom of the river," he told himself more than once. He sat beneath the window, not stirring and apparently listening to the current of tranquil life which surrounded him and the sporadic sounds of rustic isolation. Somewhere beyond the nettles someone was singing a shrill little song; a gnat seemed to echo it. Then the song stopped, but the gnat droned on: through the concerted, tiresomely plaintive buzzing of flies came the humming of a fat bumblebee which kept banging its head on the ceiling; a cockerel in the street began to crow, hoarsely sustaining the final note; a cart clattered by; a gate creaked somewhere on the estate; "Wha –at?" came the quavery sound of a woman's voice. "Well hello, little lady," said Anton to a two-year-old girl he was holding in his arms. "Bring the kvass," repeated the same woman's voice – and suddenly there was dead silence; no knocking sounds, no stirrings; the wind did not ruffle the leaves; one after another, swallows skimmed past silently over the ground and their noiseless passage brought sadness to the soul. "Now at last I've reached the very bottom of the river," Lavretsky again thought. "And always, at all times, life here is tranquil and unhurried," he thought. "Whoever comes into its sphere must submit. Here there is nothing to agitate one, nothing to trouble one. Here only he will succeed who, without hurrying, carves out his own path, as a ploughman ploughs his furrow. And what strength all round, what vigour there is in this dormant tranquillity! Here, beneath the window, a stocky burdock pushes through the thick grass; above it stretches a juicy lovage stem and lungwort throws its pink umbels still higher. Over there, farther away, rye gleams in the fields, oats are already in stalk and every leaf on every tree, and every blade of grass is widening to its full width. My best years have gone on a woman's love," Lavretsky continued his train of thought. "May the dullness of this place sober me up, soothe me and prepare me to set about my task unhurriedly." And he again began to listen to the silence, expecting nothing – yet at the same time somehow expecting something. The silence enveloped him from all sides, the sun travelled silently through a calm blue sky, across which the clouds floated silently; they seemed to know why and whither they were floating. At the same time, in other corners of the earth, seething, tumultuous life sped by; here that same life flowed by inaudibly, like water over grasses in a marsh. And right up to that evening Lavretsky could not tear himself away from the contemplation of this receding ebb tide of life; sorrow for the past melted in his soul, like snow in spring and – strange to relate – he had never before felt so deeply and strongly for his native country.

21

IN THE COURSE OF TWO WEEKS Fyodor Ivanovich put Glafira Petrovna's house in order, and cleaned up the courtyard and garden. Comfortable furniture was brought in from Lavriki and, from the town, wine, books and journals. Horses appeared in the stables – in a word, Fyodor Ivanovich equipped himself with everything he needed and began to live – not quite as a landowner, nor yet as a hermit. His days passed monotonously, but although he saw no one, he was not bored. He ran the estate diligently and attentively, travelled round the surrounding area on horseback and read. However, he did not do much reading: he preferred to listen to the stories of old Anton. Usually Lavretsky would sit by the window with a pipe of tobacco and a cup of cold tea; Anton would stand by the door, his hands behind his back, and begin his unhurried stories about the old times, those legendary times when oats and rye were sold not in measures but in large sacks, for two or three copecks a sack; when impassable forest and virgin steppe stretched in all directions, even in the direction of the town. "But now," complained the old man, who was over eighty, "everything's been cut down and ploughed up and there's no way through." Anton also talked a great deal about the mistress of the house, Glafira Petrovna: how sensible and thrifty she was; how a certain gentleman, a young neighbour, tried to ingratiate himself with her, began to drive round frequently to visit; how, for his sake, she graciously deigned to put on her best Sunday bonnet, with massacas-coloured* ribbons and a yellow dress of *trou-trou* levantine; how, subsequently, furious at her gentleman neighbour for his unseemly question: "What would you say your capital might be, ma'am?" she had ordered him to be barred from the house; and how she then ordered that after her death everything, down to the last scrap of cloth, should be left to Fyodor Ivanovich. And indeed Fyodor Ivanovich found all his aunt's effects intact, including the Sunday bonnet with the massacas-coloured ribbons and the yellow dress of *trou-trou* levantine. There turned out not to be any of the ancient papers or curious documents on which Lavretsky had counted, apart from one battered book, in which his grandfather, Pyotr Andreyevich, had inscribed the words: "Celebration in the city of St Petersburg of the peace concluded with the Turkish Empire by His Grace Prince Alexander Alexandrovich Prozorovsky",* and a recipe for a decoction for chest ailments, with the note: "This prescription was given to Praskovya Fyodorovna, wife of General Saltykov by Fyodor Avksentyevich, dean of the Church of the Life-Giving Trinity." Then there was some political news of the following kind: "No further news concerning the French tigers" and, alongside this: "*Moscow News** reports the death of Lieutenant Colonel Mikhail Petrovich Kolychov. Is he not the son of Pyotr Vasilyevich Kolychov?"* Lavretsky also found several old dream books and church almanacs and the mysterious work by Mr Ambodik; the familiar but long-forgotten *Symbols and Emblems* stirred many memories in him. In Glafira Petrovna's dressing table Lavretsky found a small packet, bound with black ribbon, sealed with black sealing wax and pushed to the very back of the drawer. In the packet, lying face to face, were pastel portraits of his father as a young man, with soft curls spilling over his forehead, long, languid eyes and a half-open mouth, and a very faded portrait of a pale woman in a white dress, with a white rose in her hand – his mother. Glafira Petrovna had never allowed anyone to paint her portrait. "I, Fyodor Ivanovich, sir," Anton would say to Lavretsky, "though in them days I weren't resident in my master's house, still remember your great-grandfather, Andrei Afanasyevich. To be sure I do: when he died I was just eighteen. Once I met him in the garden – that gave me the shivers; but he was all right, just asked me my name and sent me to get him a handkerchief from his room. He was the master, no question – no one was his boss. 'Cause

I tell you, your great-grandfather had this amazing amulet – a monk from Mount Athos gave it him. And this here monk said to him: 'This I give you, master, for your hospitality; wear it and you'll have nothing to fear.' Well, sir, you know what times was like then: whatever the master wanted to do, he did. It might happen that some gentleman took it into his head to gainsay him, but he would just look at him and say: 'You're just small fry' – that was his favourite expression. And your great-grandfather of blessed memory lived in a little wooden manor house – and what goods he left behind, silver, all sorts: all the cellars were full to the brim with them. He knew the business. That decanter, what you was good enough to praise, was his. He drank vodka from it. Then your grandfather, Pyotr Andreyevich, built a stone place for himself, but he didn't acquire any goods; everything went to pot with him, and he lived worse than his dad and took no pleasure in anything – and he got through all his money and left nothing to remember him by, not even a silver spoon. Thank the Lord Glafira Petrovna got a grip."

"But is it true," Lavretsky interrupted, "they called her an old battleaxe?"

"But who was it called her that?" Anton retorted crossly.

"By the way, sir," the old man made so bold as to ask on one occasion, "where will our mistress take up her residence?"

"I've divorced my wife," Lavretsky said forcefully. "Please don't ask about her."

"As you wish, sir," replied the old man sadly.

After three weeks had elapsed, Lavretsky rode to O— to see the Kalitins and spent the evening with them. Lemm was there; Lavretsky liked him very much. Although, thanks to his father, he did not play any instrument, he was nevertheless passionately fond of music – proper music, classical music. Panshin was not at the Kalitins' that evening. The governor had sent him somewhere out of town. Liza played alone and with great accuracy. Lemm became animated and expansive, rolled up a piece of paper and conducted. As she watched him, Marya Dmitriyevna at first laughed, then went off to bed – as she put it,

Beethoven was too trying on her nerves. At midnight Lavretsky escorted Lemm back to his apartment and sat with him until three o'clock in the morning. Lemm spoke a great deal; he no longer stooped and his eyes widened and gleamed; the very hair on his forehead stood up. No one had paid any heed to him for such a long time, but Lavretsky was clearly interested in him and questioned him solicitously and attentively. The old man was touched by this. He ended up by showing his guest his music, playing for him and singing some excerpts from his compositions in a lifeless voice, among them the whole of Schiller's ballad 'Fridolin', which he had set to music.* Lavretsky praised him, made him repeat some pieces and, as he left, invited him to stay for a few days at his house. Lemm, who accompanied him as far as the street, accepted on the spot and shook his hand warmly, but, left alone in the fresh, damp air in the first glimmerings of dawn, he looked around him, screwed up his eyes, hunched himself up and slunk back to his room like a guilty man. "*Ich bin wohl nicht klug* (That was not very clever of me)," he muttered as he lay down on his hard, short bed. He tried to plead illness when, a few days later, Lavretsky called round for him in his carriage, but Lavretsky went into his room and persuaded him. Lemm was particularly impressed by the fact that Lavretsky had ordered a piano to be brought from the town to his estate specifically for him. They set out together to the Kalitins and spent the evening with them, though not as pleasantly as before. Panshin was there, did a lot of talking about his trip and very amusingly characterized and mimicked the landowners he had met; Lavretsky laughed, but Lemm did not emerge from his corner, saying nothing, making quiet, spider-like movements and staring morosely and blankly; he only came to life when Lavretsky began to take his leave. Even when sitting in the carriage, the old man remained uncommunicative and withdrew into his shell, but the calm, warm air, a gentle breeze, the faint shadows, the smell of grass and birch buds, the peaceful glow of the starry, moonless sky, the snorting and the rhythmic hoofbeat of the horses – all the magic of the road, the spring, the night, sank into the soul of the poor German, and he was the first to speak.

22

HE BEGAN TO TALK ABOUT MUSIC, about Liza and then again about music. He seemed to enunciate more slowly when he spoke about Liza. Lavretsky turned the subject to his composition and, half in jest, offered to write a libretto for him.

"Hmm, a libretto!" Lemm responded. "No, that's not my thing: I haven't got the sort of lively imagination which is essential for opera; I've already lost my powers now... But if I could still do something, I'd be happy with a romance; of course I'd like some good words for it..."

He fell silent and for a long time sat motionless, his eyes raised skywards.

"For example," he said finally, "something like: 'Ye stars, O ye pure stars!...'"

Lavretsky turned his head slightly towards him and fixed his eyes on him.

"Ye stars, o ye pure stars," Lemm repeated, "ye look down equally on the righteous and the guilty... but only the innocent of heart – or something to that effect – understand you, or rather – love you. However, I'm not a poet, far from it! But something to that effect, something lofty."

Lemm pushed back his hat; in the delicate half-light of the bright night, his face seemed paler and younger.

"Ye stars," he continued, his voice gradually growing fainter, "ye know who loves, who is capable of love, because ye are pure and alone can console... No, that's not it at all! I'm not a poet," he said. "But something to that effect..."

"I'm sorry, but I'm not a poet either," Lavretsky observed.

"Empty daydreams!" rejoined Lemm, settling back into the corner of the carriage. He closed his eyes as if intending to go to sleep.

A few moments passed... Lavretsky renewed his attention... "Ye stars, o ye pure stars," the old man was whispering.

"Love," Lavretsky repeated to himself reflectively, and his heart grew heavy within him.

"You've written some splendid music for 'Fridolin', Khristofor Fyodorovich," he said aloud. "But what do you suppose? Once the count had brought this 'Fridolin' to his wife, surely he became her lover."

"That's what you think," replied Lemm, "because, probably, experience..." Suddenly he fell silent and turned away in embarrassment. Lavretsky gave a forced laugh, then also turned away and began to contemplate the road.

The stars were already beginning to fade and the sky was turning grey when the carriage pulled up to the entrance porch of the house at Vasilyevskoye. Lavretsky escorted his guest to his allotted room, returned to his study and sat down in front of the window. In the garden a nightingale was singing its last pre-dawn song. Lavretsky remembered that a nightingale had also been singing in the Kalitins' garden; he also remembered the quiet movement of Liza's eyes when, at the sound of the first notes, they had turned towards the dark window. He began to think about her and his heart grew calm within him. "A maiden pure," he said under his breath. "Pure stars," he added with a smile, and went peacefully to bed.

But Lemm sat for a long time on his bed with a book of handwritten sheet music on his knees. It seemed he was about to be visited by an unprecedentedly sweet melody: he was already burning with excitement, already feeling the sweet languor of its approach... but it eluded him.

"Not a poet and not a musician!" he whispered at last.

And his weary head slumped onto the pillow.

23

THE NEXT MORNING, host and guest drank tea in the garden under an old lime tree.

"Maestro!" said Lavretsky, among other things. "You will soon have to compose a solemn cantata."

"For which occasion?"

"On the occasion of the marriage of Mr Panshin and Liza. Did you notice how he danced attendance on her yesterday? Everything seems set fair for them."

"It won't happen!" exclaimed Lemm.

"Why not?"

"Because it is impossible. Although," he added after a pause, "in this world, anything is possible. Especially here in Russia."

"Let's leave Russia out of it for the moment. What do you find bad about this marriage?"

"Everything's bad. Everything. Lizaveta Mikhailovna is a right-minded, serious girl, with lofty sentiments, while he... he is, in a word, a di-let-tante."

"But surely she loves him?"

Lemm rose from the bench.

"No, she doesn't love him – that is to say she's very pure in heart and doesn't know the meaning of the word 'love'. Madame von Kalitin tells her he's a nice young man, and she listens to Madame von Kalitin, because she's still quite a child, although she's nineteen. She prays in the morning and prays in the evening – and that's very laudable – but she doesn't love him. She can love only the beautiful, and he isn't beautiful – that is to say he hasn't a beautiful soul."

Lemm uttered this whole speech cogently and passionately, walking backwards and forwards with short steps in front of the tea table, his gaze darting over the ground.

"Dearest maestro!" Lavretsky suddenly exclaimed. "It seems to me that you yourself are in love with my cousin."

Lemm broke off suddenly.

"Please," he began in an uncertain voice, "don't make fun of me like that. I'm not out of my mind: I'm staring into a dark grave, not a rosy future."

Lavretsky felt sorry for the old man and asked his forgiveness. After tea Lemm played him his cantata and, over dinner, prompted by Lavretsky himself, again began talking about Liza. Lavretsky listened to him with attention and curiosity.

"What do you think, Khristofor Fyodorovich," he said finally, "with everything in order here now and the garden in full bloom, should we invite her here for the day, along with her mother and my old auntie? Would you like that?"

Lemm bent his head over his plate.

"Invite them," he said, barely audibly.

"But not Panshin?"

"No," replied the old man, with an almost childlike smile.

Two days later Fyodor Ivanovich set off for the town to see the Kalitins.

24

HE FOUND EVERYONE AT HOME, but did not announce his intention at once, wanting to talk to Liza privately. Chance was on his side: they were left alone together in the drawing room. They talked; she had had time by now to grow used to him – and in general she was not shy with anyone. He listened to her, gazed into her eyes, mentally repeated Lemm's words and agreed with him. It sometimes happens that two people who know each other, but are not on intimate terms with one another, suddenly and rapidly, in the course of a few moments, establish an intimacy, the awareness of which is immediately expressed in their eyes, in their gentle, affectionate smiles and in their very movements. This is precisely what happened to Lavretsky and Liza. "So that's what he's like," she thought, regarding him fondly. "So that's what she's like," he likewise thought. Therefore he was not very surprised when she – not, however, without some slight hesitation – declared that she had long had it in her heart to tell him something, but was afraid of annoying him.

"Don't be afraid. Speak up," he said, standing in front of her.

Liza raised her clear eyes to his.

"You're so kind," she began, at the same time thinking: "Yes, he really is kind..." "Forgive me, I ought not be so bold as to speak to you about this... but how could you... why did you divorce your wife?"

Lavretsky shuddered, glanced at Liza and sat down beside her.

"My child," he said, "please don't touch that wound: you have gentle hands but all the same it will hurt me."

"I know," Liza went on, as if she had not heard him, "she is in the wrong and I don't want to justify her. But how can that which God has joined be put asunder?"

"Our views on that score are widely different, Lizaveta Mikhailovna," said Lavretsky rather sharply. "We will not understand one another."

Liza turned pale; her whole body trembled slightly, but she did not fall silent.

"You must forgive," she said quietly, "if you want to be forgiven in your turn."

"Forgive!" retorted Lavretsky. "You ought first to find out for whom you are seeking forgiveness. Forgive that woman and take her back into my house, that empty, heartless, creature! Who told you that she wanted to return to me? She's perfectly content with her situation, if you please... What's the point of talking about it! Her name should not be uttered by you. You're too pure and in no position even to understand such a creature."

"Why insult her?" said Liza with an effort. The tremor in her hands was becoming apparent. "It was you who left her, Fyodor Ivanovich."

"But I'm telling you," countered Lavretsky with a sudden outburst of impatience, "you don't know what sort of a creature she is!"

"So why did you marry her?" Liza whispered, lowering her eyes.

Lavretsky quickly rose from his chair.

"Why did I marry her? I was young and inexperienced at the time; I deceived myself; I was carried away by outer beauty. I didn't know women – I didn't know anything. May God grant you a happier marriage! But believe me, nothing can be taken for granted in advance."

"I too could be unlucky," said Liza (her voice was beginning to falter), "but in that case I will have to submit. I don't know how to put this, but if we don't submit..."

Lavretsky clenched his fists and stamped his foot.

"Don't be angry. Forgive me," said Liza hastily.

At that moment Marya Dmitriyevna came in. Liza stood up and tried to withdraw.

"Wait!" Lavretsky shouted after her unexpectedly. "I have a big request to make of your mother and of you: come to my house-warming party. You know I've got a piano now; Lemm is staying with me. The lilac is in bloom; you'll be able to breathe the country air and return home the same day. Do you accept?"

Liza looked at her mother, and Marya Dmitriyevna adopted a pained expression. Lavretsky, however, did not let her open her mouth and immediately kissed both her hands. Marya Dmitriyevna, always susceptible to endearments and not expecting such politenesses from the "clumsy oaf", relented and agreed. While she was thinking about fixing a day, Lavretsky went up to Liza and, still in a state of high emotion, surreptitiously whispered: "Thank you. You're a kind girl – I'm to blame..." And a blushing, happy, shy smile spread over her pale face; her eyes also smiled – until that moment she feared she had offended him.

"Can Vladimir Nikolayevich come with us?" asked Marya Dmitriyevna.

"Of course," Lavretsky replied, "but wouldn't it be best to keep it to our family circle?"

"But it seems to me..." Marya Dmitriyevna began. "All right – as you wish," she added.

It was decided to take Lenochka and Shurochka. Marfa Timofeyevna declined to go.

"My old bones can't take it, my dear," she said. "And I expect there's nowhere to sleep at your place. Anyway, I can't sleep in a strange bed. Let the young folk do the travelling."

Lavretsky did not manage to be alone with Liza again, but he looked at her in a way that made her feel both pleased and a little ashamed, as well as sorry for him. As he took his leave, he clasped her hand firmly; left alone, she became wrapped in thought.

25

When Lavretsky returned home, he was met at the door of the drawing room by a tall, thin man wearing a shabby blue frock coat; he had a lined but animated face, untidy grey whiskers, a long, straight nose and small, inflamed eyes. This was Mikhalevich, his former university friend. At first Lavretsky did not recognize him, but as soon as the man gave his name, he embraced him warmly. They had not seen each other since their Moscow days. There followed a torrent of exclamations and questions; long-buried recollections re-emerged into the light. Hurriedly smoking pipe after pipe, gulping down tea and waving his long arms about, Mikhalevich recounted his adventures to Lavretsky; there was nothing very cheerful in them and he could not boast of success in his enterprises, but he incessantly laughed a hoarse, nervous laugh. A month previously he had obtained a post in the private office of a rich tax-farmer, about two hundred miles from the town of O—, and, learning of Lavretsky's return from abroad, had made a detour in order to see his own friend. Mikhalevich spoke as tremulously as he had in his youth, ranting and raving as much as ever. Lavretsky was about to mention his own circumstances, but Mikhalevich interrupted him with a hurried mutter: "I heard, my friend, I heard – who could have expected that?" He immediately steered the conversation towards generalities.

"Tomorrow, my friend," he said, "I've got to go. Today, if you'll excuse me, we'll stay up late. I would really like to know what you are like, what your opinions and convictions are, what you've become and what life has taught you." (Mikhalevich adhered to the phraseology of the 1830s.) "As for me, I've changed a great deal, my friend: the waves of life have broken over my breast – I wonder who said that – although in all the important essentials I haven't changed. I believe in Goodness and Truth, as I always did; but not only do I believe, I have faith in them now. Yes, I have faith, I have faith. Listen, you know I write verses. There's little poetry in them, but there is truth. I'll read you my latest piece: in it I've expressed my innermost convictions. Listen."

Mikhalevich began to read his poem: it was rather long and ended with the following lines:

> To new feelings my heart wholly turned,
> Like a child in my soul I became:
> Everything I esteemed I have burned,
> And have burned everything I esteemed.

As he spoke the last two lines Mikhalevich almost broke down in tears; a slight quiver – a sign of powerful emotion – ran across his broad lips and his plain features lit up. Lavretsky listened and listened to him… and a bloody-minded spirit stirred within him: he had always been irritated by the perpetual ready-made ebullience of the Moscow student. A quarter of an hour had not elapsed before a heated argument broke out, one of those interminable arguments of which only Russians are capable. After a separation of many years, spent in two different worlds, their first move was to launch into an argument about the most abstract of topics, without any clear understanding of the other's ideas, let alone their own, latching on to words and replying with mere words; they argued as if it were a matter of life and death for both of them. They screamed and yelled so much that everyone in the house became alarmed, and poor Lemm, who from the moment of Mikhalevich's arrival had shut himself in his room, felt bewildered and even began to feel vaguely fearful.

"After this, what are you – disenchanted?" Mikhalevich shouted, sometime after midnight.

"Are disenchanted people like that?" rejoined Lavretsky. "They're all usually pale and sickly – but if you want I'll lift you up with one hand."

"All right, if you're not disenchanted, you're a sceptic. That's even worse," said Mikhalevich, his pronunciation betraying his Ukrainian origins. "What gives you the right to be a sceptic? Let's assume you've been unlucky in life; no blame attaches to you for that: you were born with a passionate, loving soul, but you were forcibly kept away from women – the first woman who came along was bound to deceive you."

"She deceived you too," remarked Lavretsky sullenly.

"Granted, granted: in that instance I was the instrument of fate. But what rubbish I'm talking. Fate doesn't come into it: it's my old habit of expressing myself inaccurately. But what does this prove?"

"It proves I've been out of joint since childhood."

"Then put yourself right! That's why you're human, that's why you're a man; you've no lack of energy! But however that may be, is it possible, is it allowable to elevate a, so to speak, private fact into a general law or immutable rule?"

"How does rule come into it?" Lavretsky interrupted. "I don't accept—"

"But it's your rule, your rule," Mikhalevich interrupted in his turn.

"You're an egoist, that's what you are!" he thundered an hour later. "You sought self-gratification, you sought happiness in life, you wanted to live for yourself alone…"

"What is self-gratification?"

"And everything has deceived you; everything has collapsed under your feet."

"What is self-gratification, I'm asking you?"

"And it was bound to collapse. For you sought support where none could be found, for you built your house on shifting sand…"

"Speak more plainly, without similes, *for* I don't understand you."

"For – all right, laugh – for you have no faith, no warmth of heart – just a piffling intellect... You're simply a pathetic, outmoded Voltairean – that's what you are!"

"I'm a Voltairean?"

"Yes, just like your father, and you don't even suspect it."

"After that," exclaimed Lavretsky, "I have every right to say you're a fanatic."

"Alas," retorted Mikhalevich sorrowfully, "unfortunately I haven't done anything to deserve such a lofty appellation."

"I've found out now what to call you," shouted Mikhalevich, still going strong, towards three o'clock in the morning. "You're not a sceptic, you're not disenchanted, you're not a Voltairean: you're a loafer, a nasty loafer, and you know it. You're not just a plain and simple loafer – they lie on the stove and do nothing, because they're incapable of doing anything. They don't even think about anything, but you've got an active mind – and yet you just lie there. You could be doing something – and you do nothing. You lie on your back with a full stomach and say: this is the life, lying like this, because whatever people do, it's all rubbish and pointless nonsense."

"But where did you get the idea that I lie around?" Lavretsky persisted. "Why do you ascribe such thoughts to me?"

"And, on top of everything, you are all, all your kind," Mikhalevich continued relentlessly, "erudite loafers. You know the Germans' weak spot, you know what's wrong with the English and the French – and your knowledge stands you in good stead, justifies your shameful indolence and your disgraceful inactivity. Some are even proud of the fact that they're clever, as they put it, yet lie around while other people busy themselves, the fools. Yes! Then again, there are in this country gentlemen – however, this isn't aimed at you – who spend their whole lives in a kind of bored trance, who accustom themselves to it and go together with it like... like mushrooms and sour cream. Oh, that bored trance – the ruin of Russians! The ghastly loafer spends his whole life intending to work..."

"But why these strictures?" Lavretsky yelled in his turn. "Doing something… Working… Rather than these strictures, you'd be better off saying what should be done, you Poltavan Demosthenes!"*

"Look what he wants now! That I won't say, my friend: everyone should know this themselves," returned Demosthenes ironically. "A landowner and a nobleman – and he doesn't know what should be done! You've no faith, otherwise you'd know. No faith – and no epiphany."

"Let me at least have a rest, damn it – let me. Let me get my bearings."

"Not a minute's rest, not a second's," replied Mikhalevich with a peremptory wave of the hand. "Not a single second! Death does not wait and nor should life."

"And when and where have people taken it into their heads to make loafers of themselves?" he shouted at four o'clock in the morning, his voice already rather hoarse. "In this country! Now! In Russia! When every individual has a duty, a great responsibility before God, before the people, before themselves! We sleep, but time is passing. We sleep…"

"Allow me to observe," said Lavretsky, "that we are not sleeping at all now, but rather preventing others from sleeping. We're exercising our throats like cockerels. Listen – it sounds as if the cocks are crowing thrice."

This shaft of wit amused Mikhalevich and calmed him down. "Till tomorrow," he said with a smile, putting his pipe away in his tobacco pouch. "Till tomorrow," said Lavretsky. But the friends went on chatting for more than an hour… However, their voices were no longer raised and their talk was quiet, sad, friendly talk.

Mikhalevich departed the next day, despite Lavretsky's efforts to detain him. Fyodor Ivanovich failed to persuade him to stay, but he talked to him to his heart's content. It turned out that Mikhalevich did not have a bean. Already the previous day Lavretsky had been sorry to observe in him all the indications and habits of long-standing poverty: his shoes were worn out, a button was missing from the back of his frock coat, his hands were strangers to gloves and bits of fluff stuck out of his hair. When he arrived he had not thought of asking if he could have a wash, and at supper he had eaten like a shark, tearing the meat with his hands and crunching the bones with his strong black teeth. It also turned out that government service had done him no good, and that he had pinned all his hopes on the tax-farmer, who had taken him on solely in order to have an "educated man" in his office. For all this, Mikhalevich was not despondent, but lived his life as a cynic, an idealist and a poet, with genuine concern and sorrow for the fate of humanity and his own mission in life – and was singularly unworried about dying of hunger. Mikhalevich was not married, but had fallen in love countless times and written poems about all his loves; he sang the praises of a mysterious black-haired *panna** with particular fervour… Admittedly there were rumours that this *panna* was actually an ordinary Jewess, well-known to many cavalry officers… but, when you think about it, isn't that neither here nor there?

Mikhalevich did not get on with Lemm: the German was unused to, and scared by, his stentorian speeches and his brusque manners… One failure immediately senses another from a distance, but in old age rarely seeks his company, and that is not in the least surprising: they have nothing in common – not even hopes.

Before his departure, Mikhalevich again had a long talk with Lavretsky, prophesied doom for him if he did not come to his senses, beseeched him to take a serious interest in the lives of his peasants and cited himself as an example, saying that he had been refined in the furnace of misfortunes. Thereupon he termed himself a happy man, comparing himself with the birds of the air and the lilies of the valley.

"Black lilies, at any rate," Lavretsky observed.

"Oh, don't play the aristocrat, my friend," Mikhalevich retorted good-humouredly. "You should rather thank God that honest plebeian blood flows in your veins. But I see you need some pure, other-worldly being who would wrest you from your apathy."

"Thank you, brother, but I've had enough of these other-worldly beings."

"Silence, cynic," said Mikhalevich in his Ukrainian accent.

Lavretsky corrected his pronunciation.

"Just so, cynic," Mikhalevich repeated, ignoring the correction and not a whit embarrassed.

Even when sitting in the tarantass, to which his flat, yellow, strangely light trunk had been carried, he was still talking; swathed in a sort of Spanish cloak, the collar of which had faded to a brownish-red colour and which had lion's-paw fastenings instead of clasps, he was still expounding his views on the fate of Russia and making aerial gestures with his swarthy hand, as if sowing the seeds of future prosperity. Finally the horses moved off... "Remember my last three words," he shouted, leaning right out and balancing himself on the pole of the tarantass. "Religion, Progress, Humanity! Goodbye!" His head, with a forage cap pulled down over his eyes, disappeared. Lavretsky was left alone in the entrance porch, gazing fixedly along the road into the distance, until the tarantass was hidden from view. "You know, perhaps he's right," he thought as he went back into the house. "Perhaps I am a loafer." Many of Mikhalevich's words had sunk inexorably into his soul, although he had argued and disagreed with him. So long as a man is good-hearted, no one can resist him.

26

TWO DAYS LATER, Marya Dmitriyevna, as promised, arrived in Vasilyevskoye with her youthful entourage. The girls at once ran off into the garden, while Marya Dmitriyevna languidly processed through all the rooms and languidly praised everything. She considered her visit to Lavretsky to be sign of great condescension, almost as an act of kindness. When Anton and Apraxeya, in the time-honoured manner of house serfs, kissed her hand, she smiled graciously and, in a subdued, nasal voice, asked for some tea. To the intense annoyance of Anton, who had donned white knitted gloves, tea was served to the lady visitor not by him but by Lavretsky's hired butler, who, in the words of the old man, had no understanding of the way things were done. However, Anton got his own way at dinner: he planted himself resolutely behind Marya Dmitriyevna's chair – and did not give up his place to anyone. The appearance of guests at Vasilyevskoye, to which he had been so long unaccustomed, both alarmed and delighted the old man: he was pleased to see that people from good families knew his master. However, he was not alone in being excited that day: Lemm was also excited. He had donned a short tobacco-coloured dress coat with a pointed tail, tied his cravat tightly, cleared his throat incessantly and made way for people with a pleasant and gracious mien. Lavretsky noted with pleasure that the rapprochement between himself and Liza was ongoing: as soon as she came in, she held her hand out to him in friendly fashion. After dinner, Lemm produced from the back pocket of his dress coat, into which he had been reaching from time to time, a small bundle of sheet music, which, pursing his lips and without saying anything, he placed on the piano. It was a romance he had composed the previous day to old-fashioned German words, which made mention of the stars... Liza immediately sat down at the piano and sight-read the piece... Alas! The music turned out to be complicated and painfully strained: it was clear that the composer had endeavoured to express something passionate and profound, but nothing had come of it. Lavretsky and Liza both felt this – and Lemm understood. Without saying a word, he put his romance back in his pocket and, in answer to Liza's offer to play it again, merely shook his head and said meaningfully: "Now – that's enough!" Hunching his shoulders and withdrawing into his shell, he left.

Towards evening the whole company went fishing. In the pond at the bottom of the garden there were lots of carp and charr. They sat Marya Dmitriyevna in a chair on the edge of the pond, spread a rug at her feet and gave her the best fishing rod. Anton, as an old and experienced angler, offered his services to her. He assiduously baited the hook with worms, slapped them, spat on them and even cast the line himself, gracefully inclining his whole body forward. That very day Marya Dmitriyevna commented on him to Fyodor Ivanovich in the following words of schoolgirl French: "*Il n'y a plus maintenant de ces gens comme ça comme autrefois*".* Lemm and the two girls went on farther, right up to the dam; Lavretsky took his place beside Liza. The fish were biting continually; the gold and silver sides of carp flashed as they were reeled through the air; there was no end to the joyful exclamations of the girls; Marya Dmitriyevna herself emitted one or two girlish shrieks. Lavretsky and Liza were the least successful: this was probably because they paid less attention than the others to the fishing and allowed their floats to drift right up to the bank. The tall russet-coloured reeds rustled quietly around them; in front of them the motionless water shone quietly, and their conversation was quiet. Liza was standing on a small raft; Lavretsky was sitting on the slanting trunk of a willow tree. Liza was wearing a white dress with a broad ribbon, also white, round the waist. Her straw hat hung on one arm while, with the other, she struggled to hold the flexible fishing rod in the correct position. Lavretsky looked at her pure, rather severe profile, at her hair, drawn back behind her ears, at her soft cheeks, which, like those of a child, had caught the sun, and thought: "Oh, how charming you look, standing by my pond!" Liza did not turn to him, but continued to look at the water, half screwing her eyes up, half smiling. The shadow of a nearby lime tree fell on them both.

"Do you know," Lavretsky began, "I've thought about our last conversation many times and come to the conclusion that you're extremely kind."

"That was not my intention..." Liza started to say, before becoming embarrassed.

"You're kind," Lavretsky repeated. "I'm a rough diamond, but I feel that everyone should love you. Take Lemm, for instance: he's quite simply in love with you."

Liza's eyebrows did not so much pucker as quiver – this always happened when she heard something unpleasant.

"I felt very sorry for him today," Lavretsky continued, "with his unsuccessful romance. To be young and a failure – that's bearable; but to grow old and not have the ability – that's hard. What's painful is that you don't sense that your ability is waning. It's difficult for an old man to bear such blows! Careful – you've got a bite... They say," Lavretsky added after a pause, "that Vladimir Nikolayevich has written a very charming romance."

"Yes," replied Liza, "it's a trifle, but not at all bad."

"And what do you think?" asked Lavretsky. "Is he a good musician?"

"It seems to me that he has a great talent for music, but so far has not studied it as much as he should have done."

"I see. But is he a good man?"

Liza laughed and shot a quick glance at Fyodor Ivanovich.

"What a strange question!" she exclaimed, pulling her line out of the water and casting it again.

"Why strange? I'm asking you about him as someone who has recently arrived, as a relative."

"As a relative?"

"Yes. After all, am I not an uncle to you?"*

"Vladimir Nikolayevich has a kind heart," said Liza. "He's clever – Maman is very fond of him."

"But are you fond of him?"

"He's a good man. Why should I not be fond of him?"

"Ah," said Lavretsky, and fell silent. A half-sorrowful, half-mocking expression passed quickly across his face. His steadfast gaze disconcerted Liza, but she continued to smile. "Well, God grant them happiness," he said finally, as if talking to himself, then turned his head away.

Liza blushed.

"You're mistaken, Fyodor Ivanovich," she said. "You're wrong to think… But don't you like Vladimir Nikolayevich?" she asked suddenly.

"No."

"Why not?"

"He seems heartless to me."

The smile vanished from Liza's face.

"You've got used to judging people harshly," she said, after a long pause.

"Me? I don't think so. Good Heavens, what right have I to judge others harshly when I myself need their indulgence? Or have you forgotten that if there's anyone who doesn't laugh at me, it's only because they're too lazy to do so? By the way," he added, "did you keep your promise?"

"What promise?"

"Did you pray for me?"

"Yes, I prayed for you, and I do pray every day. Please don't speak lightly about it."

Lavretsky began to assure Liza that that thought had not entered his head and that he profoundly respected all beliefs.

Then he launched into a disquisition on religion, on its significance in the history of humanity, on the significance of Christianity...

"One must be a Christian," Liza began, not without some difficulty, "not in order to perceive things heavenly... or... earthly, but because Man must die."

Lavretsky raised his eyes to Liza in involuntary amazement and met her gaze.

"What words you have spoken!" he said.

"The words are not mine," she replied.

"Not yours... But why did you start talking about death?"

"I don't know. I often think about it."

"Often?"

"Yes."

"To look at you now, one wouldn't think so: you have such a happy, radiant face. You smile..."

"Yes, I'm very happy now," she replied naively.

Lavretsky wanted to take both her hands and press them firmly...

"Liza, Liza," Marya Dmitriyevna shouted, "come here and see this carp I've caught."

"Coming, Maman," Liza replied, and went to her, but Lavretsky remained on his willow bough. "I talk to her as if I were not yesterday's man," he thought. As she left, Liza had hung her hat on a branch; Lavretsky regarded this hat, with its long, slightly crumpled ribbons, with a strange, almost tender feeling. Liza soon came back to him and again took up a position on the raft.

"Why does Vladimir Nikolayevich seem heartless to you?" she asked a few moments later.

"I've already told you I might be mistaken; however, time will reveal all."

Liza became thoughtful. Lavretsky began to speak about his life at Vasilyevskoye, about Mikhalevich, about Anton; he felt the need to talk to Liza, to impart to her everything that came into his heart.

She listened to him so pleasantly, so attentively; her occasional remarks and remonstrations seemed so simple and intelligent to him. He even told her so.

Liza was astonished.

"Really?" she said. "And I thought that, like my maid Nastya, I didn't have any words of my *own*. She once said to her betrothed: 'You must find it boring with me; you're always saying such nice things to me but I have no words of my own.'"

"Thank Heavens for that!" thought Lavretsky.

27

MEANWHILE THE EVENING was drawing in and Marya Dmitriyevna expressed the desire to return home. They tore the girls away from the pond with difficulty and got them ready for the journey. Lavretsky announced that he would accompany his guests halfway home and ordered his horse to be saddled. As he sat Marya Dmitriyevna in her carriage, he realized Lemm was missing: the old man could not be found anywhere. He had disappeared the moment the fishing was over. With force remarkable for one of his years, Anton slammed the carriage doors and barked: "Get going, driver!" The carriage moved off. The back seats were occupied by Marya Dmitriyevna and Liza, the front by the girls and the maid. The evening was still and warm, and the carriage windows on both sides were lowered. Lavretsky trotted beside the carriage on Liza's side, with his hand on the door – he had thrown the reins over the neck of his horse, which was moving easily – occasionally exchanging two or three words with her. The sun had set and night had fallen, but the air had even grown warmer. Marya Dmitriyevna quickly dozed off; the girls and the maid also fell asleep. The carriage bowled along quickly and smoothly; Liza leant forward; the newly risen moon shone into her face and a fragrant night breeze wafted into her eyes and cheeks. She was in love with life. Her hand rested on the carriage door alongside Lavretsky's. He too was in love with life: he was borne along through the still warmth of the night, never taking his eyes from the kind young face, listening to the ringing whispers of that young voice which spoke simple, kind words; he did not even notice that he had gone past the halfway mark. Not wanting to waken Marya Dmitriyevna, he gently squeezed Liza's hand and said: "We're friends now, aren't we?" She nodded; he pulled up his horse. The carriage rolled on, gently pitching and swaying; Lavretsky set off home at walking pace. The magic of the summer night possessed him; all around seemed unexpectedly strange and at the same time seemed so long, and so sweetly familiar; everything, both near and far – and you could see a long way, although the eye could not make out clearly much of what it saw – was tranquil; young, burgeoning life could be sensed in this tranquillity. Lavretsky's horse moved boldly, swaying rhythmically to right and left; its large black shadow accompanied it; there was something pleasantly mysterious in the clatter of its hooves, something wonderful and happy in the ringing cries of the quail. The stars were disappearing in a kind of luminous haze; the waxing gibbous moon gleamed steadily; its light suffused the sky in a grey-blue cascade and fell in a patch of smoky gold on the wispy clouds passing close by beneath; the freshness of the air made the eyes slightly moist, enveloped every limb in its caress and filled the breast in a free-flowing stream. Lavretsky enjoyed all this and savoured his enjoyment. "Well, there's life in us yet," he thought. "We've not yet been completely eaten away by…" He did not say by whom or by what… Then he began to think about Liza and about the fact that she could scarcely love Panshin; that, had he met her in different circumstances, Heaven knows what might have resulted; that he understood what Lemm felt about her although she had no words "of her own". But that wasn't true either: she did have her own words… Lavretsky remembered her words: "Don't speak lightly about it". He rode on for a long time, his eyes downcast, then straightened and slowly recited the words:

> Everything I esteemed I have burned,
> And have burned everything I esteemed…

Thereupon, however, he whipped up his horse and galloped all the way home.

CHAPTER 27

As he dismounted, he looked round himself for the last time with an involuntary smile of gratitude. Night, silent, tender night, lay on the hills and valleys; from afar, from its fragrant depths – God knows whence, whether from heaven or earth – came a calm, gentle warmth. Lavretsky made a final bow to Liza and ran up the porch steps.

The following day passed in fairly lacklustre fashion. Rain set in early in the morning; Lemm maintained his sullen look, pursing his lips ever more tightly, as if he had pledged never to open them again. On going to bed, Lavretsky took with him a whole heap of French newspapers which had lain unopened on his desk for more than two weeks. He set about casually tearing off the wrappers and running his eye over the newspaper columns which, moreover, contained nothing new. He was on the point of junking them when suddenly he leapt from the bed as if he had been stung. In a piece in one of the newspapers, Monsieur Jules, who is already familiar to us, informed his readers of some "distressing news": "That delightful and charming lady from Moscow," he wrote, "one of the queens of fashion and adornment of the Paris salons, Madame Lavretski, has died suddenly." This news, unfortunately all too true, had only just reached Monsieur Jules. He went on to describe himself as "a friend of the deceased".

Lavretsky got dressed, went out into the garden and walked up and down the same avenue of trees until morning.

28

THE NEXT MORNING, OVER TEA, Lemm asked Lavretsky to let him have some horses in order to return to town. "It's time I got down to business – that is, to lessons," the old man remarked. "Otherwise I'm just wasting time here." Lavretsky did not answer at once: he seemed distracted. "All right," he said finally, "I'll go with you myself." Without the help of a servant, groaning and getting angry, Lemm packed his small trunk, then tore up and burned several sheets of manuscript paper. The horses were brought round. On his way out of his study Lavretsky slipped into his pocket the newspaper he had read the night before. Throughout the whole journey Lemm and Lavretsky said little to one another: each was preoccupied with his own thoughts and each was glad that the other did not disturb him. They parted somewhat coolly, which, however, is often the way with friends in dear old Russia. Lavretsky took the old man to his house; the old man got out, found his trunk and, without offering his friend his hand (he was holding the trunk with both hands in front of his chest), without even looking at him, said in Russian: "Goodbye, sir!"

"Goodbye!" Lavretsky echoed, and ordered the coachman to take him to his rooms. To meet any eventuality, he had rented rooms in the town of O— After writing several letters and having a quick dinner, Lavretsky set off to the Kalitins. In their drawing room he found only Panshin, who announced that Marya Dmitriyevna would appear shortly and immediately launched into conversation with him in the most genial and affable manner. Until that day Panshin had treated Lavretsky, if not haughtily, then condescendingly; but Liza, in telling Panshin of her visit the previous day, had spoken of Lavretsky as a fine, intelligent man. That was sufficient:

the "fine man" had to be won over, and Panshin began with compliments, by describing the delight with which, as he put it, Marya Dmitriyevna's entire family had spoken of Vasilyevskoye, and then, as was his wont, deftly turning the subject to himself, began to talk about his own affairs and his views on life, society and government service. He said a couple of things about the future of Russia and about how governors should be taken in hand. At that point he cheerfully made fun of himself, adding that, among other things, he had been given the task "*de populariser l'idée du cadastre.*"* He spoke at some length, resolving all difficulties with casual self-confidence, playing with the weightiest administrative and political questions, as a juggler plays with balls. The expressions: "This is what I would do if I were the government", "As an intelligent man you will be the first to agree with me" were constantly on his lips. Lavretsky listened coldly to Panshin's harangues: he did not like this handsome, intelligent, unaffectedly refined man, with his radiant smile, polite voice and probing eyes. Panshin quickly divined, with his characteristically quick understanding of another's feelings, that he was no source of pleasure to his interlocutor; under some plausible pretext he made himself scarce, deciding that Lavretsky might well be a splendid fellow, but was uncongenial, "*aigri*" and, "*en somme*",* rather ludicrous. Marya Dmitriyevna appeared, accompanied by Gedeonovsky; then Marfa Timofeyevna came in with Liza, followed by the remainder of the household; then the lover of music, Belenitsyna, also arrived, a small, thin woman with an almost childish, careworn, but attractive face; she wore a rustling black dress and had a multicoloured fan and thick gold bracelets; her husband came too, a podgy, rubicund man with big feet and big hands, white eyelashes and a permanent smile on his thick lips. When they were visiting, his wife never spoke to him, but at home, in moments of tenderness, she would call him her little piggy-wiggy. Panshin returned: inside the house it became crowded and noisy. Such a large number of people was the last thing Lavretsky wanted. He was particularly irked by

Belenitsyna, who kept peering at him through her lorgnette. He would have left at once had it not been for Liza: he wanted to have a word or two with her in private but, unable to find a suitable occasion, he contented himself with watching, with secret delight, her every movement. Never had her face seemed more noble or more attractive. She gained much from her proximity to Belenitsyna, who fidgeted constantly on her chair, flexed her narrow shoulders, laughed girlishly and one minute screwed up her eyes and the next opened them wide. Liza sat demurely, looking straight ahead and not laughing at all. Marya Dmitriyevna sat down to play cards with Marfa Timofeyevna, Belenitsyn and Gedeonovsky; the latter played very slowly, made endless mistakes and kept blinking and mopping his face with his handkerchief. Panshin assumed a melancholy aspect, expressing himself curtly, sadly and highly meaningfully – for all the world like an artist with something to say but unable to do so – but, in spite of requests from Belenitsyna, who was very flirtatious with him – declined to sing his romance: Lavretsky inhibited him. Fyodor Ivanovich also said little; the peculiar expression on his face had struck Liza as soon as he entered the room: she immediately sensed that he had something to communicate to her but, without knowing why, she was afraid to question him. Finally, as she crossed into the main room to pour the tea, she involuntarily turned her head in his direction. He immediately followed her.

"What's the matter?" she said as she placed the teapot on the samovar.

"You've noticed something, then?" he said.

"Today you weren't the same person I've known up to now."

Lavretsky leant over the table.

"I wanted," he began, "to give you some news, but that's not possible now. However, read what's marked in pencil in this newspaper sketch," he added, giving her the copy of the newspaper he had brought with him. "I ask you to keep this confidential. I'll call in tomorrow morning."

CHAPTER 28

Liza was astounded... Panshin appeared in the doorway: she put the newspaper in her pocket.

"Have you read *Obermann*,* Lizaveta Mikhailovna?" Panshin enquired thoughtfully.

Liza gave a non-committal answer, left the room and went upstairs. Lavretsky returned to the drawing room and went up to the card table. Marfa Timofeyevna, red in the face and with her bonnet ribbons undone, began complaining to him about her partner Gedeonovsky, who, as she put it, never knew which card to lead with.

"It's clear that playing cards," she said, "is not the same as telling tales."

He continued to blink and mop his brow. Liza came into the drawing room and sat down in the corner. Lavretsky looked at her, and she looked at him – and both of them felt apprehensive. He read puzzlement and a certain secret reproachfulness in her face. He could not speak to her as he would have wished; to stay in the same room as her, a guest among other guests, was hard, and he decided to leave. As he said goodbye to her, he managed to repeat that he would come the following day, adding that he hoped he could count on her friendship.

"Do come," she said, with the same air of puzzlement in her face.

On the departure of Lavretsky, Panshin came to life: he began to give advice to Gedeonovsky, was ironically complimentary to Belenitsyna and, finally, sang his romance. But he spoke to Liza and looked at her the same way as before: meaningfully and rather sorrowfully.

Once again, Lavretsky did not sleep all night. He was neither sad nor excited and was perfectly calm; but he could not sleep. He was not even recalling the past but was simply surveying his life. His heart was beating heavily and evenly; the hours flew by and he did not even think of sleep. Only occasionally did the thought arise: "But that's not true: it's all rubbish." Then he would pause, hang his head and resume his survey of his life.

29

MARYA DMITRIYEVNA DID NOT RECEIVE Lavretsky too kindly when he came to see her the next day. "Look, he's got into the habit," she thought. She did not much care for him in any case, and Panshin, under whose influence she was, had cunningly damned him with faint praise the previous day. Since she did not regard Lavretsky as a guest and did not consider it necessary to entertain a relative, almost a member of the household, half an hour had not passed before he was walking with Liza down one of the avenues in the garden. Lenochka and Shurochka ran about in the flower bed a few paces away from them.

Liza was calm, as usual, but paler than usual. From her pocket she took the sheet of newspaper, folded small, and handed it to Lavretsky.

"That's terrible," she said.

Lavretsky did not reply.

"But perhaps it's not true," Liza added.

"That's why I asked you not to speak of this to anyone."

Liza walked on a little.

"Tell me, she began, "you're not upset, are you? Just a little?"

"I don't know myself what I'm feeling," Lavretsky replied.

"But did you love her before?"

"Yes."

"Very much?"

"Very much."

"And you're not upset by her death?"

"For me she died long ago."

"What you say is a sin… Don't be angry with me. You call me your friend. A friend can say anything. I do feel terror-stricken, really. Yesterday you looked dreadful… Do you remember how you complained about her recently? Perhaps at that very moment she was no longer with us. That's terrible. It's as if it was visited upon you as a punishment."

Lavretsky smiled bitterly.

"You think so? At least I'm free now."

Liza shuddered slightly.

"That's enough. Don't talk like that. What use is your freedom to you? You mustn't think about that now, but about forgiveness."

"I forgave her a long time ago," Lavretsky interrupted with a dismissive gesture.

"No, I didn't mean that," Liza protested, reddening. "You've misunderstood me. You must find a way to be forgiven."

"Forgiven by whom?"

"By whom? By God. Who but God can forgive us?"

Lavretsky seized her hand.

"Oh, Lizaveta Mikhailovna, believe me," he exclaimed. "I've been punished enough as it is. Believe me, I've atoned for everything."

"You can't know that," said Liza in a low voice. "You're forgetting – quite recently when you were talking to me, you did not want to forgive her."

Both walked on down the avenue in silence.

"What about your daughter?" Liza asked suddenly and halted.

Lavretsky gave a start.

"Oh, don't worry. I've already sent letters to all the appropriate places. The future of my daughter, as you call… as you put it… is assured. Don't worry."

Liza smiled sadly.

"But you're right," Lavretsky went on. "What can I do with my freedom? What use is it to me?"

"When did you get this newspaper?" said Liza, not answering his question.

"The day after your visit."

"And did you not… did you not even shed a tear?"

"No. I was shocked. But what would have given rise to tears? Weep for the past? My past has been consigned to the flames!… Her misconduct did not destroy my happiness, but merely proved to me that it had never so much as existed. What was there to weep about there? But who knows? Perhaps I would have been more upset if I'd got the news two weeks earlier…"

"Two weeks?" Liza queried. "What happened in those two weeks?"

Lavretsky made no reply, but Liza suddenly reddened even more than before.

"Yes, yes, you've guessed," Lavretsky cut in sharply. "In those two weeks I learnt what a pure womanly soul means, and my past fell away from me even more."

Liza was embarrassed and quietly joined Lenochka and Shurochka in the flower bed.

"And I'm glad that I showed you the newspaper," said Lavretsky, following her. "I'm already used to not hiding anything from you and hope that you will repay me by confiding in me in the same way."

"Do you really?" said Liza, pausing. "In that case I ought to have… But no! That's impossible."

"What is? Tell me, please do."

"Really, I don't think I should… However," Liza added, turning to Lavretsky with a smile, "why not be completely frank? Did you know I got a letter today?"

"From Panshin?"

"Yes, from him… How did you know?"

"He asked for your hand?"

"Yes," said Liza, looking directly and seriously into Lavretsky's eyes.

Lavretsky, in his turn, looked seriously at Liza.

"Well, and what reply did you give him?" he said finally.

"I don't know how to reply," returned Liza, unfolding and lowering her arms.

"What? You love him, don't you?"

"Yes, I like him. He seems to be a nice man."

"You said the same thing in the same terms three days ago. I want to know whether you love him with that powerful, passionate feeling which we're accustomed to call love?"

"As *you* understand it – no."

"You're not in love with him?"

"No. Is that really necessary?"

"What do you mean?"

"Mama likes him," Liza went on. "He's kind. I've nothing against him."

"You're still hesitating, however."

"Yes... and perhaps you – your words – are the reason for that. Do you remember what you said the day before yesterday? But this is weakness..."

"Oh, my child!" Lavretsky exclaimed suddenly, his voice trembling. "Don't indulge in sophistry. Don't dismiss as weakness the cry of your heart, which does not want to give itself away without love. Don't take upon yourself such terrible responsibility towards a man whom you do not love and yet to whom you wish to belong..."

"I'm not taking anything upon myself – I'm simply obeying," Liza began.

"Obey your heart: it alone will tell you the truth," Lavretsky interposed. "Experience, reason – that's all dust and ashes! Don't deprive yourself of the best, the only happiness on earth."

"Is it you saying this, Fyodor Ivanovich? You yourself married for love – and were you happy?"

Lavretsky wrung his hands.

"Oh, don't talk about me! You can't begin to understand everything that a callow young boy, grotesquely ill-educated, can take to be love!... However, why should I speak ill of myself? I told you just now that I have not known happiness... but no, I have been happy!"

"It seems to me, Fyodor Ivanovich," said Liza, lowering her voice (when she did not agree with her interlocutor, she always lowered her voice; besides, she was in a state of great excitement), "that happiness on earth does not depend on us..."

"Believe me, it does, it does" – he seized both her hands; Liza turned pale and gazed at him with a mixture of fear and attention – "provided we have not spoilt our lives ourselves. For some people a marriage based on love can be a misfortune, but not for you, with your placid temperament and clear soul! I beg you, don't marry without love, out of a feeling of duty or renunciation or some such... That would show lack of faith, mercenariness – and worse. Believe me – I have the right to say this: I've paid dearly for that right. And if your God..."

At that moment Lavretsky noticed that Lenochka and Shurochka were standing beside Liza and staring at him with dumb incomprehension. Releasing Liza's hands, he said hastily: "Please forgive me," and set off towards the house.

"I just have one thing to ask of you," he said, coming back to Liza. "Don't decide at once. Wait, think about what I've told you. Even if you don't believe me, even if you decide to marry for money – even then don't marry Mr Panshin: he cannot be your husband... Will you promise me not to hurry?"

Liza tried to answer Lavretsky – and said not a word, not because she had decided to "hurry", but because her heart was beating too strongly within her and a feeling akin to terror had taken her breath away.

30

As he left the Kalitins, Lavretsky met Panshin; they bowed coldly to each other. Lavretsky arrived back at his rooms and locked the door. He was experiencing feelings which he had scarcely experienced before. Was it so long ago that he had been in a state of "peaceful torpor"? Was it so long ago that he had felt himself to be, as he put it, at the very bottom of the river? What had changed his situation? What had brought him up to the surface? The most banal, inevitable, though always unexpected, of happenstances: death? Yes, but he was not so much thinking about the death of his wife or about his freedom as about the answer Liza would give to Panshin. He felt that in the course of the last three days he had begun to regard her with different eyes; he recalled how, on returning home and thinking about her in he still of the night, he had said to himself: "If only!..." That "if only", which in his mind had applied to the past, to the inconceivable, had come to pass, although not in the way he had expected – but his freedom alone was not enough. "She will obey her mother," he thought, "and marry Panshin; but even if she does refuse him – isn't it all the same to me?" As he passed in front of the mirror, he caught a glimpse of his face and shrugged his shoulders.

The day went by quickly in such thoughts; evening came on. Lavretsky set off to the Kalitins. He walked briskly, but, as he approached their house, his pace slackened. Panshin's droshky was standing in front of the entrance porch. "Well," thought Lavretsky, "I won't be an egoist," and thereupon entered the house. He met no one inside and all was quiet in the drawing room; he opened the door and saw Marya Dmitriyevna playing piquet with Panshin. Panshin bowed to him without speaking, and the mistress of the house exclaimed: "This is an unexpected pleasure!" and knitted her brows slightly. Lavretsky sat down beside her and began to examine her cards.

"Do you know how to play piquet?" she asked him, with scarcely concealed irritation, then announced that she had discarded.

Panshin had scored ninety and, politely and calmly, began to take tricks, with a grave and dignified expression on his face. Thus diplomats should play and thus he probably had played with some powerful magnate in Petersburg, in whom he wanted to inculcate a favourable impression of his reliability and maturity. "A hundred and one, a hundred and two, hearts, a hundred and three," came the measured tones of his voice, and Lavretsky could not make out whether it sounded reproachful or self-satisfied.

"May I see Marfa Timofeyevna?" he asked, noticing that Panshin had begun shuffling the cards with an even greater air of importance; there was not a trace of the artist in him now.

"I think so, yes. She's in her room, upstairs," replied Marya Dmitriyevna. "Go and enquire."

Lavretsky went upstairs and also found Marfa Timofeyevna playing cards: she was playing old maid with Nastasya Karpovna. Roska began to bark at him, but the two old ladies received him cordially; Marfa Timofeyevna in particular seemed in a good mood.

"Ah, Fedya! Come and sit down, my dear," she said. "We'll be finished in a minute. Would you like some jam? Shurochka, go and fetch the jar of strawberry jam for him. You don't want any? All right then, just sit there; but don't you go and smoke now: I can't stand that strong tobacco of yours and it makes Matros sneeze."

Lavretsky hastily made clear that he had no desire to smoke.

"Were you downstairs?" the old lady went on. "Who did you see there? Is Panshin still hanging about there? Did you see Liza? You didn't? She wanted to come up here... But here she is: talk of the devil."

Liza came into the room and, on seeing Lavretsky, blushed.

"I've come to see you for a minute, Marfa Timofeyevna..." she began.

"Why for a minute?" retorted the old lady. "Why are all you young girls so unable to settle? As you can see, I have a guest: have a chinwag with him, keep him entertained."

Liza sat down on the edge of a chair, raised her eyes to Lavretsky – and felt that she could not fail to let him know how her meeting with Panshin had finished. But how was she to do it? She felt both ashamed and awkward. It was no time since she had got to know this man who rarely went to church and who took the death of his wife so unconcernedly – and here she was confiding her secrets to him... Admittedly he was taking an interest in her; she trusted him and felt attracted to him; but all the same she felt ashamed, as if a man, a stranger, had entered her chaste, virginal room.

Marfa Timofeyevna came to her aid.

"If you won't keep him entertained," she said, "who will entertain the poor man? I'm too old for him, he's too intelligent for me and he's too old for Nastasya Karpovna: she only likes youngsters."

"How can I keep Fyodor Ivanovich entertained?" said Liza. "If he likes, I could play something for him on the piano," she added hesitantly.

"Splendid – clever girl," Marfa Timofeyevna replied. "Go downstairs, my dears; when you've finished, come back. I've lost this game, and that hurts, so I want to recoup my losses."

Liza stood up. Lavretsky followed her. As they were going downstairs, Liza paused.

"It's true what they say, that the human heart is full of contradictions. Your example should frighten me, should make me distrustful of marrying for love, but I—"

"Did you refuse him?" Lavretsky interrupted.

"No, but I didn't consent either. I told him everything, everything I felt, and asked him to wait. Are you satisfied?" she added with a quick smile and, placing her hand lightly on the banisters, ran downstairs.

"What shall I play for you?" she asked, raising the lid of the piano.

"Whatever you like," Lavretsky replied, taking a seat in such a way that he could watch her.

Liza began to play, and for a long time she did not take her eyes off her fingers. Finally, she glanced at Lavretsky and paused: his face looked so strange and wonderful to her.

"What's the matter?" she asked.

"Nothing," he replied, "I'm fine. I'm glad for you, I'm glad to see you. Do go on."

"It seems to me," said Liza a few moments later, "that if he really loved me, he wouldn't have written that letter: he should have sensed that I couldn't answer him now."

"That's not important," said Lavretsky. "The important thing is that you don't love him."

"Stop it! What are you saying? I keep seeing your late wife in my mind and you terrify me."

"How charmingly my Lisette plays, doesn't she, Woldemar?" Marya Dmitriyevna was saying to Panshin at the same time.

"Yes," replied Panshin, "very charmingly."

Marya Dmitriyevna shot a tender look at her young playing partner, but he assumed an even more important and preoccupied aspect and declared a quatorze of kings.

31

LAVRETSKY WAS NOT A YOUNG MAN; he did not deceive himself for long about the feeling instilled in him by Liza: that very day he became totally convinced that he loved her. This conviction did not bring him much joy. "Can it be," he thought, "that at thirty-five I've nothing better to do than to give my heart to a woman? But *that woman* was not the equal of Liza: Liza would not demand shameful sacrifices of me and would not distract me from my studies. She would inspire me to honest hard work, and we would both go forward towards a noble aim. "Yes," he said, concluding his reflections, "that's all very well, but the trouble is she does not want to go with me. Not for nothing did she say I terrified her. On the other hand she doesn't love Panshin either. Cold comfort!"

Lavretsky drove to Vasilyevskoye, but so boring did it seem to him that he spent less than four days there. He was also tormented by suspense: the news communicated by Monsieur Jules required confirmation, but he had not received any letters. He returned to town and passed the evening at the Kalitins. He had no difficulty in seeing that Marya Dmitriyevna was unfavourably disposed towards him, but he managed to propitiate her somewhat by losing some fifteen roubles to her at piquet, and he spent about half an hour almost alone with Liza, despite the fact that the previous evening her mother had advised her not to be too familiar with a man "*qui a un si grand ridicule*."* He detected a change in her: she appeared to have become more pensive, reproached him for his absence and asked him whether he would come to church the next day, the next day being Sunday.

"Do come," she said, before he had had time to answer. "We will pray together for the repose of *her* soul." Then she added that she did not know what to do, did not know whether she had the right to make Panshin wait any longer for her decision.

"Why so?" enquired Lavretsky.

"Because I'm already beginning to suspect what that decision will be," she said.

She announced that she had a headache and, tentatively offering Lavretsky the tips of her fingers, went upstairs to her room.

The next day Lavretsky went to church. Liza was already there when he arrived. She noticed him, although she did not turn towards him. She was praying fervently. He felt that she was praying for him, and his soul was filled with wonderfully tender emotion. He felt both happy and somewhat ashamed. The congregation standing reverently, the familiar faces, the harmonious singing, the smell of incense, the long slanting rays of sunlight from the windows, the very darkness of the walls and vaulted roof – everything spoke to his heart. He had not been in a church for a long time, had not turned to God for a long time; even now he did not utter any words of prayer, did not even pray wordlessly, although for a moment, if not with his body, then with his whole mind, he fell to his knees and humbly prostrated himself. He remembered how, every time he went to church in his childhood he would pray until he felt a kind of fresh touch upon his brow; at the time he thought it was his guardian angel receiving him and marking him as one of the anointed. He glanced at Liza... "You brought me here," he thought, "touch me, touch my soul." She was still praying quietly; her face seemed joyful to him and he again softened and asked for peace for another's soul and forgiveness for his own.

They met at the entrance to the church; she greeted him with cheerful and affectionate seriousness. The sun shone brightly on the young grass in the square in front of the church and on the colourful dresses and kerchiefs of the women. The bells of neighbouring churches boomed on high; sparrows twittered on fences. Lavretsky stood bareheaded and smiling; a light breeze ruffled his hair and the ends of the ribbons on Liza's hat. He sat Liza and Lenochka, who had come with her, in their carriage, gave all the money he had on him to beggars and quietly made his way home.

32

DIFFICULT DAYS FOLLOWED for Fyodor Ivanovich. He went about in a constant fever. Every morning he went to the post office and excitedly opened letters and newspapers: he found nothing anywhere to confirm or refute the fateful rumour. Sometimes he loathed himself: "What am I doing," he thought, "waiting for an accurate report of the death of my wife, like a raven waiting for blood!" He went to the Kalitins every day, but even there things were no easier for him. The lady of the house was clearly annoyed with him and was merely humouring him by receiving him. Panshin behaved with exaggerated politeness towards him; Lemm had taken on a misanthropic air and barely acknowledged him. Most important of all, Liza appeared to be avoiding him. Whenever she happened to find herself alone with him, she manifested, in place of her former confidence, embarrassment; she did not know what to say to him and he himself felt discomfited. In a few days Liza had become someone he did not recognize: her movements, her voice, even her laughter showed signs of hidden anxiety and an erraticism of behaviour not previously apparent. Being a true egotist, Marya Dmitriyevna suspected nothing, but Marfa Timofeyevna was beginning to keep a close eye on her favourite. Several times Lavretsky reproached himself for showing her the newspaper he had received: he was forced to admit that in his spiritual condition there was something utterly inimical to pure feeling. He supposed too that the change in Liza arose from her struggle with herself, from her doubts over the answer she should give to Panshin. Once she brought back a book, a Walter Scott novel,* which she herself had asked him for.

"Have you read this book?" he said.

"No. I'm not in the mood for books just now," she replied, making to leave.

"Wait a minute: I haven't been alone with you for so long. It's as if you're afraid of me."

"Yes, I am."

"Why, for Heaven's sake?"

"I don't know."

Lavretsky said nothing.

"Tell me," he began, "have you not decided yet?"

"What do you mean?" she said, not raising her eyes.

"You know what I mean."

Liza suddenly flared up.

"Don't ask me about anything," she said animatedly. "I don't know anything; I don't know my own mind."

And she left the room at once.

The next day Lavretsky arrived at the Kalitins after dinner and found everything being readied for a vigil service. In a corner of the dining room, on a rectangular table covered with a clean cloth, there were, leaning against the wall, small icons in gold frames with small, lustreless diamonds in the haloes. An old servant in shoes and a grey dress coat glided unhurriedly across the room, placed two wax candles in slim candleholders in front of the icons, crossed himself, bowed and quietly withdrew. The unlit drawing room was empty. Lavretsky made his way into the dining room and asked whether it was someone's name day. The whispered reply was no: the vigil had been ordered by Lizaveta Mikhailovna and Marfa Timofeyevna; they had wanted to a miracle-working icon to be carried in procession, but it had been taken to a sick man twenty miles away. Soon the priest arrived with his acolytes: he was not a young man, had a large bald patch and coughed loudly in the entrance hall; the ladies immediately filed out of the study and went up to him for his blessing. Lavretsky bowed to them in silence; they did likewise to him. The priest waited for a moment, again cleared his throat, then asked in a whispered bass voice:

"Do you wish me to begin?"

"Please begin, Father," replied Marya Dmitriyevna.

The priest began to robe; an acolyte wearing an alb asked obsequiously for a hot ember; the smell of incense arose. Maids and footmen trooped out of the entrance hall and halted in a solid phalanx in front of the doors. Roska, who had never been downstairs before, suddenly appeared in the dining room: they began to chase her out – she took fright, spun round and sat down; a footman scooped her up and took her out. The vigil service began. Lavretsky ensconced himself in a corner. His feelings were strange, almost sad. He himself could not make out very well what he felt. Marya Dmitriyevna stood in front of everyone and in front of the armchairs: she was crossing herself in ladylike fashion, elegantly and nonchalantly – now looking about her, now gazing upwards: she was bored. Marfa Timofeyevna seemed preoccupied; Nastasya Karpovna was falling to her knees and bowing her head to the ground, then rising to her feet with a kind of discreet, subdued sound. Liza did not move from the spot where she stood and did not move a muscle; from the concentrated expression on her face one could deduce that she was praying intently and fervently. When, at the end of the vigil service, the cross was placed to her lips, she also kissed the priest's big red hand. Marya Dmitriyevna invited the priest to take tea: he took off his stole, assumed a somewhat worldly air and, together with the ladies, moved into the drawing room. A not particularly animated conversation began. The priest drank four cups of tea, constantly mopping his bald patch the while, and told, among other things, of how the merchant Avoshnikov had donated seven hundred roubles towards gilding the church "cumpola" and shared with everyone an infallible remedy for freckles. Lavretsky was about to sit next to Liza, but she maintained an austere, almost severe air and did not look at him once. She seemed to be deliberately not noticing him; she was possessed by a kind of cold, solemn elatedness. For some reason Lavretsky kept wanting to smile and say something amusing; but he was inwardly perplexed and so ended by withdrawing in secret bewilderment… He felt there was a corner of Liza's soul which was barred to him.

On another occasion, Lavretsky, sitting in the drawing room and listening to Gedeonovsky's wheedling but weighty harangues, suddenly, and without knowing why, turned and caught a profound, attentive, questioning look in Liza's eyes… This enigmatic gaze was directed at him. Lavretsky later thought about it the whole night through. He was not like a boy in love – sighing and longing did not suit him, nor did Liza arouse that sort of feeling in him – but love at any age brings with it suffering – and he experienced suffering to the full.

33

ONCE, AS WAS HIS CUSTOM, Lavretsky was at the Kalitins. A hot, enervating day had been followed by such a splendid evening that Marya Dmitriyevna, despite her loathing of draughts, ordered all the windows and doors giving onto the garden to be opened and announced that she wouldn't be playing cards, that it was a crying shame to play cards in such weather and that one should enjoy nature. Only Panshin remained of the guests. Under the influence of the evening and reluctant to sing in front of Lavretsky but feeling an access of artistic feelings, he launched into poetry. He read well, but too deliberately and with unnecessary refinement, several poems by Lermontov (at that time Pushkin had not yet become fashionable), then suddenly, as if ashamed of his effusions, apropos of the well-known 'Meditation',* to excoriate the modern generation, not missing the opportunity meanwhile to set out how he would do things his way if he had the power. "Russia," he said, "lags behind Europe: she must catch up. It is asserted that we are young – that's rubbish and, besides, we lack inventiveness. Khomyakov* himself admits that we didn't even invent the mousetrap. Consequently we are forced willy-nilly to borrow from other people. We are sick, says Lermontov, and I agree with him; but we are sick, because we have only become half European; we must use what damaged us to cure ourselves." ("*Le cadastre*," thought Lavretsky). "The best brains – *les meilleures têtes* – among us have long been convinced of this: all peoples are essentially the same; merely introduce good institutions and the matter is settled. Certainly one may make some allowance for the existing way of life of a people – that is our business, the business of state functionaries" – he almost said statesmen – "but, in case of need, don't worry: the institutions will refashion the way of life." Marya Dmitriyevna warmly supported Panshin. "Look what a clever man I have talking in my house," she thought. Liza, leaning back against the window, said nothing; Lavretsky also said nothing; Marfa Timofeyevna, playing cards in the corner with her friend, muttered quietly to herself. Panshin paced the room and spoke eloquently, but with concealed exasperation; he seemed to be berating not an entire generation but a few people known to him. In a lilac bush in the Kalitins' garden a nightingale had made its home; its first evening notes rang out during pauses in the eloquent speech; the first stars were beginning to appear in the pink sky above the motionless tops of the lime trees. Lavretsky stood up and began to take issue with Panshin; an argument began. Lavretsky defended the youthfulness and independence of Russia: he sacrificed himself and his generation – but interceded on behalf of the new men, their desires and their convictions; Panshin made sharp and irritable rejoinders, declaring that intelligent people must refashion everything, and finally went so far as to forget both his status as a *kammerjunker* and his official career and call Lavretsky a reactionary conservative, and even to refer – admittedly very obliquely – to his false position in society. Lavretsky did not get angry or raise his voice (he recalled that Mikhalevich also called him reactionary – but a reactionary Voltairean) and calmly demolished all Panshin's points. He demonstrated the impossibility of dramatic changes or high-handed refashioning from on high by officialdom – refashioning which was not justified either by patriotic sentiment or genuine belief in an ideal, even a negative ideal; as an example he cited his own education, demanding above all recognition of and humility before the expression of popular will – humility without which courage in the face of falsehood is impossible. Finally he did not seek to refute the accusation – well deserved in his view – of having frivolously wasted time and energy.

"This is all well and good!" an exasperated Panshin exclaimed finally. "Here you are, back in Russia, so what do you intend to do?"

"Plough the land," Lavretsky replied, "and try to plough it as well as possible."

"That is undoubtedly very laudable," Panshin replied, "and I've been told that you've already made great progress in that direction. But you must agree that not everyone is capable of that kind of activity."

"*Une nature poétique*," said Marya Dmitriyevna, "cannot plough of course... *et puis*, it is your vocation, Vladimir Nikolayevich, to do everything *en grand*."*

This was too much even for Panshin: his eloquence faltered, and so too did the conversation. He tried to change the subject to the beauty of the starry sky and the music of Schubert – but the whole thing somehow lacked coherence. He ended up suggesting to Marya Dmitriyevna that they play piquet. "What! On an evening like this?" was her feeble rejoinder; however she ordered cards to be brought in.

Panshin snapped open a new pack, while Liza and Lavretsky, as if in cahoots, both stood up and stationed themselves beside Marfa Timofeyevna. Suddenly they both felt so contented that they were even afraid to stay together – yet at the same time both felt that the embarrassment felt by them in recent days had disappeared and would not return. The old woman patted Lavretsky surreptitiously on the cheek, slyly screwed up her eyes, shook her head several times and added in a whisper: "You've put one over the brainbox. Thank you." Everything fell quiet in the room; all that could be heard was the faint crackling of the wax candles, the knocking of a hand on the table, an exclamation or the adding-up of scores and, pouring through the windows in a broad torrent, together with a dewy coolness, the powerful, audaciously loud song of the nightingale.

34

LIZA HAD NOT SAID A SINGLE WORD during the quarrel between Lavretsky and Panshin, but she followed it closely and was entirely on Lavretsky's side. Politics did not interest her much, but the self-confident tone of the worldly official (he had never before expressed himself in this way) repelled her; his contempt for Russia offended her. It had never entered Liza's head that she was a patriot, but she felt at ease with Russians. The Russian mindset delighted her; she found no problem in talking for hours with the bailiff of her mother's estate when he came to town, talking to him as her equal, without any lordly condescension. Lavretsky sensed all this; he would not have spoken simply to counter Panshin's arguments: he spoke only for Liza's sake. They said nothing to each other; even their eyes rarely met; but both realized that they had grown close that evening, realized that they liked and disliked the same things. On only one point did they part company, but Liza secretly hoped to bring Lavretsky to God. They sat beside Marfa Timofeyevna and seemed to be following her game; indeed, they were following it, yet both their hearts were swelling and nothing escaped them: it was for them that the nightingale sang, the stars shone and the trees quietly whispered, lulled by sleep and the gentle warmth of summer. Lavretsky gave himself over entirely to the wave which swept over him – and rejoiced. But no words can convey what was going on in the pure soul of the girl; it was a mystery even to her and she wished it to remain a mystery to everyone else. No one knows, has seen or ever will see how a seed, summoned to life and florescence in the bosom of the earth, swells and matures.

Ten o'clock struck. Marfa Timofeyevna went upstairs to her room with Nastasya Karpovna; Lavretsky and Liza took a turn round the room, halted in front of the open door into the garden and looked first into the endless darkness and then at each other – and smiled; it seemed they would have joined hands and talked to their heart's content. They returned to Marya Dmitriyevna and Panshin, who had started a game of piquet. The last "king"* was finally completed and the mistress of the house rose, groaning and sighing, from her well-cushioned easy chair; Panshin took his hat, kissed Marya Dmitriyevna's hand, observed that nothing was preventing some lucky people from sleeping or enjoying the night, but that he would have to sit up till morning over stupid papers, bowed coldly to Liza (he had not expected that, in answer to his proposal, she would ask him to wait, and was therefore cross with her) and withdrew. Lavretsky followed him out to the gate, where they went their separate ways. Panshin woke up his coachman by prodding him in the neck with the end of his stick, climbed into his droshky and drove away. Lavretsky was unwilling to go home: he walked out of the town into the fields. The night was calm and bright, although there was no moon; for a long time Lavretsky wandered through dewy grass. Then he came across a narrow path and set off along it. It brought him to a long fence with a wicket gate in it. Without knowing why, he tried to force it: it creaked faintly and opened, as if it had anticipated the touch of his hand. Lavretsky found himself in a garden; he took a few steps along a lime-tree avenue and suddenly halted in astonishment: he had recognized the Kalitins' garden.

He immediately sought a dark patch of shade thrown by a thick hazelnut bush and for a long time stood motionless and in wonderment, shrugging his shoulders.

"There's a reason for this," he thought.

All around everything was quiet; from the direction of the house there came not a sound. He went carefully forward. There, at a bend in the avenue, the whole house suddenly presented its dark façade to him; a light glimmered in just two of the upstairs windows: in Liza's room a candle burned behind the white curtain; in Marfa Timofeyevna's bedroom the icon lamp flickered with a red flame before the icon and gave off an even reflection from the gold frame; downstairs the door onto the balcony gaped wide open. Lavretsky sat down on a wooden bench, rested his head on his hand and began to look at this door and at Liza's window. In the town midnight struck; in the house small clocks delicately chimed twelve; the watchman drummed his board. Lavretsky was not thinking or expecting anything: he enjoyed feeling himself to be near Liza, enjoyed sitting on a bench in her garden where she too had frequently sat... The light in Liza's room went out: "Goodnight, my dearest girl," Lavretsky whispered, continuing to sit motionless and not taking his eyes of the darkened window.

Suddenly a light appeared in one of the downstairs windows, moved to a second window, then a third... Someone was walking through the rooms with a candle. "Can it be Liza? It can't be!..." Lavretsky half-rose... There was a glimpse of a familiar figure, and Liza appeared in the drawing room. Wearing a white dress, her plaits hanging over her shoulders, she went quietly up to the table, bent over it, put her candle down and began looking for something. Then, turning her face to the garden, she approached the open door and halted on the threshold, a slight, graceful figure in white. A thrill of excitement ran through Lavretsky's veins.

"Liza!" The word escaped almost inaudibly from his lips.

She shuddered and peered into the darkness.

"Liza!" Lavretsky repeated more loudly, emerging from the shadows of the avenue. Liza raised her head in alarm and stumbled backwards: she had recognized him. He called out her name a third time and held out his hands towards her. She moved away from the door and stepped into the garden.

"Is it you?" she said. "You're here?"

"It's me... me. Hear me out," whispered Lavretsky, and, seizing her hand, he led her to the bench.

She followed him without resisting; her pale face, her fixed look and all her movements expressed ineffable bewilderment. Lavretsky seated her on the bench; he stood in front of her.

"I didn't think of coming here," he began. "Something brought me here... I... I... I love you," he said in involuntary terror.

Liza looked slowly up at him; it seemed that it was only at that moment that she understood where she was and what was happening to her. She tried to stand up, was unable to and covered her face with her hands,

"Liza," said Lavretsky. "Liza," he repeated, bowing down to her feet...

Her shoulders began to shake slightly, and she pressed the fingers of her pale hands more tightly to her face.

"What's the matter?" said Lavretsky, hearing a gentle sobbing. His heart missed a beat... He understood what these tears meant. "Do you really love me?" he whispered, and touched her knees.

"Stand up," came her voice. "Stand up, Fyodor Ivanovich. What are we doing?"

He stood up and sat down beside her on the bench. She was no longer crying, but was looking at him attentively with her moist eyes.

"I'm afraid – what are we doing?" she repeated.

"I love you," he said again, "and am ready to devote my whole life to you."

She again shuddered, as if she had been stung, then raised her eyes heavenwards.

"It's all in the hands of God," she said.

"But you do love me, Liza? We will be happy, won't we?"

She lowered her eyes; he gently drew her to himself until her head rested on his shoulder... He moved his head away a little and touched her pale lips.

* * *

CHAPTER 34

Half an hour later, Lavretsky was already standing in front of the wicket gate. He found it locked and was forced to jump over the fence. He returned to the town and walked through its sleeping streets. A feeling of great and unexpected joy filled his soul – all his doubts had ceased. "Be gone, dark spectre of my past," he thought. "She loves me; she will be mine." Suddenly he fancied that some sort of wonderful, exultant sounds had poured forth in the air above his head. He paused: the sounds rang out even more magnificently, streaming in a powerful torrent of melody, in which it seemed all his happiness spoke and sang. He looked round: the sounds were coming from the two upper windows of a small house.

"Lemm!" Lavretsky yelled, and ran to the house. "Lemm! Lemm!" he repeated loudly.

The sounds stopped and the figure of the old man, bare-chested and wearing a dressing gown, appeared in the window.

"Aha!" he said with dignity. "Is that you?"

"Khristofor Fyodorovich, what marvellous music that is! For Heaven's sake let me in."

The old man, without saying a word but with a majestic wave of the hand, threw the key to the door into the street. Lavretsky hurried upstairs, entered the room and was about to embrace Lemm. The latter, however, peremptorily indicated a chair and said in his halting Russian: "Please to sit down and listen this." He sat down at the piano, looked proudly and sternly about him and began to play. It was a long time since Lavretsky had heard anything like it: the sweet passionate melody gripped his heart from the first note; it was full of light, full of languorous inspiration, happiness and beauty; it swelled and died away; it touched on everything dear, everything mysterious, everything holy on earth; it emanated immortal sorrow and rose heavenwards to die. Lavretsky straightened and stood, pale and frozen with delight. These sounds bored right into his soul, so recently shaken by the happiness of love; they themselves were ablaze with love. "Play it again," he whispered as soon as the last chord had sounded. The old man cast an aquiline look at him, thumped his chest and said unhurriedly in his native tongue: "I have done this, for I am a great musician," and again played his marvellous composition. There were no candles in the room; light from the newly risen moon fell obliquely through the windows; the sentient air vibrated resonantly; the wretched little room seemed a sanctum and the old man's head rose, high and inspired, in the silvery half-light. Lavretsky went up to him and embraced him. Lemm did not respond to his embrace and even fended him off with his elbow; for a long time, not moving a muscle, he went on looking as sternly, almost rudely, as before; only a couple of times did he grunt: "Aha!" At last his transformed features mellowed, relaxed and, in answer to Lavretsky's warm congratulations, he first gave a little smile, then burst into tears, sobbing quietly, like a child.

"It's surprising," he said, "that you should have come at this precise time, but I know, I know everything."

"You know everything?" said Lavretsky in embarrassment.

"You heard me," replied Lemm. "Surely you realize that I know everything."

Lavretsky could not get to sleep before morning: he sat up all night on his bed. Liza too did not sleep: she was praying.

35

THE READER KNOWS HOW Lavretsky grew up and developed; let us say a few words about Liza's upbringing. She was ten when her father died, but he had taken little interest in her. Inundated with business affairs, constantly preoccupied with increasing his capital, bilious, acerbic and impatient, he lavished money on teachers and governors, on clothes and other needs of children; but he could not stand, as he put it, "fussing over squalling kids" – and in any case he had no time to fuss over them: he worked, wrestled with his business affairs, slept little, occasionally played cards and again worked. He compared himself to a horse harnessed to a threshing machine. "My life has slipped past a bit quick," he said on his deathbed, a bitter smile on his parched lips. Marya Dmitriyevna did not, in essence, take much more interest in Liza than her husband, although she boasted to Lavretsky that she had raised her children alone; she dressed her up like a doll, stroked her head when guests were present and to her face called her a clever girl and a darling – and that was all. Any sort of constant care wearied the lady of leisure. During her father's lifetime Liza was in the hands of a governess, Mademoiselle Moreau from Paris, but after his death she passed into the care of Marfa Timofeyevna. The reader knows Marfa Timofeyevna; Mademoiselle Moreau was a tiny, wrinkled creature with birdlike ways and a bird brain. In her youth she had led a very dissipated life, but in her old age she had retained only two passions – sweetmeats and cards. When she had eaten enough, was not playing cards and not chattering, her face took on an almost deathlike expression: she would sit, look, breathe – and yet it was clear that she did not have a single thought in her head. Nor could she be termed kind-hearted – birds are not usually kind. Whether as a consequence of her misspent youth, or of the Paris air which she had inhaled deeply since childhood – there dwelt in her something akin to tawdry universal scepticism which usually expressed itself in the words: "*Tout ça c'est des bêtises*."* She spoke incorrect French, but pure Parisian jargon, did not retail gossip and was not capricious – what more could one wish for from a governess? She had little influence on Liza; the influence on her of her nanny Agafya Vlasyevna was all the greater because of this.

This woman's story was remarkable. She came from a peasant family. At the age of sixteen she was married off to a muzhik. However, she was very different from her peasant sisters. Her father was the village elder for some twenty years, made a great deal of money and spoilt her. She was exceptionally beautiful, was the most elegant dresser in the whole district, was bright, articulate and bold. Her master, Dmitry Pestov, Marya Dmitriyevna's father, a quiet, modest man, saw her one day on the threshing floor, spoke to her and fell passionately in love with her. She was soon widowed; although he too was married, Pestov took her into his house and dressed her like a household serf. Agafya immediately adapted to her new situation, as if she had lived that way all her life. She grew pale and filled out; beneath her muslin sleeves her arms became "floury white" like those of a lady from the merchant class. The samovar never left the table; she would wear nothing apart from silk and velvet and would sleep on feather beds. This idyllic life went on for some five years, but then Dmitry Pestov died; his widow, a kind-hearted lady, out of respect for her late husband, did not want to behave dishonourably towards her rival, especially since Agafya had never forgotten herself in her presence. However, she got rid of her by marrying her off to a cowherd. Some three years passed. One hot summer's day the mistress paid a visit to her cattle yard. Agafya regaled her with such splendid cold cream, behaved so modestly and was herself so well turned out, happy and content with everything that her mistress declared her forgiven and allowed her back into the house; some six months later she had become so attached to her that she promoted her to housekeeper and entrusted the entire household to her. Agafya again came into her own, again grew plump and white-skinned; the mistress had full confidence in her. Thus another five years or so passed. Misfortune twice descended on Agafya. Her husband, whom she had made a footman, began to drink and to absent himself from the house and ended up by stealing six of the mistress's silver spoons and hiding them, for the time being, in his wife's trunk. The theft was discovered. He was sent back to the cattle yard, and Agafya suffered the indignity, not of being dismissed but of being demoted from housekeeper to seamstress and ordered to wear a kerchief instead of a mob cap. To everyone's surprise Agafya accepted this reversal with meek humility. She was already over thirty, her children had all died and her husband did not live long. It was time for her to take stock of her situation and she did so. She became very taciturn and devout, did not miss a single service of matins or vespers and gave away all her fine dresses. For fifteen years she lived quietly, humbly, moderately, arguing with no one, yielding to everyone. If anyone was rude to her, she would merely bow and thank them for teaching her a lesson. The mistress had long since forgiven her, restored her to her good graces and given her a mob cap from her own head; she, however, did not want to take off her kerchief and continued to go about in a dark-coloured dress. After the death of her mistress she became even more placid and humble. Russians are easily scared and easily make attachments, but to gain their respect is difficult: it is not quickly given and not to everyone. Everyone in the house very much respected Agafya; no one mentioned her former sins, as if they had been buried in the earth together with the old master.

Once he had become Marya Dmitriyevna's husband, Kalitin wanted to hand over the running of the household to Agafya, but she refused "on account of temptation". He shouted at her; she bowed low and went out. Kalitin was an intelligent man and understood people; he understood Agafya too and did not forget her. When he moved to the town, he installed her, with her agreement, as nanny to Liza, who was just five.

At first Liza was frightened by the serious and stern face of the new nanny, but she soon got used to her and became extremely fond of her. She herself was a serious child – her features recalled Kalitin's angular and regular profile; only her eyes were not her father's: they shone with a calm attentiveness and goodness which is rare in children. She did not like playing with dolls, did not laugh loudly or at length and behaved properly. She was not one for reflecting deeply, but when she did, it was always to some purpose: after remaining silent for a time she would usually end up by turning to someone older than herself with a question which showed that her brain had been at work on some new impression. She soon got over childish mispronunciations and before she was four was speaking absolutely clearly. She was afraid of her father; her feelings towards her mother was difficult to define – she was not afraid of her but nor did she warm to her; however, she did not warm to Agafya either, although she was the only one she loved. Agafya and she were inseparable. They made an odd couple. Sometimes Agafya, all dressed in black, with a dark-coloured kerchief on her head, her face thin and transparent as wax, but still beautiful and expressive, would be sitting bolt upright, knitting a stocking; at her feet, on a little armchair, would sit Liza, also doing some sort of work or listening, her bright eyes upraised, to the stories Agafya told her. Agafya told her not fairy tales but, in a measured, level voice, the Life of the Virgin most Pure, and the lives of hermits, saints and holy women martyrs. She would tell Liza how the saints lived in the wilderness, how they were saved, how they endured hunger and privation – and did not fear monarchs, how they proclaimed Christ, how the birds of the air brought them food and how the beasts obeyed them; how, in the places where their blood fell, flowers grew up. "Wallflowers?" Liza, who was very fond of flowers, asked on one occasion… Agafya spoke to Liza very seriously and humbly, as if she felt it was not for her to utter such high-flown and holy words. Liza listened to her – and the image of an omnipresent and omniscient God permeated her soul with a certain sweet power, filling her with pure, reverential fear, while Christ became for her something close, familiar, almost kindred. Agafya also taught her how to pray. Sometimes she would wake Liza up at dawn, quickly get her dressed and take her secretly to matins. Liza would follow her on tiptoe, scarcely breathing. The cold and half-light of the morning, the chill and the emptiness of the church, the very mysteriousness of all these unexpected sorties, the cautious return home and back to bed – this whole mixture of the forbidden, the strange and the sacred – had a profound effect on the little girl and penetrated the very depths of her being. Agafya never passed judgement on anyone and never scolded Liza for getting into mischief. When she was displeased about something, she simply kept silent, and Liza understood this silence. With the quick perceptiveness of a child, she understood equally well when Agafya was displeased with other people – with Marya Dmitriyevna or with Kalitin himself. For just over three years, Agafya looked after Liza. She was succeeded by Mademoiselle Moreau, but the frivolous French woman, with her dry ways and her exclamations of "*Tout ça c'est des bêtises*", could not drive out her beloved nanny from Liza's heart: the seeds sown had put down roots that were too deep. Moreover, although Agafya had stopped looking after Liza, she remained in the house and often saw her young charge, who trusted her the same as ever.

Agafya, however, did not get on with Marfa Timofeyevna when she moved into the Kalitin house. The impatient and self-willed old lady did not like the stern solemnity of the former "peasant woman". Agafya asked permission to go on a pilgrimage and did not return. There were dark rumours that she had gone into an Old Believer monastery.* But the trace left by her in Liza's soul was not erased. As before, she went to communion as if she were going to a festival, took pleasure in praying with a kind of restrained and shy burst of enthusiasm, which was a source of no little surprise to Marya Dmitriyevna. Marfa Timofeyevna too, although not constraining Liza in any way, nevertheless tried to moderate her zeal and did not allow her to fall to her knees and bow her head to the ground: "Not an aristocratic habit," she said. Liza was a good, that is to say assiduous pupil; God had not endowed her with particularly brilliant abilities or a great mind. She achieved nothing without hard work. She played the piano well, but only Lemm knew how much effort this had cost her. She was not a great reader, nor did she have "her own words". She did have her own ideas and a firmly set path. Not for nothing did she resemble her father: he too did not ask other people what he should do. So she grew up – tranquilly and unhurriedly – and had now reached the age of nineteen. She was very attractive, without realizing it. Her every movement betrayed an involuntary, somewhat awkward gracefulness; her voice had the silvery ring of inviolate youth; the slightest pleasurable sensation brought a winning smile to her lips and gave a deep lustre and a certain secret affectionateness to her luminous eyes. Totally imbued with a sense of duty and a fear of offending anyone, with a kind and gentle heart, she loved everyone, and no one in particular; she loved God alone, ecstatically, timidly, tenderly. Lavretsky was the first to disrupt her calm inner life.

Such was Liza.

36

THE NEXT DAY, SOON AFTER NOON, Lavretsky set off for the Kalitins. On the way he encountered Panshin, who galloped past him on horseback, his hat pulled right down over his eyebrows. At the Kalitins, for the first time since he had made their acquaintance, Lavretsky was not received. Marya Dmitriyevna was "having a snooze", so the footman reported: "Her Ladyship" had a headache. Marfa Timofeyevna and Lizaveta Mikhailovna were not at home. Lavretsky went for a walk round the garden in the vague hope of meeting Liza, but saw no one. He returned two hours later and received the same answer, in addition to which the footman gave him a kind of oblique look. Lavretsky felt it was unseemly to enquire three times on the same day, so decided to make a quick visit to Vasilyevskoye, where he had business to attend to in any case. On the way there he drew up various plans, each one more elaborate than the next. However, when he got to his aunt's village, gloom descended on him. He fell into conversation with Anton; the old man seemed deliberately to have nothing but dismal thoughts on his mind. He told Lavretsky how, before her death, Glafira Petrovna had bitten her own hand; after a pause, he said with a sigh: "Every human, sir, is committed to devouring itself." It was already late when Lavretsky set off on his return journey. The sounds of the previous day took hold of him and the image of Liza arose in his soul in all its meek clarity; he was deeply affected by the thought that she loved him – and drove up to his town house in a calm and happy frame of mind.

The first thing that struck him on coming into the entrance hall was the smell of patchouli, which he loathed; there too stood several tall trunks and travel bags. The face of his valet, who came hastily out to meet him, seemed strange. Taking no account of his impressions, he crossed the threshold of the drawing room... A lady rose from the sofa to greet him; she was wearing a black silk dress with flounces and, raising a cambric handkerchief to her pale face, she took a few steps forward, bowed her carefully coiffed and perfumed head – and fell at his feet... Only then did he recognize her: the lady was his wife.

This took Lavretsky's breath away... He leant against the wall.

"Théodore, don't send me away!" she said in French, and her voice cut like a knife through his heart.

He looked at her uncomprehendingly and yet could not help noticing that she had become both pale and stout.

"Théodore," she continued, occasionally raising her eyes and carefully twisting her surprisingly beautiful fingers with their polished pink nails, "Théodore, I am guilty before you, deeply guilty. More than that, I'm criminally guilty. But hear me out. I'm tormented by remorse; I've become a burden to myself; I could not bear my situation any longer. How many times I've thought of turning to you, but I feared your anger. I've decided to sever all links with the past... *puis j'ai été si malade* – I've been so ill," she added, running her hand across her forehead and cheek, "that I took advantage of the rumour about my death and abandoned everything. Day and night I hurried here non-stop; for a long time I hesitated to appear before you, my judge – *paraître devant vous, mon juge* – but I finally made up my mind to come and see you, remembering how kind you've always been. In Moscow I found out your address. Believe me," she went on, quietly rising from the floor and seating herself on the very edge of an armchair, "I've often thought of death, and I would have found enough courage in me to take my own life – life is now an unbearable burden for me – but the thought of my daughter, my little Adochka,* prevented me. She's here, asleep in the next room, poor child! She's tired. You'll see her. She at least is not guilty before you, but I am so unhappy, so unhappy," cried Madame Lavretsky, bursting into floods of tears.

CHAPTER 36

Lavretsky finally collected himself; he moved away from the wall and turned towards the door.

"Are you leaving?" said his wife in desperation. "Oh, that's cruel! Without saying a single word to me, not even a reproach... This contempt is killing me. It's terrible!"

Lavretsky stopped.

"What do you want to hear from me?" he said in a toneless voice.

"Nothing, nothing," she replied animatedly. "I know I have no right to demand anything – believe me, I'm in my right mind. I don't hope – I don't dare hope – for your forgiveness; I only make so bold as to ask you to order me what to do and where to live. Like a slave I will carry out your order, whatever it may be."

"I've no orders to give you," Lavretsky returned in the same voice. "You know that everything's finished between us... now more than ever. You may live where you like – and if your pension isn't enough—"

"Oh, don't say such horrible things," Varvara Pavlovna interrupted. "Have pity on me, if only... if only for the sake of this angel..." And, so saying, Varvara Pavlovna rushed out headlong into another room and immediately returned with a small, elegantly dressed little girl in her arms. Thick light-brown curls fell round a pretty rosy little face and large black sleepy eyes; she was both smiling and half-closing her eyes against the light and had one chubby arm round her mother's neck.

"*Ada, vois, c'est ton père*,"* said Varvara Pavlovna, pushing the curls from the child's eyes and giving her a big kiss. "*Prie-le avec moi.*"*

"*C'est ça papa*?"* said the little girl in a childish lisp.

"*Oui, mon enfant, n'est-ce pas que tu l'aimes*?"*

But this had all become too much for Lavretsky.

"In what melodrama is there just such a scene as this?" he muttered and went out.

Varvara Pavlovna stood where she was for some time, then, with a slight shrug of the shoulders, took the little girl off to another room, undressed her and put her to bed. Then she got out a book, sat down by the lamp, waited about an hour and finally went to bed herself.

"*Eh bien, madame*?" asked her French maid, brought in by her from Paris, as she unlaced her stays.

"*Eh bien, Justine*," she replied, "he's aged a lot, but I think he's as kind as ever. Give me my gloves for the night and lay out my high-necked grey dress for tomorrow – and don't forget the lamb chop for Ada... I admit they're difficult to find here, but we must try."

"*À la guerre comme à la guerre*,"* replied Justine, and extinguished the candle.

37

FOR MORE THAN TWO HOURS Lavretsky wandered the streets of the town. The memory of the night spent in the suburbs of Paris came to his mind. His heart was breaking, and in his brain, blank and seemingly stunned, the same dark, ugly, evil thoughts revolved. "She's alive; she's here," he whispered with a constantly growing sense of bemusement. He felt that he had lost Liza. He was choked with bile: the blow had been too sudden. How could he have believed the idle chit-chat of a newspaper sketch, a scrap of paper? "Well, if I hadn't believed it," he thought, "what difference would it have made? I would not have known that Liza loved me; she herself would not have known it." He could not drive the image of his wife, her voice, her eyes, out of his mind… and cursed himself, cursed everything on earth.

Exhausted, he went to see Lemm before dawn. For a long time he could get no answer to his knocking; finally the old man's head appeared in a nightcap at a window; his sour, wrinkled face was quite unlike the austere, inspired face which, twenty-four hours previously, had looked regally down on Lavretsky from the height of its artistic grandeur.

"What do you want?" Lemm asked. "I can't play every night. I've taken a decoction."

Clearly, however, Lavretsky's face looked strange: the old man shielded his eyes with his hand, looked at his nocturnal visitor and let him in.

Lavretsky entered the room and sank down on a chair; the old man halted in front of him, wrapping his shabby coloured dressing gown around him, hunching himself up and chewing his lips.

"My wife has come back," said Lavretsky. He raised his head and suddenly burst into a fit of involuntary laughter.

Lemm's face expressed astonishment, but he did not even smile, merely wrapping himself more tightly in his dressing gown.

"Of course, you don't know," Lavretsky went on. "I imagined... I read in the newspaper that she was no longer with us."

"O-oh – did you read that recently?" Lemm asked.

"Yes."

"O-oh," the old man repeated, raising his eyebrows high. "And she's come here?"

"Yes. She's at my house now – I... I'm an unlucky man."

And he again gave a wry smile.

"You're an unlucky man," Lemm repeated slowly.

"Khristofor Fyodorovich," Lavretsky began, "will you undertake to deliver a note?"

"Hmm. May I know to whom?"

"To Lizav—"

"Yes, yes, I understand. All right. But when will I have to deliver the note?"

"Tomorrow, as early as possible."

"Hmm. I could send my cook, Catherine. No, I'll go myself."

"And you'll bring the answer back to me?"

"Yes, I will."

Lemm sighed.

"Yes, my poor young friend: you are indeed an unhappy young man."

Lavretsky wrote a quick note to Liza informing her of his wife's arrival and asking her to arrange a meeting with him. Then he threw himself onto the narrow sofa, his face to the wall, while the old man got into bed, where he tossed and turned for a long time, coughing and gulping down his decoction.

Morning came and both men got up. They directed strange looks at one another. At that moment Lavretsky wanted to kill himself. Catherine the cook brought them some dreadful coffee.

CHAPTER 37

The clock struck eight. Lemm put on his hat and, saying that he was not giving a lesson at the Kalitins until ten o'clock, but would find a suitable pretext, he set off. Lavretsky again threw himself onto the sofa and again bitter laughter welled up from the depths of his soul. He thought about how his wife had driven him out of the house; he pictured Liza's situation to himself, closed his eyes and clasped his hands behind his head. At last Lemm returned, bringing with him a scrap of paper on which Liza had pencilled the following words: "We cannot see each other today; maybe tomorrow evening. Goodbye." Lavretsky thanked Lemm drily and perfunctorily and went home.

He found his wife having breakfast; Ada, her hair in ringlets and wearing a little white dress with blue ribbons, was eating a lamb-chop. As soon as Lavretsky entered the room, Varvara Pavlovna stood up and approached him, a look of submissiveness on her face. He asked her to follow him into his study, locked the door behind him and began to pace up and down; she sat down, modestly placed one hand upon the other and proceeded to follow him with her still lovely, though slightly made-up eyes.

For a long time Lavretsky was unable to speak: he felt he was not in control of himself and saw clearly that Varvara Pavlovna was not at all afraid of him, but was pretending that she was about to faint.

"Listen, madam," he began finally, breathing heavily and occasionally clenching his teeth, "there is no point in our pretending to one another; I don't believe in your remorse and, even if it were sincere, to be reconciled with you, to live with you is impossible for me."

Varvara Pavlovna pursed her lips and narrowed her eyes. "This is revulsion," she thought. " It's all over! I'm not even a woman for him."

"Impossible," Lavretsky repeated, buttoning his coat to the top. "I don't know why you favoured me with your presence – probably because you'd run out of money."

"Alas! You insult me," Varvara Pavlovna whispered.

"Be that as it may – you're still my wife, unfortunately. I can't turn you out, so this is what I propose. You can go to Lavriki this very day, if you like, and live there; there's a very nice house there, as you know. You will receive everything you need, over and above your pension. Do you agree?"

Varvara Pavlovna raised an embroidered handkerchief to her face.

"I've already told you," she said, her lips twitching nervously, "that I'll agree to anything you think fit to do with me. On this occasion it only remains for me to ask one thing of you: will you allow me at least to thank you for your magnanimity?"

"No gratitude, please. It's better that way," Lavretsky said hastily. "So," he continued, going up to the door, "I can count on—"

"I'll be in Lavriki as soon as tomorrow," said Varvara Pavlovna, rising respectfully from her chair. "But, Fyodor Ivanovich…" (She no longer called him Théodore.)

"What do you want?"

"I know I have in no way deserved your forgiveness: can I at least hope that with time—"

"Ah, Varvara Pavlovna," Lavretsky interrupted, "you're an intelligent woman, but I am no fool either. I know that you have absolutely no need of that. I forgave you a long time ago, but there was always a gulf between us."

"I shall know how to submit," answered Varvara Pavlovna, bowing her head. "I have not forgotten my guilt. I would not have been surprised to learn that you were even pleased at the news of my death," she added meekly, indicating with a small gesture of her hand the newspaper lying on the table, forgotten by Lavretsky.

Fyodor Ivanovich shuddered: the piece in the newspaper had been marked in pencil. Varvara Pavlovna gazed at him even more abjectly. She looked very beautiful at that moment. A grey Parisian dress gracefully hugged her supple waist, the waist almost of a seventeen-year-old, her delicate soft neck, wrapped in a white collar, her bosom rising and falling evenly, her hands bereft of bracelets and rings – her whole figure, from her glossy hair to the tip of her barely visible ankle boot, was so elegant…

Lavretsky cast a malevolent glance over her, almost exclaimed: "*Brava!*" almost punched her in the head, then went out. An hour later he had already set off for Vasilyevskoye; two hours later Varvara Pavlovna had ordered the best carriage in town to be hired for her, put on a straw hat with a black veil and a modest mantilla, handed Ada over to Justine and set off to the Kalitins. As a result of questioning the servants she had ascertained that her husband went to see them every day.

38

THE DAY OF THE ARRIVAL of Lavretsky's wife in the town of O—, an unhappy day for him, was also a painful day for Liza. No sooner had she come downstairs to greet her mother when the clatter of horse's hooves sounded outside the window and, with secret trepidation, she saw Panshin ride into the yard. "He's appeared so early for a definite answer," she thought – and she was not mistaken. After spending a brief time in the drawing room, he suggested she go into the garden with him and demanded to know his fate. Liza summoned up her courage and declared that she could not be his wife. He heard her out, standing sideways on to her, his hat pulled down over his forehead. Politely, but in an altered voice, he asked her whether that was her last word and whether he had given some cause for such a change of mind in her. Then he pressed his hand to his eyes, gave a brief, convulsive sigh and withdrew his hand from his face.

"I did not want to tread a well-worn path," he said tonelessly. "I wanted to find a companion for myself according to the dictates of my heart. But, clearly, that is not going to happen. Farewell, dream!" He bowed deeply to Liza and went back into the house.

She hoped he would leave at once, but he went to the study to talk to Marya Dmitryievna and stayed there about an hour. As he left, he said to Liza: "*Votre mère vous appelle; adieu à jamais...*",* mounted his horse and galloped away from the porch at top speed. Liza went in to see Marya Dmitriyevna and found her in tears: Panshin had told her of his misfortune.

"Why have you been the death of me? Why have you been the death of me?" Thus the aggrieved widow began her complaints.

"Who else do you want? What's wrong with him as a husband for you? He's a *kammerjunker* not a fortune-hunter. In Petersburg he could marry any lady-in-waiting. I had such hopes, such hopes! Is it long since you changed your mind about him? This didn't come out of a clear blue sky. Is this to do with that ninny? A fine adviser you've found!"

"But he, my dearest," Marya Dmitriyevna went on, "how respectful he was, how attentive, in the very midst of his sorrow! He promised not to abandon me. Oh, I'll not get over this. Oh, I've got a killing headache. Send Palashka to me. You'll be the death of me if you don't think again, do you hear?" And having called her daughter an ingrate a time or two, Marya Dmitriyevna dismissed her.

Liza went to her room. But before she had time to recover from the explanations with Panshin and her mother, another storm broke over her head: it came from the direction she least expected. Marfa Timofeyevna came into her room and immediately slammed the door behind her. The old woman's face was pale, her mob cap was askew, her eyes gleamed, her hands and lips trembled. Liza was astonished: she had never seen her intelligent, rational aunt in such a state.

"This is a pretty pickle we're in, madam," Marfa Timofeyevna began in a tremulous, fitful whisper. "A pretty pickle! Who taught you to behave like this, my dear... Give me some water – I can't speak."

"Calm down, Auntie. What's the matter?" said Liza, giving her a glass of water. "After all, it seems to me you yourself didn't much take to Monsieur Panshin."

Marfa Timofeyevna put her glass to one side.

"I can't drink: I'll knock my remaining teeth out. What's Panshin got to do with it? Where does Panshin come in? You'd much better tell me, my dear, who taught you to make night-time assignations?"

Liza turned pale.

"Please don't try to talk your way out of it," Marfa Timofeyevna continued. Shurochka saw everything herself and told me. I told her not to gossip, but she doesn't lie."

"I'm not going to talk my way out of it, Auntie," said Liza, scarcely audibly.

"Aha! So that's how it is, my dear: you made an assignation with that old sinner, the wretch?"

"No."

"How did it happen then?"

"I went down to the drawing room for a book: he was in the garden – and called to me."

"And you went? How nice. Do you love him or something?"

"I love him," Liza answered in a quiet voice.

"Good Heavens! She loves him!" Marfa Timofeyevna snatched the mob cap off her head. "Does she love a married man? She does!"

"He told me..." Liza began.

"What did the dear man tell you? What was it?"

"He told me that his wife had died."

Marfa Timofeyevna crossed herself.

"God rest her soul," she whispered. "She was an empty-headed thing, so help her. So he's a widower then? I see he's losing no time. He's killed off one wife and now he's after a second. Butter wouldn't melt in his mouth. Only this is what I would say to you, niece: in my time, when I was young, such escapades would turn out badly for giddy girls. Don't be angry with me, my dear: only fools get angry at the truth. I gave orders to refuse him entry today. I like him a lot, but I'll never forgive him this. Well, well, a widower! Give me some water. As for sending Panshin packing, well done you. But don't sit up at nights with men – they're all old goats. Don't grieve me in my old age or you'll find I'm not always nice – I can bite too... A widower!"

Marfa Timofeyevna went out, but Liza sat down in the corner and burst into tears. Bitterness filled her soul: she had not deserved such humiliation. Love had not made itself felt as happiness for her: for the second time since the previous evening she wept. This new and unexpected feeling had only just been engendered in her heart, but already how heavy the price she had paid for it, how crude the touch of alien hands on her cherished secret! She felt shame, bitterness and pain, but had neither doubt nor fear – and Lavretsky had become even dearer to her. As long as she had lacked understanding of herself she had hesitated, but after that meeting, after that kiss, she could no longer hesitate: she knew she was in love, that she had fallen in love honourably and seriously, had committed herself firmly and for life, and was not afraid of threats – she felt that this union could not be broken by force.

39

Marya Dmitriyevna was very alarmed when she was informed of the arrival of Varvara Pavlovna Lavretsky; she did not even know whether she should receive her, being afraid of offending Fyodor Ivanovich. Finally curiosity got the better of her. "After all," she reflected, "she's a relative too." And, seating herself in an armchair, she said to the footman: "Show her in!" Several moments passed; the door opened; Varvara Pavlovna went quickly, and almost noiselessly, up to Marya Dmitriyevna and, not allowing her to rise from the armchair, almost sank to her knees before her.

"Thank you kindly, Auntie," she began in Russian, her voice quiet and emotional. "Thank you kindly; I did not hope for such indulgence on your part: you're an angel of kindness."

So saying, Varvara Pavlovna unexpectedly seized one of Marya Dmitriyevna's hands and, squeezing it lightly in her pale-lilac Jouvin gloves,* brought it obsequiously to her full, rosy lips. Marya Dmitriyevna was completely nonplussed, seeing such a beautiful, exquisitely dressed woman almost at her feet; she did not know how she should act: she wanted to withdraw her hand and offer her a seat and say something affectionate to her; she ended up by half-rising and kissing Varvara Pavlovna on her smooth, fragrant forehead. Varvara Pavlovna was completely bowled over by this kiss.

"*Bonjour.* How do you do?" said Marya Dmitriyevna. "Of course I never imagined… however, of course I'm pleased to see you. You understand, my dear, that it's not for me to act as judge between husband and wife—"

"My husband is right in every respect," Varvara Pavlovna interrupted. "I alone am guilty."

"These are very laudable sentiments," replied Marya Dmitriyevna. "Very. Have you been here long? Have you seen him? Do sit down, please."

"I arrived yesterday," answered Varvara Pavlovna, meekly taking a chair. "I saw Fyodor Ivanovich and spoke with him."

"Aha! Well, what did he say?"

"I was afraid that my unforeseen arrival would arouse his anger," Varvara Pavlovna continued, "but he favoured me with his presence."

"That is to say, he didn't... Yes, yes. I understand," said Marya Dmitriyevna. "He only appears somewhat uncouth, but he's soft-hearted really."

"Fyodor Ivanovich has not forgiven me; he didn't want to hear me out... But he was kind enough to nominate Lavriki as my place of domicile."

"Aha! A very nice estate!"

"I'm setting off there as soon as tomorrow, in compliance with his wishes, but I considered it my duty to visit you first."

"I'm very, very grateful to you, my dear. One should never forget one's relatives. Do you know, I'm surprised how well you speak Russian. *C'est étonnant.*"*

Varvara Pavlovna sighed.

"I've been abroad too long, Marya Dmitriyevna, I know; but my heart was always Russian and I haven't forgotten my native land."

"Good, good. That's the most important thing. However, Fyodor Ivanovich didn't expect you at all... Yes, trust my experience: *la patrie avant tout...** Oh, do please show me, what is that charming mantilla you're wearing?"

"Do you like it?" said Varvara Pavlovna, slipping it off her shoulders. "It's a very simple little thing from Madame Baudran."*

"That's clear straight away. From Madame Baudran... How nice and how tasteful! I'm sure you've brought lots of delightful things with you. I'd love to have a look at them."

"My entire toilette is at your disposal, dearest Auntie. With your permission I can show one or two things to your maid. I have a girl with me from Paris – a remarkable seamstress."

"You're very kind, my dear. But, really, I'm ashamed."

"Ashamed," Varvara Pavlovna echoed reproachfully. "If you want to make me happy, treat me as your own property!"

Marya Dmitriyevna melted completely.

"*Vous êtes charmante*,"* she said, "but why don't you take off your hat and gloves?"

"What? You will allow me?" asked Varvara Pavlovna, lightly clasping her hands in a show of emotion.

"Of course. You will have dinner with us, I hope. I… I will introduce you to my daughter." Marya Dmitriyevna became a trifle uneasy. "Well, I suppose it's all right," she thought. "She's a bit under the weather today."

"*Ô, ma tante*,* that is kind of you!" Varvara Pavlovna exclaimed, raising her handkerchief to her eyes.

A pageboy announced the arrival of Gedeonovsky. The old windbag came in, bowing all round and smirking. Marya Dmitriyevna introduced him to her guest. At first he was embarrassed, but Varvara Pavlovna treated him with such a mixture of coquettishness and respect that he blushed to the roots of his hair; anecdotes, scandal and compliments began to flow like honey from his lips. Varvara Pavlovna listened to him and began gradually to join in the conversation. She modestly recounted tales of Paris, of her travels, of Baden-Baden; once or twice she made Marya Dmitriyevna laugh and each time she followed this with a sigh and seemed to reproach herself mentally for inappropriate jollity. She requested permission to bring Ada; she took off her gloves and demonstrated with her smooth hands, which had been washed in soap *à la guimauve*,* how and where flounces, ruches, lace and choux were being worn; she promised to bring a bottle of the new English perfume "Victoria Essence"* and was as delighted as a child when Marya Dmitriyevna agreed to accept it as a gift. She sobbed at the remembrance of the feeling she had experienced when she had heard Russian church bells for the first time: "They struck me to the depths of my heart," she said.

At that moment Liza came in.

Since that moment, since the very moment when, frozen with horror, she had read Lavretsky's note, Liza had been bracing herself for a meeting with his wife; she had a presentiment that she would see her. She had decided not to avoid her, as a punishment for what she called her "criminal hopes". The sudden crisis in her destiny had shaken her to the core; in some two hours her face had grown haggard, but she had not shed a single tear. "Serves me right!" she said to herself, suppressing, not without difficulty and trouble, certain bitter and evil impulses in her soul, which she herself found frightening. "Well, I must go," she thought as soon as she learnt of Lavretskaya's arrival, and go she did... For a long time she stood in front of the drawing room door before plucking up courage to open it. With the thought "I am guilty before her", she crossed the threshold and forced herself to look at her and smile. As soon as she saw her, Varvara Pavlovna went to meet her, bowing to her perfunctorily but nevertheless respectfully. "Allow me to introduce myself," she began in an ingratiating tone. "Your mother has been so indulgent towards me that I hope you too will be... kind." The expression on the face of Varvara Pavlovna when she uttered this last word, her cunning smile, her cold and, at the same time, tender look, the movement of her arms and shoulders, her very dress – indeed her whole being – aroused such a feeling of revulsion in Liza that she could not answer her and had to force herself to offer her hand. "This young lady despises me," thought Varvara Pavlovna, gripping Liza's cold fingers tightly, and, turning to Marya Dmitriyevna, she said in an undertone: "*Mais elle est délicieuse!*"* Liza reddened slightly: she detected mockery and offensiveness in this exclamation, but decided not to trust her impressions and so sat down with her embroidery work by the window. Even then

Varvara Pavlovna did not leave her in peace: she came up to her and began to praise her taste and artistic skill… Liza's heart began to beat violently and painfully: she could scarcely retain mastery over herself, scarcely remain seated. It seemed to her that Varvara Pavlovna knew everything and was secretly triumphing over her and mocking her. Fortunately for her, Gedeonovsky began talking to Varvara Pavlovna and distracted her attention. Liza bent over her embroidery and surreptitiously watched her. "That woman," she thought, "was loved by *him*." But she immediately dismissed the very thought of Lavretsky: she feared losing control of herself, feeling that her head was spinning gently. Marya Dmitriyevna began to talk about music.

"I've heard, my dear," she began, "that you are a remarkable virtuosa."

"I haven't played for a long time," Varvara Pavlovna replied, immediately sitting down at the piano and boldly running her fingers over the keyboard. "May I?"

"Please do."

Varvara Pavlovna gave a masterly rendition of a brilliant and difficult étude by Herz.* She had a very strong and agile touch.

"A sylphide!" exclaimed Gedeonovsky.

"Extraordinary!" agreed Marya Dmitriyevna. "Well, Varvara Pavlovna," she said, addressing her by name for the first time, "I admit you've surprised me – you should give concerts. We have a musician here, an old man, a German, rather eccentric, very knowledgeable. He gives Liza lessons; he'll be simply crazy about you."

"Is Lizaveta Mikhailovna also a musician?" asked Varvara Pavlovna, slightly turning her head towards her.

"Yes, she doesn't play badly and she loves music. But what's that compared with you? But there is one young man here: you ought to meet him. He has the soul of an artist and composes most charmingly. Only he can fully appreciate you."

"A young man?" said Varvara Pavlovna. "Who is he? Some impoverished soul?"

"Goodness gracious no. He's a gentleman much in demand here, and not only here – *et à Pétersbourg*. A *kammerjunker*, received in the best circles. You may well have heard of him: Panshin, Vladimir Nikolayevich. He's here on official business – a future minister, if you please!"

"And an artist?"

"The soul of an artist, and such an amiable person. You'll see him. All this time he's been coming here very frequently. I've invited him for this evening – I *hope* he will come," Marya Dmitriyevna added with a brief sigh and a bitter, crooked smile.

Liza understood the significance of this smile, but she had other things to think of.

"And he's young?" repeated Varvara Pavlovna, modulating effortlessly from key to key.

"Twenty-eight – and the most fetching of looks. *Un jeune homme accompli*,* if you please."

"One might say a model young man," Gedeonovsky remarked.

Suddenly Varvara Pavlovna began to play a noisy Strauss waltz* which began with such a powerful and rapid trill that Gedeonovsky even shuddered; in the very midst of the waltz she suddenly switched to a sad motif and ended with the aria from *Lucia*: 'Fra poco…'* She considered that cheerful music was not appropriate to her situation. The aria from *Lucia*, in which the accents fall on emotive notes, greatly affected Marya Dmitriyevna.

"What heartfelt music," she said to Gedeonovsky in an undertone.

"A sylphide," Gedeonovsky repeated, raising his eyes heavenwards.

The dinner hour arrived. Marfa Timofeyevna came downstairs when the soup was already on the table. She behaved very brusquely to Varvara Pavlovna, responding to her compliments in monosyllables and making no eye contact with her. Varvara Pavlovna herself soon realized that she would get no joy out of this old woman and gave up trying to converse with her. On the other hand, Marya Dmitriyevna became even more affable towards her guest; her aunt's impoliteness had angered her. However, Marfa Timofeyevna did not only avoid Varvara Pavlovna's look, she also avoided Liza's, even though Liza's eyes were shining. She sat as if petrified, all yellow and pale, with lips clamped tight – and ate nothing. Liza seemed calm, and indeed she was: her soul was more tranquil; a strange numbness had settled on her, the numbness of the condemned. Varvara Pavlovna spoke little over dinner: she seemed to have grown shy again, allowing her face to assume an expression of modest melancholy. Only Gedeonovsky enlivened the conversation with his stories, although he kept looking apprehensively at Marfa Timofeyevna and clearing his throat – he did this every time he was about to tell an untruth in her presence – but she did not stop him or interrupt him. After dinner it turned out that Varvara Pavlovna was a great lover of preference; this pleased Marya Dmitriyevna so much that she even became sentimental and thought to herself: "What a fool Fyodor Ivanovich must be, however, not to be able to understand a woman like that!"

She sat down to play cards with her and Gedeonovsky, while Marfa Timofeyevna took Liza upstairs to her room, saying that she looked off-colour and must have a headache.

"Yes, she's got a terrible headache," said Marya Dmitriyevna, turning to Varvara Pavlovna and rolling her eyes. "I sometimes get migraines like that myself..."

"You don't say," responded Varvara Pavlovna.

Liza entered her aunt's room and sank down exhausted onto a chair. Marfa Timofeyevna gave her a long, silent look, then quietly fell to her knees in front of her – and began, just as silently, to kiss each of her hands in turn. Liza leant forward, reddened – and burst into tears, but she did not help Marfa Timofeyevna to her feet, nor did she remove her hands: she felt she had no right to remove them, had no right to prevent the old woman from expressing her remorse and sympathy, or from asking forgiveness for what had happened the day before.

Marfa Timofeyevna could not have enough of kissing these poor, pale, enfeebled hands – and silent tears poured from her eyes and from Liza's eyes. Matros the cat, lying in a broad armchair, purred next to a ball of wool and a half-knitted stocking; the elongated flame of the icon lamp barely flickered before the icon; in the next room, behind the door, stood Nastasya Karpovna. She too was wiping her eyes with a checked handkerchief rolled up into a little ball.

40

MEANWHILE, DOWNSTAIRS in the drawing room, the game of preference was continuing; Marya Dmitriyevna had won and was in a good mood. A servant came in and announced the arrival of Panshin.

Marya Dmitriyevna dropped her cards and started fidgeting about in her armchair; Varvara Pavlovna looked at her with a half-smile, then turned her eyes to the door. Panshin appeared wearing a black dress coat, buttoned to the top, and a high English collar. "It was hard for me to obey – but, as you can see, I've come." This was the expression on Panshin's unsmiling, newly shaven face.

"Good Heavens, Woldemar," exclaimed Marya Dmitriyevna. "You used to come in unannounced before."

Panshin answered Marya Dmitriyevna with a single look, bowed politely to her but did not kiss her hand. She introduced him to Varvara Pavlovna; he stepped back a pace, bowed to her equally politely, but with a hint of refinement and respect, and sat down at the card table. The preference soon ended. Panshin enquired about Lizaveta Mikhailovna, learnt that she was not too well and expressed his regret. Then he began to talk to Varvara Pavlovna, diplomatically fashioning and weighing every word and respectfully listening to the full extent of her answers. But the seriousness of his diplomatic tone had no effect on Varvara Pavlovna and did not communicate itself to her. On the contrary, she looked him in the eye with cheerful attentiveness, spoke jauntily to him and her delicate nostrils quivered as if with suppressed laughter. Marya Dmitriyevna began to extol Varvara Pavlovna's talent; Panshin politely inclined his head, insofar as his collar allowed him to do so, and declared that he had been "certain of that from the outset". He then almost managed to bring the conversation round to Metternich.* Varvara Pavlovna narrowed her velvety eyes, saying in an undertone: "You're an artiste too, *un confrère*."* She then added in an even quieter voice: "*Venez!*"* and nodded her head in the direction of the piano. This one, casually uttered word – "*Venez*" – changed in an instant, as if by magic, Panshin's whole appearance. His preoccupied demeanour vanished; he smiled, became animated, unbuttoned his dress coat and, repeating: "What sort of an artiste am I, alas! I hear that you are a true artiste", he followed Varvara Pavlovna to the piano.

"Get him to sing his romance – about how the moon floats by," exclaimed Marya Dmitriyevna.

"Do you sing?" said Varvara Pavlovna, favouring him with a rapid, radiant look. "Do sit down."

Panshin began to make excuses.

"Do sit down," she repeated, tapping the back of the chair insistently.

He sat down, coughed, tugged at his collar and sang his romance.

"*Charmant*," said Varvara Pavlovna. "You sing splendidly. *Vous avez du style*.* Do sing it again."

She went round the piano and stood right in front of Panshin. He repeated the romance, adding a melodramatic tremolo to his voice. Varvara Pavlovna watched him attentively, leaning her elbows on the piano and holding her white hands at the level of her lips.

Panshin finished.

"*Charmant, charmante idée*," she said with the calm assurance of a connoisseur. "Tell me, have you written anything for the female voice, for a mezzo-soprano?"

"I hardly do any writing at all," replied Panshin. "I only wrote this one in my spare time… But do you sing?"

"I do."

"Oh, do sing us something," said Marya Dmitriyevna.

Varvara Pavlovna pushed her hair back from her flushed cheeks and shook her head.

"Our voices must suit one another," she said, turning to Panshin. "Let's sing a duet. Do you know 'Son geloso',* or 'Là ci darem', or 'Mira la bianca luna'?"*

"I once sang 'Mira la bianca luna'," Panshin replied, "but I've long since forgotten it."

"Never mind, we'll go through it sotto voce. Allow me."

Varvara Pavlovna sat down at the piano. Panshin stood beside her. They sang the duet sotto voce, during which time Varvara Pavlovna corrected him several times, then they sang it out loud, then they twice repeated: "*Mira la bianca lu... u... una.*" Varvara Pavlovna's voice had lost its freshness, but she used it very adroitly. At first Panshin was nervous and sang slightly flat, but then he warmed up and, if his singing was not irreproachable, he moved his shoulders, swayed his whole body to and fro and, from time to time, raised his arm, like a real singer. Varvara Pavlovna played two or three little things by Thalberg* and gave a coquettish rendition of a French arietta. Marya Dmitriyevna was already at a loss how to express her pleasure; several times she wanted to send for Liza. Gedeonovsky was equally tongue-tied, merely shaking his head, but suddenly he yawned unexpectedly and barely managed to cover his mouth with his hand. This yawn did not escape Varvara Pavlovna: she suddenly turned her back on the piano, said: "*Assez de musique comme ça.** We'll talk", and folded her arms. "*Oui, assez de musique,*" Panshin echoed cheerfully, then started a conversation with her – an animated, light-hearted conversation in French. "Exactly like in the best Paris salon," thought Marya Dmitriyevna as she listened to their allusive, witty speech. Panshin had a sense of complete satisfaction; his eyes shone; he smiled. At first he drew his hand across his face, knitted his brows and sighed spasmodically whenever he happened to meet Marya Dmitriyevna's eye; then, however, he forgot about her completely and gave himself over to enjoying semi-social, semi-artistic chatter. Varvara Pavlovna showed herself to be quite the philosopher: she had a ready answer for everything, did not hesitate over anything or doubt anything. It was evident that she had conversed frequently and at length with clever people of various kinds. All her thoughts and feelings revolved round Paris. Panshin steered the conversation towards literature; it turned out that she, like him, read nothing but French books. George Sand disgusted her; she respected Balzac, although she found him wearisome; in Scribe and Sue she saw great students of the heart; she adored Dumas and Féval; in her heart she preferred Paul de Kock* to all of them but, naturally, she never so much as mentioned his name. In point of fact, literature interested her very little. Varvara Pavlovna very skilfully avoided anything which reminded people, however distantly, of her position; her words contained no mention of love: on the contrary, they spoke of a puritanical approach to the delights of the passions, of disillusionment and humility. Panshin argued with her; she did not agree with him... But, strange to relate, at the same time as words of often severe condemnation fell from her lips, the sound of these words was caressing and tender and her eyes said... what exactly her lovely eyes were saying was difficult to ascertain. But her words were not strict, not clear and not sweet. Panshin tried to understand their secret meaning, tried himself to speak with his eyes, but felt that he achieved nothing. He was conscious of the fact that Varvara Pavlovna, as a genuine foreign lioness, outranked him socially, and he was not therefore fully his own master. Varvara Pavlovna had the habit, during a conversation, of lightly touching the sleeve of her interlocutor: these momentary contacts greatly excited Vladimir Nikolayevich. Varvara Pavlovna possessed the ability to get on easily with everyone; not two hours had passed and already it seemed to Panshin that he had known her for ever, while Liza, the same Liza whom, after all, he loved and to whom he had proposed the previous evening, was vanishing, as it were, in the mist. Tea was served; the conversation became even more relaxed. Marya Dmitriyevna rang for the pageboy and ordered Liza to be told to come downstairs if her head was better. On hearing Liza's name, Panshin began to discuss self-sacrifice and the question of whether men or women were more capable of it. Marya Dmitriyevna at once became agitated and began to assert that women were more capable of it; she declared that she would prove this in two words, got confused and ended up by making some rather weak comparison. Varvara took the book of music, partially hid herself behind it and, leaning towards Panshin and nibbling a biscuit, with a placid smile on her lips and in her eyes, said in an undertone: "*Elle n'a pas inventé la poudre, la bonne dame.*"* Panshin was not a little frightened and surprised by Varvara Pavlovna's boldness, but he did not realize how much contempt for him himself lay behind these effusions and, forgetting Marya Dmitriyevna's kindnesses and devotion, forgetting the dinners she had given him and the money which she had lent him, he replied (wretched man) with the same little smile and the same undertone: "*Je crois bien*"* – and not even "*Je crois bien*" but "*J'crois ben.*"

Varvara Pavlovna cast a friendly glance towards him and stood up. Liza came in: Marfa Timofeyevna had tried in vain to detain her and she had decided to endure her ordeal to the end. Varvara Pavlovna went to meet her together with Panshin, whose face had resumed its former diplomatic expression.

"How are you feeling?" he asked Liza.

"Better now, thank you kindly," she replied.

"We've been doing a bit of music making here; it's a pity you didn't hear Varvara Pavlovna. She sings superbly, *en artiste consommée.*"*

"Come here, *ma chère*," came the voice of Marya Dmitriyevna.

Immediately, and with the submissiveness of a child, Varvara Pavlovna went up to her and sat down on a small stool at her feet. Marya Dmitriyevna had called her over in order to leave her daughter alone with Panshin, if only for a moment: she still secretly hoped that Liza would think again. In addition, a thought had come into her head which she wanted to put into words without delay.

"Do you know," she whispered to Varvara Pavlovna, "I want to try to reconcile you with your husband; I can't answer for my success but I will try. He holds me in high esteem, you know."

Varvara Pavlovna slowly raised her eyes to Marya Dmitriyevna and gracefully clasped her hands.

"You would be my saviour, *ma tante*," she said in a sorrowful voice. "I don't know how to thank you for all your kindnesses. But I am too guilty before Fyodor Ivanovich; he cannot forgive me."

"But is it possible that you... really did..." Marya Dmitriyevna began inquiringly.

"Don't ask me," Varvara Pavlovna cut in, lowering her eyes. "I was young and foolish... However, I don't want to justify myself."

"Well, all the same, why not try? Don't despair," replied Marya Dmitriyevna. She wanted to pat her cheek, but looked her in the eye – and her courage deserted her. "A modest woman, modest – and indeed a lioness," she thought.

"Are you ill?" Panshin was saying meanwhile to Liza.

"Yes, I'm not well."

"I understand you," he said after a fairly prolonged pause. "Yes, I understand you."

"What do you mean?"

"I understand you," Panshin repeated meaningfully, simply not knowing what to say.

Liza was embarrassed, then thought: "Let it pass!" Panshin assumed an air of mystery and fell silent, looking sternly to one side.

"However, it seems eleven o'clock has struck," remarked Marya Dmitriyevna.

The guests took the hint and began to make their farewells. Varvara Pavlovna had to promise that she would come to dinner the following day and bring Ada; Gedeonovsky, who had almost fallen asleep sitting in the corner, volunteered to see her home. Panshin bowed ceremonially all round, but at the entrance porch, as he saw Varvara Pavlovna into her carriage, he squeezed her hand and called "*Au revoir!*" after her. Gedeonovsky took his seat beside her; throughout the whole journey she amused herself by placing, apparently accidentally, the end of her foot against his leg. He became flustered and paid her compliments; she giggled and made eyes at him whenever the light from a street lamp fell into the carriage. The waltz that she had played rang in her head and excited her; wherever she happened to be, she only had to imagine lanterns, a ballroom, figures spinning to the sound of music, for her soul to catch fire, her eyes to grow strangely dim, a smile to hover over her lips and something gracefully bacchanalian to pervade her whole body. When she arrived home, Varvara Pavlovna jumped lightly out of the carriage – only lionesses can jump like that – turned to Gedeonovsky and suddenly burst into loud laughter right under his nose.

"A very pleasant person," thought the State Councillor as he made his way back to his apartment, where his servant was waiting for him with a bottle of embrocation. "It's a good job I'm a steady sort. But what was she laughing at?"

Marfa Timofeyevna spent the whole night sitting at the head of Liza's bed.

41

Lavretsky spent a day and a half at Vasilyevskoye and, for almost the whole of that time, wandered around its environs. He could not remain in one place for a long time; anguish gnawed at him; he experienced all the ceaseless torments of impetuous, violent, yet impotent impulses. He recalled the feeling which had seized his soul the day after his arrival in the country, recalled his intentions at the time and experienced a strong sense of disgust with himself. What could have torn him away from what he recognized as his duty, the sole task of his future life? The thirst for happiness – yet again the thirst for happiness! "It's clear Mikhalevich was right," he thought. "You wanted to know happiness twice in life," he told himself, "but you forgot that if it visits a man just once, it is a luxury, an unmerited favour. It was incomplete, spurious happiness, you will say. Well, demonstrate what right you have to complete, genuine happiness. Look about you: who is blessed with happiness or enjoyment? Look, there's a peasant going to mow; perhaps he's satisfied with his lot... Well then, would you like to change places with him? Remember your mother: how negligible were her demands, yet what was her portion? Clearly you were merely boasting to Panshin when you told him that you'd come back to Russia to plough the land: you came back to chase young girls in your old age. The news of your freedom arrived and you abandoned everything, forgot everything, ran off like a boy after a butterfly..." The image of Liza constantly presented itself to him amid his reflections; he banished it with difficulty, as he did another persistent image, that of other impassively wily, beautiful and hateful features. Old Anton noticed that his master was not himself; after sighing several times behind the door, and several more times in the doorway, he plucked up courage to approach Lavretsky and advise him to have a nice warm drink. Lavretsky shouted at him and ordered him out, then apologized to him; however, this made Anton even sadder. Lavretsky could not sit in the drawing room: he fancied that his great-grandfather Andrei was gazing down from the canvas at his spineless descendant. "You! You're just small fry," his twisted lips appeared to be saying. "Is it possible that I won't be able to cope, that I'll give in to this... rubbish?" (Badly wounded soldiers in wartime always call their wounds rubbish. If a man can't deceive himself, he's not for this world.)

"Am I really just a callow youth? Well, yes: I glimpsed the possibility of lifelong happiness close up, I almost had it in my hands – and suddenly it vanished; it's the same in roulette: if the wheel turns just a little more, the pauper may perhaps become a rich man. If it doesn't, it doesn't and that's it. I'll get down to work, gritting my teeth, and I'll tell myself to keep silent, because it's not the first time I've had to take myself in hand. And why did I run away? Why am I sitting here like an ostrich, with my head in the sand? To look disaster in the face is terrible? Nonsense! Anton!" he yelled. "Order the tarantass to be got ready." "Yes," he thought, "I must tell myself to keep silent, I must keep myself on a tight rein..."

It was with such deliberations that Lavretsky tried to assuage his grief, but it was too great and too strong. And, when he got into the tarantass to drive to town, even Apraxeya, who had long since lost the ability not only to think, but to feel, shook her head and followed him sadly with her eyes. The horses broke into a gallop; Lavretsky sat motionless and erect and gazed motionlessly down the road ahead of him.

42

Liza had written to Lavretsky the day before, asking him to come and see her that evening; but he went first to his own apartment. He did not find either his wife or his daughter at home; from the servants he learnt that both had gone to the Kalitins. This news both astounded him and enraged him. "It's clear that Varvara Pavlovna has decided not to let me live," he thought, his heart rancorous and agitated. He began to pace backwards and forward, thrusting aside with hand or foot any children's toys or female appurtenances which got in his way; he summoned Justine and told her to clear up all this "junk". "*Oui, monsieur*," she said with a grimace and began to tidy the room, bending elegantly and with her every movement making Lavretsky feel that she considered him an uncouth boor. He contemplated with loathing her haggard, but still "piquant" and mocking Parisian face, her white oversleeves, her silk apron and tiny little cap. He dismissed her finally and, after much hesitation (Varvara Pavlovna had not yet returned), decided to go to the Kalitins – not to see Marya Dmitriyevna (he would not have entered her drawing room for anything, that drawing room where his wife was), but to see Marfa Timofeyevna; he remembered that the backstairs led straight from the servants' entrance to her quarters. Lavretsky decided to take that route. A chance circumstance helped him: in the yard he met Shurochka, and she conducted him to Marfa Timofeyevna. He found her alone, which was unusual for her. She was sitting in the corner, bent, capless, her arms folded across her bosom. On seeing Lavretsky, the old lady became very alarmed, leapt to her feet and began to wander hither and thither about the room, as if looking for her cap.

"Ah, there you are," she said, avoiding his eyes and fussing about. "Well, hello. Well, what do you think? What's to be done? Where were you yesterday? All right, she's come back. Yes indeed. Well we must... somehow or other."

Lavretsky sank onto a chair.

"Well, sit down, sit down," the old lady went on. "Did you come straight upstairs? Yes, of course you did. So what now? Have you come to look at me? Thank you."

The old lady fell silent. Lavretsky did not know what to say to her, but she understood him.

"Liza... Yes, Liza was here just now," continued Marfa Timofeyevna, tying and untying the strings of her reticule. "She's not very well. Shurochka, where are you? Come here, my dear. Why can't you stay put? And I've got a headache. It must be because of that there singing and music."

"What singing, Auntie?"

"What do you mean? We had some – what do you call them – duets. And all in Italian: *ci-ci* and *cia-cia*. Real magpies. They hold those notes as if their lives depended on it, that Panshin and that wife of yours. And how quickly everything's been sorted out: kept in the family, no standing on ceremony. And, it has to be said: a dog looking for a home won't come to grief when there's folk as won't chase it away."

"All the same, I confess I hadn't expected that," Lavretsky replied. "That needed a great deal of boldness."

"No, my dear, it's not boldness, but calculation. And good luck to her! They say you're sending her to Lavriki. Is that true?"

"Yes, I'm signing that estate over to Varvara Pavlovna."

"Has she asked for money?"

"Not so far."

"Well, it won't be long coming. But it's only now I've been able to get a good look at you. Are you well?"

"Yes."

CHAPTER 42

"Shurochka," Marfa Timofeyevna cried suddenly, "go and tell Lizaveta Mikhailovna – or no, ask her rather... she's downstairs, isn't she?"

"She's downstairs, ma'am."

"Right – then ask her where she's put my book. She knows."

"Yes, ma'am."

The old lady again began bustling about and opening drawers in a chest of drawers. Lavretsky sat motionless in his chair.

Suddenly light footsteps were heard on the stairs – and Liza came in.

Lavretsky stood and bowed; Liza halted by the door.

"Liza, my dear Lizochka," said Marfa Timofeyevna fussily, "where did you put my book? My book – where did you put it?"

"What book, Auntie?"

"My book, for Heaven's sake! By the way, I didn't call you... Well, never mind. What are you doing downstairs? Here's Fyodor Ivanovich who's come to see us. How's your head?"

"It's nothing."

"You keep saying it's nothing. What's happening there downstairs? Music again?"

"No – they're playing cards."

"Yes, she's losing no time, is she? Shurochka, I can see you want to run about the garden. Off you go."

"But I don't, Marfa Timofeyevna."

"Don't argue, please. Off you go. Nastasya Karpovna has gone into the garden on her own – go and join her. Be nice to me in my old age." Shurochka went out. "But where's my cap? Where's it got to, really?"

"Let me look for it," said Liza.

"You stay where you are – my legs haven't fallen off yet. It must be in my bedroom."

And, throwing a sideways glance at Lavretsky, Marfa Timofeyevna withdrew. She was about to leave the door open, but suddenly turned and closed it.

Liza leant back in her armchair and quietly put her hands to her face; Lavretsky remained where he was.

"So this is how we were to see each other again," he said finally.

Liza took her hands away from her face.

"Yes, she said in a toneless voice, "we've soon been punished."

"Punished," said Lavretsky. "What've you been punished for?"

Liza raised her eyes to him. They expressed neither grief nor anxiety; they seemed smaller and dimmer. Her face was pale; her slightly parted lips had also turned pale.

Lavretsky's heart leapt with love and pity.

"You've written to me that it's all over," he whispered. "Yes, it is all over – before it had started."

"We must forget all this," said Liza. "I'm glad you've come; I wanted to write to you, but it's better this way. Only we must make the most of these moments. It remains for both of us to do our duty. You, Fyodor Ivanovich, must be reconciled with your wife."

"Liza!"

"I beg you to do this: only that way can everything that has happened be erased. Think about it – and don't refuse me."

"Liza, for Heaven's sake, you're asking the impossible. I am prepared to do anything you command; but to be reconciled with her *now*!... I agree to everything; I've forgotten everything – but I can't compel my heart... For pity's sake, that's cruel."

"I'm not demanding of you what you say I am: don't live with her if you are unable to – but be reconciled," Liza replied, again putting her hand over her eyes. "Remember your daughter – do it for me."

"All right," said Lavretsky through gritted teeth. "Let's suppose I do that; I will thereby be doing my duty. Well, what about you? In what does your duty consist?"

"I know the answer to that."

Lavretsky suddenly shuddered.

"Do you not intend to marry Panshin?"

Liza gave a barely perceptible smile.

"Oh no!" she said.

"Oh Liza, Liza!" Lavretsky cried. "How happy you might have been!"

Liza again looked at him.

"Now you yourself can see, Fyodor Ivanovich, that happiness depends not on ourselves, but on God."

"Yes, because you…"

The door from the neighbouring room burst open and in came Marfa Timofeyevna with her cap in her hand.

"I had a job finding it," she said, standing between Lavretsky and Liza. "I'd put it down myself. That's old age for you, alas! However, youth isn't any better. So, are you going to Lavriki yourself with your wife?" she added, turning to Fyodor Ivanovich.

"Go with her to Lavriki? Me? I don't know," he said after a short pause.

"Aren't you going downstairs?"

"Not today."

"Very well. You know best. But I think you, Liza, ought to go downstairs. Oh, good Heavens above, I've even forgotten to feed the bullfinch. Stay there – I'll be back in a minute."

With that Marfa Timofeyevna ran out without putting her cap on.

Lavretsky quickly went up to Liza.

"Liza," he began beseechingly, "we are parting for ever; my heart is breaking – give me your hand as I take my leave."

Liza raised her head. Her tired eyes, their light almost extinguished, rested on him…

"No," she said, taking back the hand she had already extended. "No, Lavretsky" – it was he first time she had called him this – "I won't give you my hand. What's the point? Please go away, I beg you. You know I love you… yes, I do love you," she added with an effort, "but no… no."

And she raised her handkerchief to her lips.

"At least give me that handkerchief."

The door creaked… The handkerchief slipped onto Liza's knees. Lavretsky grabbed it before it fell to the floor, stuffed it quickly into his side pocket and, turning round, exchanged glances with Marfa Timofeyevna.

"Lizochka, I think your mother is calling you," said the old lady.

Liza at once stood up and went out.

Marfa Timofeyevna again sat down in her corner. Lavretsky began taking his leave of her.

"Fedya," she said suddenly.

"What is it, Auntie?"

"Are you an honourable man?"

"How do you mean?"

"I'm asking you: are you an honourable man?"

"I hope so, yes."

"Hmm. Give me your word of honour that you're an honourable man."

"With pleasure. But what's this for?"

"I know what it's for. And you too, my boy, if you think about it, and after all you're not stupid, will understand yourself what I'm asking you this for. But now, goodbye, old thing. Thank you for visiting me. Remember what you said, Fedya, and kiss me. Oh, my dear, I know it's hard for you; but after all it's not easy for anyone. That's why I used to envy flies: there's something, I thought, that enjoys living in the world. But one night I heard a fly whining in the clutches of a spider. No, I thought, the storms of life hit them too. What can one do, Fedya? But remember what you said. Off you go."

Lavretsky left by the back door and was already approaching the gate when a servant caught him up.

"Marya Dmitriyevna asked me to request you to pay her a visit," he announced.

"Tell her, my man, that I can't just now..." Lavretsky began.

"She asked me to request you very firmly," the servant went on. "She asked me to say that she is alone."

"But have the guests gone?" asked Lavretsky.

"They have, sir," replied the servant with a grin.

Lavretsky shrugged his shoulders and set off after him.

43

Marya Dmitriyevna was alone in her study, sitting in a Voltaire armchair and sniffing eau de Cologne; a glass orange-blossom water stood on a small table beside her. She was agitated and appeared scared of something.

In came Lavretsky.

"You wanted to see me," he said, bowing coldly.

"Yes," replied Marya Dmitriyevna, taking a sip of water. "I was told you went straight through to Auntie, so I gave orders for you to be asked to come here: I need to talk things over with you. Take a seat, please." Marya Dmitriyevna drew breath then continued: "You know your wife has come back."

"That is known to me," said Lavretsky.

"Yes, well, what I meant to say was: she came to me and I received her; that's what I want to explain myself about to you, Fyodor Ivanovich. I, thank the Lord, have earned, I may say, universal respect, and nothing on earth will make me do anything improper. Although I foresaw that it would be unpleasant for you, I nevertheless took the decision not to refuse her, Fyodor Ivanovich: she's a relative of mine – through you. Put yourself in my position: what right have I to refuse her entry to my house. Do you agree?"

"You're worrying needlessly, Marya Dmitriyevna," Lavretsky replied. "You did absolutely the right thing; I'm not at all angry. I have no intention of depriving Varvara Pavlovna of the possibility of seeing her friends; I didn't come and see you today purely because I didn't want to meet her. That's all there was to it."

"Oh, how pleasant it is to hear that from you, Fyodor Ivanovich," exclaimed Marya Dmitriyevna. "However, I always expected that of your noble sentiments. But it's no surprise that I'm worrying:

I'm a woman and a mother. And your wife… of course I cannot judge you or her – I told her as much to her face; but she's such a nice lady that she can afford nothing but pleasure."

Lavretsky gave a wry smile and toyed with his hat.

"And this is what I meant to say to you, Fyodor Ivanovich," Marya Dmitriyevna continued, moving slightly towards him. "If you had seen how modestly she behaves, how respectful she is! It was even touching, really. And if you had heard how she refers to you! I am, she said, wholly guilty before him; I was unable, she said, to appreciate him; he's not a human being, she said, but an angel. Really, that's what she said: an angel. Her remorse was such that… God knows, I've never seen such remorse!"

"But satisfy my curiosity on one point, Marya Dmitriyevna," said Lavretsky. "I'm told Varvara Pavlovna sang at your house – did she sing in the throes of remorse – or what?"

"Oh, you should be ashamed of talking like that! She sang and played merely in order to please me, because I pressed her, almost ordered her, to do so. I could see that it was hard for her, very hard; I wondered how to distract her – and I heard that she was very talented! Believe me, Fyodor Ivanovich, she's completely devastated. Just ask Sergei Petrovich: a woman brought low, *tout à fait*,* so how can you say that?"

Lavretsky merely shrugged his shoulders.

"And then, what a little angel you have in Adochka. What a delightful little girl! How sweet and intelligent she is; how well she speaks French – and she understands Russian: she called me 'Auntie' in Russian! And do you know, as for being shy, like almost all children are at her age, there's no sign of that at all. She's so like you, Fyodor Ivanovich, it's quite terrifying. Her eyes, her eyebrows… well it's you all over. I must confess I don't much like small children, but I've simply fallen in love with your daughter."

"Marya Dmitriyevna," said Lavretsky suddenly, "allow me to ask you why you're favouring me with all this."

"Why?" Marya Dmitriyevna again sniffed eau de Cologne and sipped water. "I'm saying it, Fyodor Ivanovich, because… after all I'm a relative of yours and I take a very keen interest in you… I know that you have the kindest of hearts. Listen, *mon cousin*, when all's said and done I'm a woman of experience and I'm not going to waste my breath! Forgive your wife. Forgive her." Marya Dmitriyevna's eyes suddenly filled with tears. "Just think: youth, inexperience… well, maybe a bad role model: she did not have a mother who could put her on the right path. Forgive her, Fyodor Ivanovich: she's been punished enough."

Tears began to roll down Marya Dmitriyevna's cheeks; she did not wipe them away: she liked crying. Lavretsky sat as if on hot coals. "Good Lord," he thought, "what sort of torture is this! What a day I've had!"

"You don't answer," said Marya Dmitriyevna again. "How am I to take that? Can you be so cruel? No, I don't want to believe that. I sense that my words have convinced you. Fyodor Ivanovich, God will reward you for your kindness; now take your wife from my hands…"

Lavretsky rose reluctantly from his chair; Marya Dmitriyevna also rose and, going quickly behind a screen, led out Varvara Pavlovna. Pale, half-alive, her eyes cast down, she seemed to have renounced all thoughts or will of her own and to have put herself entirely in the hands of Marya Dmitriyevna.

Lavretsky took a step backwards.

"You were here!" he cried.

"Don't blame her," said Marya Dmitriyevna hastily. "She didn't want to stay at all, but I told her to and put her behind the screen. She assured me that it would make you even angrier, but I wouldn't even listen to her – I know you better than she does. So take your wife from my hands – go on, Varya, don't be afraid, fall on your knees before your husband" – she tugged her by the arm – "and my blessing—"

"Wait, Marya Dmitriyevna," Lavretsky interrupted in a toneless but strong voice. "You probably like scenes of sensibility" – Lavretsky was not mistaken: since her boarding school days Marya Dmitriyevna had retained a passion for a certain theatricality – "they amuse you, but other people come off badly from them. However, I'm not going to talk to you: you're not the main character in *this* scene. What do *you* want of me, madam?" he added, turning to his wife. "Have I not done everything I could for you? Don't tell me you didn't engineer this meeting: I won't believe you – and you know that I can't believe you. What is it you want? You're intelligent – you do nothing without purpose. You must understand that I can't countenance living with you as I did before, not because I'm angry with you but because I've changed. I told you so the day after you arrived, and you yourself, at the present moment, know in your heart that you agree with me. But you want to rehabilitate yourself in the eyes of the world: it is not enough for you to live in my house – you want to live under the same roof as me. Isn't that so?"

"I want you to forgive me," said Varvara Pavlovna, not raising her eyes.

"She wants you to forgive her," echoed Marya Dmitriyevna.

"Not for myself, but for Ada," whispered Varvara Pavlovna.

"Not for her, but for your Ada," echoed Marya Dmitriyevna.

"Fine. Is that what you want?" said Lavretsky with an effort. "All right, I'll agree to that too."

Varvara Pavlovna cast a swift look at him and Marya Dmitriyevna exclaimed: "Well, thank the Lord!" and again drew Varvara Pavlovna forward by the arm. "Accept from me—"

"Wait, I tell you," Lavretsky interrupted. "I consent to live with you, Varvara Pavlovna," he continued, "that is, I will bring you to Lavriki and live with you, as long as I have the strength to do so, and then I'll go away, and make occasional brief visits. You see, I don't want to deceive you, but don't make any more demands. You yourself would have laughed if I'd carried out the wish of our respected relative, pressed you to my heart and started reassuring you that... that the past never happened, that the felled tree would blossom again. But I can see I have to submit. You will misunderstand that... but no matter. I repeat... I will live with you... or no, I can't promise that... will resolve my differences with you and again regard you as my wife..."

"At least give her your hand on that," said Marya Dmitriyevna, whose tears had long since dried.

"I have at no time deceived Varvara Pavlovna," Lavretsky retorted. "She'll believe me as it is. I will take her off to Lavriki – and remember, Varvara Pavlovna: our pact will be considered broken as soon as you leave there. And now allow me to go."

He bowed to both ladies and hurriedly withdrew.

"You're not taking her with you?" Marya Dmitriyevna called after him.

"Leave him alone," Varvara Pavlovna whispered to her, and immediately embraced her, began to thank her, kiss her and call her her saviour.

Marya Dmitriyevna condescendingly accepted these tokens of her affection, but in her heart she was not pleased with Lavretsky, nor with the whole scene she had arranged. There was little sensibility in it: in her opinion Varvara Pavlovna should have thrown herself at her husband's feet.

"How did you fail to understand me?" she maintained. "Didn't I say: fall at his feet?"

"It's better this way, my dear auntie: don't worry – everything's fine," Varvara Pavlovna insisted.

"Well, he really is as cold as ice," remarked Marya Dmitriyevna. "Granted, you didn't cry, but I was in floods of tears in front of him. He wants to lock you up in Lavriki. Does that mean you won't even be able to come and see me? All men are heartless," she said in conclusion, shaking her head meaningfully.

"On the other hand, women can appreciate goodness and magnanimity," said Varvara Pavlovna, sinking quietly to her knees before Marya Dmitriyevna, wrapping her arms round her ample waist and pressing her face to her. Her face bore a surreptitious smile, but Marya Dmitriyevna's tears began to flow again.

Lavretsky meanwhile went home, shut himself in his butler's room, threw himself on the sofa and lay there till morning.

44

THE NEXT DAY WAS SUNDAY. The ring of bells for early Mass did not wake Lavretsky up – he had not closed his eyes all night – but reminded him of another Sunday when he, at Liza's request, had gone to church. He rose hastily; some secret voice told him that he would see her there again. He left the house quietly, asking the servants to tell Varvara Pavlovna that he would return by dinner time, and strode off in the direction that the monotonously sorrowful sound of the bells was calling him. He arrived early: there was almost no one in the church; an acolyte was reading the hours on the *solea*:* his voice droned on in measured fashion, rising and falling and occasionally interrupted by bouts of coughing. Lavretsky took his place near the entrance. Worshippers arrived one by one, halted, crossed themselves and bowed to all sides; the footsteps rang out in the empty silence, reverberating loudly from the vaulted roof. An infirm old woman in a shabby hooded coat was kneeling near Lavretsky and praying assiduously: her toothless, wizened, yellow, face was expressive of intense emotion; her red eyes looked fixedly upwards at the icons on the iconostasis: a bony hand kept emerging from her coat and making the sign of the cross, slowly and firmly. A peasant with a thick beard and gloomy face, dishevelled and crumpled, entered the church, fell on both knees and immediately began to cross himself rapidly, throwing back and shaking his head after each bow. Such bitter sorrow was evidenced in his face, in all his movements, that Lavretsky decided to approach him and ask what the matter was. The peasant recoiled and stared at him with a mixture of anger and fear… "My son is dead," he gabbled and again began to bow… "What can replace the consolation of the church for such people?" thought Lavretsky, trying to pray himself, but his heart had grown heavy and hardened and his thoughts were far off. He was still waiting for Liza, but Liza did not come. The church had begun to fill up; still she was not there. The Mass began, the acolyte read the gospel and the bells were rung for the prayer to the Virgin; Lavretsky moved forward a little – and suddenly saw Liza. She had arrived before him, but he had not noticed her; squeezed into the space between the wall and the *kleros*,* she was neither looking about her nor stirring. Lavretsky did not takes his eyes off her throughout the rest of the Mass: he was saying goodbye to her. The congregation began to disperse, but she remained standing in her place: it seemed she was waiting for Lavretsky to go. Finally, she crossed herself one final time and set off, without turning round; she had one maid with her. Lavretsky followed her out of the church and caught up with her in the street; she was walking very quickly, her head bowed and her veil lowered over her face.

"Good morning, Lizaveta Mikhailovna," he said loudly and with forced casualness. "May I accompany you?"

She said nothing; he set off alongside her.

"Are you pleased with me?" he asked her, lowering his voice. "Did you hear what happened yesterday?"

"Yes, yes," she said in a whisper. "It's good."

And she started to walk even faster.

"Are you pleased?"

Liza merely nodded her head.

"Fyodor Ivanovich," she began in a calm, but faint voice. "I wanted to request this of you: don't come and see us any more. Go away as soon as possible; we can meet again later – some time, a year from now. But now, do this for me – do as I request, for God's sake."

"I'm prepared to obey you in everything, Lizaveta Mikhailovna, but is it possible that we must part like this? Is it possible that you won't say a single word to me?..."

"Fyodor Ivanovich, here you are walking beside me now... But you're so far away from me, so far. And not only you but..."

"Finish your sentence, I beg you!" Lavretsky exclaimed. "What do you mean?"

"You'll hear, perhaps... but whatever happens, forget... no, don't forget me, remember me."

"Me forget you..."

"Enough. Goodbye. Don't follow me."

"Liza..." Lavretsky began.

"Goodbye! Goodbye!" she repeated, lowering her veil even more and almost breaking into a run.

Lavretsky watched her go and, his head lowered, set off back along the street. He bumped into Lemm, who was also walking along with his hat pulled down over his nose and his eyes fixed on his feet.

They regarded one another in silence.

"Well, what have you to say?" said Lavretsky at last.

"What have I to say?" rejoined Lemm gloomily. "Nothing. Everything is dead and we are dead – *Alles is tot und wir sind tot.* Are you going to the right?"

"I am."

"I'm going to the left. Goodbye."

* * *

The next morning, Fyodor Ivanovich and his wife set off for Lavriki. She travelled in front in a carriage, together with Ada and Justine; he followed in a tarantass. Throughout the whole journey the pretty little girl did not move away from the carriage window; she was fascinated by everything: the peasant men, the peasant women, the peasant houses, the wells, the shaft bows, the harness bells and the vast number of rooks. Justine was equally fascinated; Varvara Pavlovna laughed at their remarks and exclamations. She was in a good mood. Before leaving O— she had had things out with her husband.

"I understand your position," she told him, and he was able to conclude, from the intelligent expression in her eyes, that she completely understood his position. "But at least in fairness to me, admit that I am easy to live with: I won't hassle or constrain you. I wanted to safeguard Ada's future – I don't need anything else."

"Yes, you've achieved all your goals," said Fyodor Ivanovich.

"There's only one thing I dream of now: burying myself for ever in some remote spot. I will always remember your beneficence—"

"That's enough!" he interrupted.

"And I will be able to respect your independence and your privacy," she said, completing her pre-prepared sentence.

Lavretsky bowed low to her. Varvara Pavlovna realized that, in his heart of hearts, her husband was thanking her.

The following day, towards evening, they arrived at Lavriki; a week later Lavretsky departed for Moscow, leaving his wife some five thousand roubles to live on; the day after Lavretsky's departure, Panshin, whom Varvara Pavlovna had begged not to forget her in her isolation, appeared. She could not have received him more cordially, and till late at night the house's high rooms and the garden itself resounded to the sound of music, singing and cheerful French talk. Panshin stayed for three days as Varvara Pavlovna's guest; as he took his leave and squeezed her lovely hands, he promised to return soon – a promise which he kept.

45

LIZA HAD HER OWN SMALL ROOM on the first floor of her mother's house, a clean, bright room with a white bed, pots of flowers in the corners and, in front of the windows, a small desk, a pile of books and a crucifix on the wall. The room was nicknamed "the nursery": Liza was born in it. On returning from the church, where Lavretsky had seen her, she tidied up more carefully than usual, dusted everywhere, re-examined and retied with ribbon all her copybooks and letters from girl friends, locked all the drawers, watered the flowers and touched every flower with her hand. She did all this without hurrying or making a noise, with a certain calm, earnest tenderness on her face. Finally, she halted in the middle of the room, looked slowly about her, went up to the table, above which hung the crucifix, sank to her knees, rested her head on her clasped hands and remained motionless.

Marfa Timofeyevna came in and found her in this position. Liza did not notice her arrival. The old lady tiptoed out through the door and coughed loudly several times. Liza hastily stood up and wiped her eyes in which bright, unshed tears were glistening.

"I see you've again tidied up your little cell," said Marfa Timofeyevna, bending low over a pot containing a single rose. "What a glorious smell!"

Liza looked thoughtfully at her aunt.

"What a word you've used there!" she whispered.

"Which word? Which?" the old lady replied animatedly. "What do you mean? It's terrible," she said, again throwing down her cap and seating herself on Liza's bed. "I can't cope with it: today's the fourth day when I feel I've been stewing in a cauldron. I can no longer pretend that I don't notice anything and can't see you growing pale, desiccated, weepy. I just can't."

"But what's the matter, Auntie?" said Liza. "I'm all right..."

"All right?" exclaimed Marfa Timofeyevna. "Tell that to other people, but not me! All right! And who was on their knees just now? Whose eyelashes are still wet with tears? All right! But just look at yourself. What've you done with your face? Where've you put your eyes? All right! Do you think I don't know everything?"

"It'll pass, Auntie. Give it time."

"It'll pass – yes. But when? Good Lord in heaven! Did you really love him so much? But he's an old man, Lizochka, isn't he? I don't dispute he's a good man. He doesn't bite. But what does that mean? We're all good people; there's more fish in the sea, so there'll always be plenty of that commodity about."

"I tell you: it'll all pass. It has already all passed."

"Lizochka, listen to what I have to say to you," said Marfa Timofeyevna, seating Liza beside her on the bed and smoothing first her hair, then her kerchief. "It only seems to you, in the heat of the moment, that there's no help for your grief. Oh, my dear, it's only for death that there's no cure! Just tell yourself: I won't give in, so there! You'll be surprised, then, how quickly and easily it passes. Just be patient."

"Auntie," Liza replied. "It's already over – everything is over."

"Over! What do you mean: over? Your nose has even grown sharp and pointed, but you say it's over. Some 'over'!"

"Yes, it's over, Auntie. If only you will come to my aid," said Liza with a burst of animation, flinging herself round Marfa Timofeyevna's neck. "Dearest Auntie, be my friend, help me, don't be angry, understand me..."

"But what's all this about? What's it about, my dear? Don't frighten me, please. I shall cry out in a minute. Don't look at me like that – rather tell me what it's all about!"

"I... I want..." Liza hid her face in Marfa Timofeyevna's bosom... "I want to go into a convent," she said in a flat voice.

The old lady almost leapt from the bed.

"Cross yourself, my dear Lizochka. Think again, and may the Lord be with you," she spluttered at last. "Lie down, my darling, have a little sleep; this is all the result of sleeplessness, my dear."

Liza raised her head; her cheeks were flaming.

"No, Auntie," she said, "don't say that. I've made my decision; I've prayed and I've asked God's advice. Everything is finished; my life with you is finished. This trial is not in vain and it's not the first time I've thought about it. Happiness was not for me; even when I had hopes of happiness, my heart still ached. I know everything, both my own sins and those of others, and how Papa made his money; I know everything. This all must be atoned for, atoned for by prayer. I'm sorry for you, I'm sorry for Mama and Lenochka, but there's nothing for it. I feel that I don't belong here any longer; I've already said goodbye to everything, bowed to everything in the house for the last time. Something is calling me away; I feel sick at heart and want to shut myself away for ever. Don't try to detain me or dissuade me. Help me, or I'll go off alone…"

Marfa Timofeyevna listened to her niece with horror.

"She's ill, she's delirious," she thought. "We must send for the doctor, but which doctor? Gedeonovsky spoke highly of one recently; he's always talking rubbish – but perhaps he was right this time." But when she became convinced that Liza was neither ill nor delirious, when Liza persistently answered all her protestations in the same way, Marfa Timofeyevna grew frightened and was genuinely distressed.

"But, after all, you don't know, my darling," she began, in an attempt to talk her round, "what life in a convent is like. Why, they'll feed you on sour hemp oil, my love, and clothe you in the thickest of thick linen. They'll make you walk about in the cold. You won't be able to stand all this, Lizochka. This is all Agafya's doing: she led you astray. But, after all, she began by living life to the full – you do the same. At least let me die in peace, then do what you like. Who ever saw the like of it, going into a convent for the sake of some old goat – God forgive me – for the sake of a man? Now, if your heart aches so much, go and pray to a saint, have prayers said, but don't you put a black hood over your head, my little one, my pet..."

And Marfa Timofeyevna wept bitterly.

Liza tried to console her, wiped away her tears and herself wept, but she remained unbending. In desperation Marfa Timofeyevna tried to employ the threat of telling her mother everything... but that did not help either. It was only as a result of redoubled entreaties on the part of the old lady that Liza agreed to defer her plan for six months; in exchange Marfa Timofeyevna had to give her word that if, after six months, she had not changed her mind, she would help Liza and would work to obtain the consent of Marya Dmitriyevna.

* * *

With the arrival of the first frosts, Varvara Pavlovna, despite her promise to bury herself in some remote spot, obtained money and moved to Petersburg, where she rented a modest but attractive apartment, found for her by Panshin, who had left O— province before her. In the latter part of his sojourn in O—, he had completely fallen out of favour with Marya Dmitriyevna; he had suddenly stopped visiting her and was almost never away from Lavriki. Varvara Pavlovna had enthralled him, literally enthralled him – there is no other way to describe her unlimited, irrevocable, irresistible power over him.

Lavretsky spent the winter in Moscow; in the spring of the following year came the news that Liza had taken the veil in the B— convent, in one of the most remote regions of Russia.

Epilogue

Eight years passed. Spring again arrived... But let us first say a few words about the fate of Mikhalevich, Panshin, Madame Lavretsky – and then take our leave of them. After prolonged wanderings, Mikhalevich finally found his true *métier*: he got a post as chief usher in a government teaching establishment. He is very satisfied with his lot and his pupils "adore" him, although they also tease him. Panshin has moved swiftly up the ranks and is already angling to become a head of department. He stoops somewhat when he walks: the St Vladimir Cross,* which he wears round his neck, weighs him down. The functionary in him has gained preponderance over the artist; his still young-looking face has become sallow, his hair has thinned and he no longer sings or draws, but takes a covert interest in literature: he's written a comedy playlet with a proverb for a title, and since all writers nowadays infallibly depict someone or something, so he has depicted a coquette in his play and reads it discreetly to two or three lady well-wishers. He has not, however, married, although he has had many good opportunities to do so: the fault for this lies with Varvara Pavlovna. As for her, she is permanently resident in Paris, as before; Fyodor Ivanovich has given her a promissory note in his name and bought his freedom from her, from the possibility of her descending on him a second time. She has aged and filled out, but is still charming and elegant. Everyone has their ideal: Varvara Pavlovna has found hers in the dramas of Monsieur Dumas *fils*.* She visits the theatre assiduously, where consumptive and sentimental camellias* are depicted; to be Madame Doche* seems to her the height of human happiness: she once said that she desires no better future for her daughter. It is to be hoped that fate will spare Mademoiselle Ada such happiness: from being a rosy-cheeked, plump child she has turned into a weak-chested, pale little girl; her nerves are already shattered. The number of Varvara Pavlovna's suitors has diminished, but not dwindled to nothing; some of them she will probably maintain until the end of her days. The most ardent of them recently has been a certain Zakurdalo-Skubyrnikov, a bewhiskered retired guards officer, a man of about thirty-eight and possessed of an unusually strong physique. French visitors to Madame Lavretsky's salon call him "*le gros taureau de l'Ukraine*";* Varvara Pavlovna never invites him to her fashionable soirées, but he enjoys her favours to the full.

And so... eight years passed. Once again the breath of spring's radiant happiness filled the sky; once again spring smiled on earth and men; once again everything blossomed, sang and fell in love under its caress. The town of O— had changed little in the course of these eight years, but the house of Marya Dmitriyevna had, as it were, grown younger: its recently painted walls wore a welcoming white and the glass in the open windows shone crimson in the setting sun; from these windows the light and joyful sound of resonant young voices and ceaseless laughter were borne onto the street: it seemed the whole house was seething with life and brimming over with gaiety. The mistress of the house herself had long since gone to her grave: Marya Dmitriyevna died some two years after Liza took the veil; nor did Marfa Timofeyevna long outlive her niece: they lie together in the town cemetery. Nastasya Karpovna has also gone. For several years the old lady went faithfully every week to pray over her friend's mortal remains... Then her time came and her bones were also laid in the damp earth. But Marya Dmitriyevna's house did not pass into other hands, did not go out of the family; the nest was not destroyed: Lenochka, who had turned into a graceful and beautiful young woman, and her betrothed, a fair-haired hussar officer; Marya Dmitriyevna's son who had just got married in Petersburg and come with his young wife to spend the spring in O—; his wife's sister, a sixteen-year-old schoolgirl with rosy cheeks and limpid eyes; Shurochka, now grown up and pretty – these were the young people whose talk and laughter resounded round the walls of the Kalitin house. Everything in it had changed to suit the new occupants. Beardless house serfs, full of fun and high spirits, had replaced the stolid old men of former days; where once the portly Roska had padded solemnly around, two setters rushed frantically around, jumping over the sofas; in the stables, wiry palfreys, dashing shaft horses, mettlesome trace horses with plaited manes and Don saddle horses had been bred; the times for breakfast, dinner and supper were all mixed up and conflated; as the neighbours put it, "unheard of arrangements" were under way.

On the evening of which we have just spoken, the occupants of the Kalitin house (the eldest of whom, Lenochka's betrothed, was just twenty-four), were engaged in a slightly complicated but, to judge by their concerted laughter, highly amusing game. They were running through the rooms, trying to catch one another; the dogs were also running and barking, and the canaries, in their cages hanging in front of the windows, vied with each other to give voice, thus augmenting the general hubbub with their loud chatter and furious trilling. At the very height of these deafening fun and games, a mud-splattered tarantass drew up to the gate, and a man of about forty-five, in traveller's garb, climbed out and stopped in amazement. He stood motionless for some time, surveyed the house with an attentive eye, went through the wicket gate into the yard and slowly climbed the steps of the porch. No one greeted him in the entrance hall, but the door of the drawing room was flung open, and from it emerged a hot-and-bothered Shurochka, followed, a moment later, by a whole group of young people, who rushed out, shouting loudly. They stopped suddenly and fell quiet on seeing a stranger; but the bright eyes directed at him were just as friendly and the fresh faces did not stop laughing. Marya Dmitriyevna's son went up to the visitor and enquired cordially what it was he wanted.

"I am Lavretsky," said the visitor.

A concerted shout went up in reply – not because all these young people were highly delighted with the arrival of a distant and almost forgotten relative, but simply because they were prepared to rejoice loudly at any suitable opportunity. They immediately surrounded Lavretsky; Lenochka, as an acquaintance from the old days, was the first to introduce herself, assuring him that, given a little more time, she would definitely have recognized him. She then introduced the rest of the company, using for each of them, even her betrothed, the affectionate diminutive form of their name. The whole crowd moved through the dining room and into the drawing room. In both rooms the wallpaper was new, but the furniture was the same; Lavretsky recognized the piano; even the same embroidery frame stood, in the same position by the window – and with almost the same unfinished embroidery on it as eight years previously. They sat him in a comfortable armchair, and they all sat decorously round him. Questions, exclamations, stories tumbled out.

"We haven't seen you for a long time," remarked Lenochka naively, "and we haven't seen Varvara Pavlovna either."

"As if we would have!" her brother chimed in hastily. "I took you off to Petersburg, but Fyodor Ivanovich has been living in the country all the time."

"Yes, and since then Mama has died."

"And Marfa Timofeyevna," said Shurochka.

"And Nastasya Karpovna," returned Lenochka, "and Monsieur Lemm…"

"What? Is Lemm dead too?"

"Yes," replied young Kalitin, "he went off to Odessa – they say someone enticed him there – he died there too."

"You don't know whether he left any music behind?"

"I don't know – it's not very likely."

Everyone fell silent and looked at each other. A cloud of sorrow descended on all the young faces.

"But Matroska's still alive," said Lenochka suddenly.

"And Gedeonovsky," added her brother.

At the name of Gedeonovsky there was a sudden bust of general laughter.

"Yes, he's still alive and fibbing just like he used to," Marya Dmitriyevna's son continued. "And just imagine: yesterday this madcap" – he indicated the schoolgirl, his wife's sister – "put pepper in his snuffbox."

"You should have seen him sneeze!" exclaimed Lenochka, and once again unrestrained laughter rang out.

"We had news of Liza recently," said young Kalitin, and again everything around went silent. "She's well and her health is gradually improving now."

"Is she still in the same convent?" asked Lavretsky, not without effort.

"Yes."

"Does she write to you?"

"No, never: people bring us news." A sudden, profound silence fell. Everyone thought, "An angel is passing."

"Would you like to come into the garden?" said Kalitin, turning to Lavretsky. "It's looking very nice now, although we've rather let it go."

Lavretsky went out into the garden, and the first thing he saw was the very same bench on which he had once spent several happy, unrepeatable moments: it was blackened and warped with age, but he recognized it and that feeling seized his soul which has no equal in either sweetness or bitterness – the feeling of lively regret for vanished youth and for happiness once possessed. He made his way down the avenues together with the young people; the limes had aged somewhat and grown up in the last eight years, and their shade had become thicker. At the same time all the bushes had shot up, the raspberries were growing vigorously and the hazel grove was denser; from everywhere came the scent of fresh brushwood, timber, grass and lilac.

"This would be a good place to play puss in the corner," Lenochka suddenly cried, going into a small grassy clearing, surrounded by lime trees. "And, by the way, there are five of us."

"But have you forgotten Fyodor Ivanovich?" remarked her brother. "Or aren't you counting yourself?"

Lenochka blushed slightly.

"But at his age, can Fyodor Ivanovich—" she began.

"Please, play away," Lavretsky hastily chimed in. "Don't pay any attention to me. I'll be happier if I know that I'm not holding you back. There's no point in your trying to entertain me: old people have something to occupy themselves with which you don't yet know about and which no diversion can replace: memories."

The young people heard Lavretsky out with respectful and slightly mocking attentiveness – as if a lesson were being taught by a teacher – then suddenly dashed off away from him and into the clearing; four of them took up positions by trees, one in the centre – and the fun began.

Lavretsky meanwhile returned to the house, went into the dining room, approached the piano and touched one of the keys; a faint, but pure note rang out and reverberated secretly in his heart: this was the note with which that inspired melody had begun and with which, so long before, on that happiest of nights, the late Lemm had so enthused him. Then Lavretsky moved into the drawing room and stayed there for a long time. In this room, where he had seen Liza so frequently, her image rose more vividly before him. He seemed to feel traces of her presence all around him, but missed her most agonizingly and unendurably. In his grief there was none of the silence brought on by death. Liza was still alive somewhere, somewhere remote and far-off; he thought of her as a living being and did not recognize the girl he had once loved in the blurred, pale spectre clad in a nun's habit and surrounded by smoky waves of incense. Lavretsky would not have recognized himself if he had been able to look at himself in the same way as he mentally looked at Liza. In the course of these eight years a turning point had been reached in his life which few experience, but without which it is impossible to remain a decent human being to the end; he genuinely had ceased to think about his own happiness or self-interest. He had mellowed and – why hide the truth? – had aged, not only in face and body, but in soul; to keep the heart young into old age, as some say they can, is both difficult and almost risible. He who has not lost his faith goodness, the constancy of the will and the desire for activity, can be satisfied. Lavretsky had the right to be satisfied: he had become a really good landowner, had really learnt how to plough the earth and had not toiled for himself alone. As far as he was able, he had safeguarded and secured the welfare of his peasants.

Lavretsky went out of the house and into the garden, sat down on the familiar bench and – in that beloved spot, facing the very house where for the last time he had stretched out his hands towards the cherished cup in which the golden wine of pleasure seethes and sparkles – he, a lonely, homeless wanderer, to the accompaniment of the joyous cries of a younger generation which had already supplanted him, surveyed his life. His heart grew sad, but not heavy and not bitter within him: there was cause for regret, but nothing to be ashamed of. "Play, enjoy yourselves, grow, you youthful forces," he thought and there was no bitterness in his thoughts. "Your life is before you and your lives will be easier: you won't have to find your own path, as we have had to; you won't have to struggle, to fall and stand up again in the darkness. Our concern was to survive intact – but how many did not! You must do what has to be done, you must work, and the blessing of us old men will be upon you. But it remains for me, after this day and the sensations it brought, to make my final bow to you and, albeit sorrowfully, but without envy or any dark feelings, to say, in sight of the end and of an expectant God: 'Greetings, lonely old age! Burn out, useless life!'"

Lavretsky stood up quietly and quietly exited; no one noticed him and no one tried to detain him; in the garden behind the solid green wall of lime trees, the joyous cries rang out louder than ever. He got into his tarantass and ordered his coachman to drive home, sparing the horses.

* * *

"How does it end?" the dissatisfied reader may perhaps ask. "What happened to Lavretsky then? Or to Liza?" But what can be said of people who are still alive but have already left the stage? Why return to them? They say that Lavretsky visited the remote convent to which Liza had retired and saw her. Passing from kleros to kleros, she passed by close to him, passed by with the hurried, meek tread of a nun – and did not look at him; only the lashes of the eye turned towards him fluttered slightly, only her haggard face was bowed still lower and the fingers of her clasped hands, entwined with the rosary, clasped even closer together. What did they both think or feel? Who knows? Who can tell? There are such moments in life, such feelings… One can merely indicate them – and pass by.

Note on the Text

This translation is based on the text used by Patrick Waddington for his edition of *Dvoryanskoye gnezdo* (Oxford: Pergamon, 1969). That text in its turn was based the Russian text published in Volume 7 of the twenty-eight-volume edition of Turgenev's *Complete Collected Works*, published in Moscow and Leningrad in 1964.

Notes

p. 3, *the provincial town of O—*: Oryol, Turgenev's birthplace.
p. 5, *State Councillor*: Fifth of the fourteen Civil Service ranks in Imperial Russia.
p. 7, *Lenochka*: Affectionate diminutive form of Yelena.
p. 7, *Fedya*: Affectionate form of Fyodor.
p. 9, *great-nephew*: Lavretsky is more a third cousin than a great-nephew to Marya Dmitriyevna. She and Lavretsky call each other "cousins" in Chapter 7.
p. 11, *Woldemar*: French version of the name Vladimir.
p. 11, *Eh bien, eh bien, mon garçon*: "Easy, boy, easy" (French).
p. 11, *Prenez garde, prenez garde*: "Be careful, be careful" (French).
p. 13, *English Clubs of both capitals*: The English Club in Moscow, founded in 1772, was extremely fashionable. Its Petersburg equivalent was less prestigious.
p. 13, *c'est même très chic*: "It's even very chic" (French).
p. 13, *Volodka*: Affectionate diminutive form of Vladimir.
p. 14, *un charmant garçon*: "A charming boy" (French).

p. 14, *kammerjunker*: The lowest rank of courtier.

p. 15, *overture to Oberon*: *Oberon* is an 1826 opera by Carl-Maria von Weber (1786–1826). Panshin is referring to the very popular piano version of the overture.

p. 21, *Shakespeare in Schlegel's translation*: The translations from Shakespeare by August-Wilhelm Schlegel (1767–1845) are classics of German literature.

p. 21, *Yelizaveta*: This is the full form of Liza's given name. She is, however, usually called Lizaveta.

p. 31, *Vasily II*: Grand Prince of Muscovy (1415–62; reigned 1425–62). Sometimes known as Basil the Blind.

p. 31, *Bezhetsk Upland*: Upland area in the north-east part of Tver province, the possession of which was long disputed between Novgorod and Moscow.

p. 32, *sprinkle it with flour... torture*: Turgenev puns on the Russian word *muka* which, depending on how it is stressed, means both *flour* and *torture*.

p. 32, *Jean-Jacques Rousseau*: Major figure of the French Enlightenment (1712–78).

p. 32, *fine fleur*: "flower" (French).

p. 32, *à la Richelieu*: The Duke of Richelieu (1696–1788), godson of Louis XIV, was said to chew ambergris pastilles as a stimulant.

p. 32, *Petitot*: Jean Petitot (1607–91), Swiss artist who worked mainly in France.

p. 33, *the very beginning of the reign of Alexander I*: Tsar Alexander I (reigned 1801–25) came to the throne with the intention of reforming the corrupt system of promotion in the civil service and military.

p. 33, *Voltaire... Diderot*: Voltaire was the pen name of François-Marie Arouet (1694–1778), a major figure of the French Enlightenment, whose writings were extremely popular, and sometimes banned, in Russia. His contemporary Denis Diderot (1713–84) was the most prominent of the French Encyclopedists.

p. 33, *Raynal… Helvétius*: Guillaume Raynal (1713–96) was a French historian and radical political thinker. Claude-Adrien Helvétius (1715–71) was a French philosopher.

p. 34, *Comment vous portez-vous*: "How are you?" (French).

p. 35, *à la Titus hairstyle*: A short hairstyle used in 1789 by the French actor François-Joseph Talma (1763–1826) for the role of Titus in Voltaire's play *Brutus* (1730).

p. 36, *five hundred paper roubles*: First introduced in 1769, paper roubles were worth considerably less than silver roubles. They were abolished in 1843.

p. 37, *la Déclaration des droits de l'homme*: Truncated title of the *Declaration of the Rights of Man and of the Citizen*, a fundamental document of the French Revolution of 1789.

p. 37, *Lépine watch*: Jean-Antoine Lépine (1720–1814) was watchmaker to Louis XV, Louis XVI and Napoleon. Turgenev misspells his name in the original Russian.

p. 37, *Theodore Stratelates*: Legendary Greek saint and martyr. Lavretsky's given name Fyodor is the Russian form of Theodore. The saint's feast day was 26th January by the Russian calendar of the nineteenth century; that would also be Lavretsky's name day.

p. 38, *Treaty of Tilsit*: Peace treaty between Russia, France and Prussia, signed in July 1807. The events are described in Tolstoy's *War and Peace*.

p. 40, *Vanka*: Affectionate diminutive of the name Ivan.

p. 42, *Malasha*: Affectionate form of the name Malanya.

p. 44, *Ochakov*: Turkish fortress, now in southern Ukraine, taken by the Russians after a long siege in 1788.

p. 44, *In recto virtus*: "Virtue in rectitude" (Latin).

p. 45, *Symbols and Emblems*: Book published in 1788 by Nestor Maximovich-Ambodik (1744–1812). This was an expanded version of a book first published in 1691 in Amsterdam.

p. 46, *the Parcae*: In Roman mythology, the three female personifications of Fate.

p. 47, *But then came 1825 and with it a great deal of grief*: Reference to the Decembrist uprising of December 1825 and its repercussions.

p. 49, *Glasha… Glashka*: Affectionate forms of the name Glafira.

p. 51, *Mochalov*: Pavel Stepanovich Mochalov (1800–48). Celebrated tragedian.

p. 53, *Institute*: The Smolny Institute, a prestigious girls' school in Petersburg, founded by Catherine II in 1764.

p. 53, *Old Stables Street*: Russian: *Starokonyushennaya ulitsa*. Major Moscow thoroughfare. It is now termed a lane (*pereulok*) rather than a street.

p. 54, *ribbon of St Anne*: The Order of St Anne, a common mark of distinction in Tsarist Russia, was founded in 1735.

p. 54, *Empress's cipher*: Monogrammed certificate awarded by the Tsarina to the best pupils.

p. 55, *Desprez's*: Camille Desprez was a Frenchman who became a celebrated Moscow wine merchant, with premises on Petrovka Street.

p. 56, *Meine Tochter macht eine schöne Partie*: "My daughter is making a good match" (German).

p. 57, *Alcides*: One of the names of Hercules.

p. 58, *Tsarskoye Selo*: Residence of the Tsar and court, some thirty miles from Petersburg. Now called Pushkin.

p. 60, *Mme de —, cette grande dame russe si distinguée, qui demeure Rue de P…*: "Madame de —, the very distinguished Russian lady who lives on the Rue de P…" (French).

p. 60, *Mademoiselle Mars… Mademoiselle Rachel had not yet appeared*: Mademoiselle Mars and Mademoiselle Rachel were the stage names of the actresses Anne Boutet (1779–1847) and Elisa Félix (1820–58) respectively.

p. 60, *Odry in Les Ruines*: Jacques-Charles Odry (1781–1853) was a French clown and comic actor. A composition dating from 1838 by Thalberg (see fourth note to p. 166) bore the title *Les Ruines*. Whether Odry had any connection with this is doubtful.

p. 60, *Mme Dorval's acting*: Marie Dorval (née Delauney) (1798–1849) was a French actress.

p. 60, *Liszt*: Franz Liszt (1811–86) was a Hungarian composer who spent most of his life in Paris.

p. 61, *Baden-Baden*: Fashionable spa town in Saxony. Both Turgenev and Pauline Viardot had houses there at one time.

p. 62, *Puskin*: Ernest is clearly unaware of the correct spelling and pronunciation of the name of Russia's national poet.

p. 62, *Aged husband, baleful husband*: These words are spoken by Zemfira in Pushkin's long poem *The Gypsies* (1824). The poem was dramatized by V.A. Karatygin and set to music by A.N. Verstovsky in 1832.

p. 63, *Varya*: Affectionate form of the name Varvara.

p. 68, *Madame Bolus*: The *pension* run by this lady is mentioned in Act 2 of Turgenev's play *A Month in the Country* (1855).

p. 68, *Matros*: The cat's name translates as "Sailor". The diminutive form of his name – Matroska – appears in the Epilogue.

p. 70, *Ivan the Terrible's Book of Remembrance*: This was a record of those who died in the reign of Ivan IV (reigned as Tsar 1547–84), and for whom prayers were ordained by the Church.

p. 73, *Robert Peel*: Sir Robert Peel (1788–1850), UK Prime Minister 1834–35 and 1841–46.

p. 81, *massacas-coloured*: A colour close to magenta.

p. 82, *Alexander Alexandrovich Prozorovsky*: Field Marshal (1733–1809). The Peace with Turkey was concluded in 1774.

p. 82, *Moscow News*: Russian: *Moskovskie Vedomosti*. Newspaper founded in 1756 and published until 1917.

p. 82, *Lieutenant Colonel Mikhail Petrovich Kolychov... Pyotr Vasilyevich Kolychov*: There was an actual personage of this name (*c*.1750–95). His father was actually Pyotr Stepanovich.

p. 84, *Schiller's ballad 'Fridolin'*: This is the title of a Russian translation of Schiller's ballad 'Der Gang nach dem Eisenhammer' ('The Walk to the Iron Foundry', 1797).

p. 96, *Demosthenes*: Prominent Greek statesman, famous for his oratory (382–322 BC)

p. 97, *panna*: "Young lady" (Polish).

p. 100, *Il n'y a plus maintenant de ces gens comme ça comme autrefois*: "Nowadays there aren't any people like that any more, as there were in former times" (French).

p. 102, *am I not an uncle to you*: Lavretsky is actually a third cousin once removed to Liza.

p. 109, *de populariser l'idée du cadastre*: "To popularize the idea of the cadastre" (French). Waddington describes a cadastre as "a complete record of lands, dwellings and inhabitants of a territorial unit, drawn up for purposes of rates and property tax".

p. 109, *aigri... en somme*: "Embittered... in short" (French).

p. 111, *Obermann*: Novel by Étienne Pivert de Senancour (1770–1846), published in 1804.

p. 121, *qui a un si grand ridicule*: Marya Dmitriyevna speaks imperfect French. The gist of her meaning here is "who has got himself into a very ridiculous situation".

p. 124, *Walter Scott novel*: The novels of Sir Walter Scott (1771–1832) were extremely popular throughout Europe. The novel referred to here is probably *Heart Of Midlothian* (1818), the heroine of which is noted for her piety. It was translated into French in 1818 and into Russian in 1825.

p. 128, '*Meditation*': Russian: '*Duma*'. Notably pessimistic poem by M. Lermontov (1814–41), written in 1838 and highly critical of the poet's contemporaries.

p. 128, *Khomyakov*: Alexei Stepanovich Khomyakov (1804–60). Slavophile poet and thinker. He made the claim about the mousetrap in an article published in 1846.

p. 130, *en grand*: "On a large scale" (French).

p. 132, *king*: Waddington notes: "When piquet is played *à écrire* i.e. in a series, each of the twelve rounds is called a 'king'".

p. 138, *Tout ça c'est des bêtises*: "That's all drivel" (French).

p. 141, *Old Believer monastery*: Old Believers were people who did not, and still do not, accept the reforms introduced by Patriarch Nikon and his successors between 1652 and 1666.

p. 144, *Adochka*: Affectionate diminutive of the name Ada.

p. 145, *Ada, vois, c'est ton père*: "Ada, look, it's your father" (French).

p. 145, *Prie-le avec moi*: "Entreat him with me" (French).

p. 145, *C'est ça papa?*: "Is that Papa?" (French).

p. 145, *Oui, mon enfant, n'est-ce pas que tu l'aimes?*: "Yes, my child, you love him, don't you?" (French).

p. 146, *À la guerre comme à la guerre*: The meaning of this can be paraphrased as "When there's a war on, act accordingly" (French).

p. 152, *Votre mère vous appelle; adieu à jamais*: "Your mother is calling you; farewell for ever" (French).

p. 156, *Jouvin gloves*: Gloves made by a leading firm of glove-makers based in Grenoble.

p. 157, *C'est étonnant*: "It's astonishing" (French).

p. 157, *la patrie avant tout*: "Your country before everything" (French).

p. 157, *Madame Baudran*: Truncated form of Maison de Modes Alexandre et Baudran, a leading Parisian modiste shop.

p. 158, *Vous êtes charmante*: "You are charming" (French).

p. 158, *Ô, ma tante*: "Oh, Auntie" (French).

p. 158, *à la guimauve*: "Marshmallow-scented" (French).

p. 158, *Victoria Essence*: Turgenev, whose English was less than perfect, writes "Victoria's essence", a mistranslation of *Essence de Victoria*. The reference is to *Victoria regia* (now known as *Victoria amazonica*), a type of water lily from which a once popular perfume was manufactured.

p. 159, *Mais elle est délicieuse*: "But she is delectable" (French).

p. 160, *Herz*: Heinrich (Henri) Herz (1806–88) was an Austrian-born composer who lived mainly in Paris.

p. 161, *Un jeune homme accompli*: "An accomplished young man" (French).

p. 161, *a noisy Strauss waltz*: Waddington notes that this "noisy" waltz "should strictly be by Johann Strauss the elder (1804–49), though Turgenev's readers would doubtless think first of Johann the younger (1825–99), who gave dazzling concerts at St Petersburg late in 1856".

p. 161, *Lucia: 'Fra poco'*: 'Fra poco a me ricovero' ('Soon I will be sheltered', Italian). Aria from *Lucia di Lammermoor* (1835) by Gaetano Donizetti (1797–1848).

p. 165, *Metternich*: Prince Klemens von Metternich (1773–1859) was the Austrian Foreign Minister from 1809 to 1848.

p. 165, *un confrère*: "A colleague" (French).

p. 165, *Venez*: "Come!" (French).

p. 165, *Vous avez du style*: "You have style" (French).

p. 166, *'Son geloso'*: 'Son geloso del zefiro errante' ('I am jealous of the wandering breeze', Italian). From Act 1 of *La sonnambula* (1831) by Vincenzo Bellini.

p. 166, *'Là ci darem'*: 'Là ci darem la mano' ('There we will give each other our hands', Italian). From Mozart's *Don Giovanni* (1787).

p. 166, *'Mira la bianca luna'*: 'Look at the white moon' (Italian). From Gioachino Rossini's *Soirées musicales* (1835).

p. 166, *Thalberg*: Sigismond Thalberg (1812–71), a Swiss-born Austrian pianist and composer.

p. 166, *Assez de musique comme ça*: "That's enough of music" (French).

p. 167, *George Sand… Paul de Kock*: George Sand was the pen name of Amantine-Lucile-Aurore Dudevant, née Dupin (1804–76), a French writer known primarily for her so-called rustic novels. Honoré de Balzac (1799–1850) was a prolific French novelist. Eugène Scribe (1791–1861) was a French dramatist. Eugène Sue (1804–57) was a French novelist. Alexandre Dumas *père* (1802–70) was a prolific French novelist. Paul Féval (1817–87) was a French novelist. Paul de Kock (1793–1871) was a prolific and, in his day, extremely popular French novelist.

p. 168, *Elle n'a pas inventé la poudre, la bonne dame*: "The good lady isn't the brightest button in the box" (French).

p. 168, *Je crois bien*: "I can well believe it" (French).

p. 168, *en artiste consommée*: "Like a consummate artiste" (French).

p. 180, *tout à fait*: "Completely" (French).

p. 185, *solea*: The raised and railed-off platform before the iconostasis in an Orthodox church.

p. 186, *kleros*: One of the two choirs in an Orthodox church.

p. 193, St Vladimir Cross: Mark of the Order of St Vladimir, instituted in 1782 for continuous civil and military service.

p. 193, *Monsieur Dumas fils*: Alexandre Dumas *fils* (1824–95). French novelist and playwright.

p. 193, *consumptive and sentimental camellias*: Women who resembled the consumptive heroine of *La Dame aux camélias* (1848) by Dumas *fils* became known as "camellias".

p. 193, *Madame Doche*: Eugénie Doche (née Plunkett). Belgian-born actress who made her name in Dumas's *La Dame aux camélias*.

p. 194, *le gros taureau de l'Ukraine*: "The fat Ukrainian bull" (French).

Extra Material

on

Ivan Turgenev's

A Nest of the Gentry

Ivan Turgenev's Life

Birth and Background

Ivan Sergeyevich Turgenev was born in the Russian city of Oryol on 9th November 1818 (all dates in this section follow the Gregorian calendar). His mother, the wealthy Varvara Petrovna Lutovinova, according to many reports was an extremely capricious and cruel woman. Her baronial estate of Spasskoye contained twenty villages, and she had control of five thousand serfs; she is reported to have had some of her serfs deported to Siberia because they did not take their hats off in her presence, and to have regularly inflicted corporal punishments on them. She came into her inheritance at the age of twenty-six, and three years later married a twenty-three-year-old army officer, Sergei Turgenev, from an ancient family of aristocrats who had fallen on hard times: he possessed only one village and had just a hundred and thirty serfs. He married her presumably for her money: he seems to have taken very little interest in her afterwards, spending his time in numerous affairs with women, mainly serf girls at Spasskoye and his own estate, Turgenevo.

Ivan Turgenev had an older brother, Nikolai, who was born in 1816, and a younger brother, Sergei, who was born in 1821; very little is known about this last child, but it appears he was partially paralysed, epileptic and mentally retarded; he died in his teens.

Childhood

Varvara Petrovna's already unpleasant personality became, it seems, progressively worse as a result of her husband's philandering, and Ivan recounted later that he and Nikolai had been whipped and beaten almost daily during their childhoods, frequently as a result of a whim on their mother's part.

As in most Russian upper-class families of the time, French was spoken as the language of preference; indeed, Russian was considered among this class to be a barbaric language. Therefore Turgenev was from an early age fluent in French, and also acquired a good knowledge of German from private tutors. Fortunately for his career as a writer in Russian, his parents almost totally ignored their sons, leaving Ivan ample time to roam around the locality getting to know the peasants and play with their children. It was from them that Turgenev learnt spoken Russian: he later claimed that he was taught to read and write Russian by his father's valet.

Move to Moscow

By 1827 the whole family had moved to Moscow, where the boys were enrolled at a private academy. However, after a couple of years, Nikolai was transferred to the Military Officer Training School in Petersburg, and Ivan was brought back home to have his education completed by tutors who would prepare him for the university entrance exams. By the age of eleven, Turgenev was being given lessons in French, German, Maths and Philosophy, and already trying his hand at writing poetry and dramas in the "sublime" style of pre-Pushkin Russian authors.

University and Ill Health

Turgenev entered Moscow University in 1833, but lasted there only one term. Just before entering university, he had been bedridden for some months by an unknown illness, probably of a hypochondriac nature, and having missed too much time from his initial term he was transferred in autumn 1835 to the Philological Faculty of Petersburg University. On 11th September of that year, when Turgenev was only sixteen, his father died.

Although intending to become a university academic, probably in Philosophy, he was already writing Romantic poetic dramas in the manner of Byron. When he sent one of them to a leading literary magazine, it was rejected, but with some encouraging words from the editor, and in 1838 he did have two poems published in this periodical. As part of his studies, he had now begun to learn English, and he attempted to translate extracts from *King Lear*, *Othello* and Byron's *Manfred*. Besides English, Turgenev was devoting a great deal of his time to studying Latin and Ancient Greek. He also took private lessons in painting and drawing, and became an accomplished artist and caricaturist.

Stay in Berlin

Turgenev graduated from the Faculty of History and Philology in June 1837. His mother thought that the true fount of all learning was outside Russia, so in May 1838 she sent him to do extra study in the subject at the University of Berlin. On the crossing from Stettin to Berlin the ferry caught fire, and Turgenev offered some of the sailors large bribes to let him embark on a lifeboat before anybody else, including women and children – an incident that was to haunt and embarrass him for the rest of his life.

In Berlin he devoted himself intensively to the study of Philosophy, History, Latin and Greek. He fell under the spell of Hegel's philosophy, and soon became involved in the seething discussion groups regularly held by the students. There were a large number of young Russians studying in Germany: the vast majority of these were social progressives who wanted a total transformation of the social and political situation at home – often by violent revolutionary means, including assassination. Among the people he met in Berlin was Mikhail Bakunin, one of the founders of the Russian anarchist movement. Although Turgenev held intense philosophical discussions with him, and was at first attracted by Bakunin's charismatic personality, he managed to keep his distance intellectually and maintain a moderate stance in regard to the methods of achieving social change. Some contemporary critics claimed that the figure of Rudin, the eponymous hero of Turgenev's first novel, was a portrait – in fact, a caricature – of Mikhail Bakunin.

Return to Russia

In the spring of 1841 Turgenev returned to Russia. In the meantime, his mother's mansion at Spasskoye had been burnt down by a fire, apparently caused by a peasant woman performing a propitiatory ritual with hot coals. Only one wing was left, and Turgenev had to be content with one room there until the end of the summer. In the winter of that year, his elder brother Nikolai married one of his mother's parlour maids. Varvara Petrovna immediately stopped his allowance, and Nikolai was forced to resign his officer's commission in the army and get a lowly job in the civil service. She severed all contact with him for many years. Ivan enrolled again at Petersburg University and began to study for a Master's in Philosophy which would have enabled him to gain a university post. He moved into his brother's flat and, after a period of intense studies, passed the exams successfully in June 1842. He then travelled to Moscow to apply for the vacant Chair of Philosophy at Moscow University.

Love Life

However, he never submitted this application, as Turgenev's personal life underwent a dramatic change. In May 1842 he had had a brief affair with a sempstress employed by his mother. She became pregnant by him, and his mother threw them out of the house. He found a room for her in Moscow, and settled an allowance on her. She soon bore him a daughter who was given the humble peasant name of Pelageya. At the same time, Turgenev met in Moscow Bakunin's sister Tatyana, who was even more imbued with Hegelian ideals than her brother. She claimed that, though she loved Turgenev, she simply wanted to be his "sister" and his "friend". This Platonic relation lasted for two years, by which time it seems Turgenev had become thoroughly disillusioned with Tatyana, Bakunin, Hegelianism and philosophy in general.

Parasha and the Birth of a Literary Career

Turgenev gave up any ambition of becoming an academic, and took a civil-service job at the Home Office. But he also began now to devote more time to writing, and one of his first mature works was a long narrative poem entitled *Parasha*. The poem, written in clear and simple language, in imitation of Pushkin, tells the tale of a love affair among ordinary peasant folk. The Romantic subjects and flowery style of his younger years had been left behind – as it turned out, for ever. *Parasha* was published in 1843 at the author's own expense, and the renowned critic Belinsky described it as one of the most remarkable productions of the year. Following this, Turgenev and Belinsky became close friends, and the critic introduced the author into the literary circles of Petersburg and Moscow.

Reprimanded by his office superiors for being often late for work or not turning up at all, Turgenev decided to resign his job and devote himself entirely to literature. His mother, in disgust, cut off his allowance and all contact with him for several years.

During this period, Turgenev had to live on practically nothing, in unheated rooms, even during the Russian winter.

Pauline Viardot

In 1843 occurred an event that was to prove the decisive turning point of Turgenev's life, and that caused him to spend much of the rest of his life outside Russia. The world-renowned Spanish opera singer Pauline Viardot, née García, visited Petersburg to sing at its opera houses. She was married to Louis Viardot, a man twenty years older than herself. Turgenev met her for the first time in November 1843, and became immediately infatuated with her. This passion was to remain with him for the rest of his life, making it difficult for him to form a stable relationship with any other woman. During Pauline's first visit to Russia, Turgenev had only a brief contact with her, as she was constantly monopolized by her many other long-standing admirers. Turgenev was able to see Pauline again when she came back to sing in Petersburg the following year, but he was once more almost ignored by her, though he inveigled himself into a long and animated conversation with her husband.

Travels Abroad

In February 1845 Turgenev went abroad, allegedly to consult an eminent oculist, but in fact to follow the Viardots to Paris, having received an invitation from Pauline to spend a short time at her country chateau of Courtavenel. He was by now writing affectionate letters to her; her letters to him were far more intermittent and reserved.

Turgenev spent much of the next few years abroad. While in France in 1845, he began to write, from his own experiences, stories of Russian peasant life, portraying the cruelty suffered by serfs from their landowners. These sketches, for the most part originally printed in Russian literary journals, were finally collected and published in volume form in August 1852 as *Memoirs of a Hunter.*

Turgenev once again saw Pauline singing in Petersburg in 1846, and then left Russia with the Viardots in early 1847. From then on, for the rest of his life, he would spend long periods of time with Pauline and her husband in France, Germany and Britain, always remaining on friendly terms with her husband. There is little evidence as to whether Pauline and Ivan ever consummated their relationship. Paul, the child born to

Pauline in 1857, may well have been Turgenev's son, although she frequently had other lovers.

Turgenev was in Paris for the latter part of the 1848 revolution. The first upheaval had seen the monarchy being overthrown and replaced by a bourgeois government. Afterwards there had been further turmoil on the streets when the workers, in their turn, tried to obtain concessions from the new administration. Turgenev, while declaring at first his full sympathy with those who brought down the monarchy and then with those who tried to establish a more democratic government, was sickened by the needless violence of the intellectual revolutionaries who incited the working classes to man the barricades, leading to many of them being slaughtered by government troops.

Return to Russia

In the summer of 1850, Turgenev finally left Paris and went back to Russia. In the preceding years he had written most of the sketches for *Memoirs of a Hunter* as well as several plays, which are generally considered to be among his weaker works, with the exception of *A Month in the Country*. The play, heavily cut by the censor, was published in a drastically altered version in January 1855 and premiered in its fuller, uncensored version in Moscow only in 1872.

While Turgenev was in France, his mother had repeatedly appealed to him to return home, and when he refused, she had devised a vicious way of punishing him, forcing his daughter Pelageya, now seven years old, to work in the kitchen with the other servants. When he returned home and discovered the situation, Turgenev immediately withdrew Pelageya from Spasskoye, and wrote to Pauline Viardot asking whether the singer could accept his daughter into her family. Pauline accepted, and Pelageya was dispatched to France, promptly renamed Paulinette, provided with tutors and brought up as a French lady.

Mother's Death and Inheritance

Varvara Petrovna became suddenly ill and died on 10th December 1850. The estates and wealth were divided between Ivan and his elder brother Nikolai, leaving the writer with the whole of Spasskoye. Proving the sincerity of his democratic ideals, he emancipated all his serfs and gave them reasonable financial severance payments – a move that was considered revolutionary at the time. If they wished to remain on his land they could pay him a moderate rent and farm it for their own profit, rather than having to turn over most of their produce to him.

Imprisonment and Exile

In March 1852 the famous writer Gogol had died, and Turgenev published a brief obituary in the press. Although by the end of his life Gogol had become profoundly reactionary and Turgenev's article contained nothing of a political nature, but simply spoke glowingly of his works, the Tsarist government reacted angrily and sentenced Turgenev to a month in prison. At the end of that term, he was sent back to Spasskoye for a two-year period of house arrest. Turgenev spent this time writing, reading and hunting on his estate. In April 1853, he wrote to the Crown Prince Alexander acknowledging his guilt and asking for permission to leave the estate in order to consult doctors. The permission was finally granted by the Tsar in November that year, meaning that Turgenev had only served sixteen months of his sentence. However, he was kept under police surveillance until 1856.

In August 1852 *Memoirs of a Hunter* had appeared in volume form, and it was an instant success. One alarmed aristocrat described it as "an incendiary work", and the Tsar, Nicholas I, dismissed the censor who had authorized its publication.

First Novel

Turgenev now began to experiment with longer forms, such as novellas and novels. On 17th June 1855, he sat down to write his first novel, *Rudin*, and completed it in only seven weeks. It was published, with considerable additions, in the January and February 1856 issues of the literary journal *Sovremennik* (*The Contemporary*).

Illness and Despair

In 1856 Turgenev spent the summer at Spasskoye, then travelled to France to be with the Viardots. His time there was embittered by the realization that Pauline was having an affair with the artist Ary Scheffer. Possibly as a result of Viardot's unfaithfulness, Turgenev was often ill with what appears to be some kind of psychosomatic illness, of which a major symptom was agonizing pains in his bladder. He suffered from this illness for many years afterwards, and there is speculation he may have become impotent as a result of it. He and Pauline had a big argument towards the end of 1856, and his affliction became even worse, plaguing him for another sixteen months or so. Turgenev lost his interest in writing and was plunged into despair, possibly suffering a mild nervous breakdown. He spent most of this period lodging in Paris, with occasional visits to Germany, Britain and Italy. On a visit to London in May 1857, he had repeated contact with such luminaries as Disraeli, Thackeray, Macaulay and Carlyle: by this time his English was competent enough for him to engage in long conversations on literature and politics with those he met there.

In October 1856 Turgenev began to write *A Nest of the Gentry*. Owing to his mental and physical sufferings, work proceeded very slowly, and the novel was completed only in the autumn of 1858. It was published in January 1859 in *Sovremennik* and was an immediate success. On a brief return to Russia, Turgenev found himself lionized in literary society.

In June 1858, Viardot's lover, Ary Scheffer, died suddenly. Although Turgenev wrote to her a couple of times soon afterwards expressing his condolences, he did not send her any more letters until April 1859, just before he returned to France, perhaps because relationships between them had greatly deteriorated. Even when he did return, he saw little of Viardot, and she kept him at a distance.

On the Eve

During this period, Turgenev was able to begin a new novel, *On the Eve*, which was almost finished by the time he went back to Russia in October 1859. It was published in the January and February 1860 editions of the periodical *Russkiy Vestnik* (*Russian Herald*). Generally approved by the critics for its style, the novel was criticized by some for the absence of any social viewpoint and for not attempting to stimulate readers to improve the social conditions surrounding them.

Fathers and Children and the Critical Backlash

Between May 1860 and May 1861, Turgenev spent most of his time in France, except a brief visit to Britain and a few weeks on the Isle of Wight in August 1860. It was here that, as he swam off the beach at Ventnor, the first idea for his next novel, *Fathers and Children*, occurred to him. He swiftly set about drawing up the characters, and then working out a detailed story around this germ of an idea. The first draft of the novel was completed at Spasskoye on 11th August 1861; then, in September that year, on his return to Paris he began revising it extensively. Published in Russia in February 1862, *Fathers and Children* unleashed a torrent of abuse from all sides that Turgenev simply had not anticipated. The right-wing press vilified him for daring to take the radical and free-thinking younger generation as its heroes, while the radicals saw the representatives of this generation in the novel, particularly the young doctor Bazarov, as caricatures of themselves. Incidentally, Bazarov describes himself as a "nihilist", a word which, although not unknown in Russian before, was popularized by Turgenev with this novel: following its publication, many of the younger generation ostentatiously adopted this label for themselves. In Turgenev's usage, it implies not so much somebody who believes in nothing, but a person who takes none of the commonly accepted beliefs on trust, subjecting everything to analysis by intensive reasoning. Years later, Turgenev wrote to a correspondent that he regretted giving what he called the "reactionary rabble" this word to beat the younger generation with.

Move to Baden-Baden

Viardot and her husband had in the meantime moved to a villa near the fashionable German spa town of Baden-Baden, so in 1863 Turgenev settled in this town too, living there until 1871, with the exception of a few brief visits back to Russia. In the spring of 1862, Viardot had resumed contact with him, possibly because she wanted him to help her select a number of Russian poems she could set to music and use his influence to sell them for her in Russia.

Problems with Russian Authorities

At this time, Turgenev was still under suspicion from the Russian authorities. On a visit to England in May 1862, he had met up with a number of Russian radicals based in London, and discussed their ideas with them. This became known in Russia, and he was summoned back there to be tried for his association with these people or face the risk of having all his property confiscated. He wrote a letter to the Tsar in person, in which he said that he had never expressed his political opinions by violent means, but had explained them in all moderation in his works. Back in Russia, in September 1863 he appeared before a court consisting of members of the Senate, and all charges were immediately dropped. Herzen and Bakunin, however, two of the revolutionaries based in London, in their publications accused Turgenev of having compromised himself by writing to the Tsar, and have betrayed his old ideals. To make up for the contempt with which he was regarded by some of his Russian contemporaries, Turgenev became acquainted with famous French authors such as Gustave Flaubert, whom he first met in January 1863.

Smoke

In 1862, Turgenev had started drafting detailed plans and character sketches for another novel, *Smoke*. He began writing it in November 1865, and finished it in January 1866. After lengthy discussions with the editorial board of the *Russian Herald* as to the work's political and moral content, the book was published in March 1867. *Smoke* takes place largely outside Russia, and one of its major characters, a Russian called Potugin, who is vaguely reminiscent of Turgenev, is a passionate Westernizer contemptuous of the Russian mentality. Not surprisingly, this provoked a storm in Russia, where the press accused Turgenev of a total lack of patriotism.

Move to England

The Franco-Prussian War of 1870–71, and the resulting growth of aggressive anti-French feelings in Germany, meant that Pauline Viardot, whose husband was French, no longer felt safe living there. The family moved to England in the autumn of 1870, and settled there till the end of the war. Turgenev, although as a Russian he had no reason to feel unsafe in Germany, faithfully followed them to London in November 1870, where he stayed for almost a year. He spent what Henry James – whom he met in Paris four years later – called a "lugubrious" winter in London.

While in England Turgenev was introduced into the leading artistic circles. There he met, among other literary figures, Tennyson, Dante Gabriel Rossetti and Ford Madox Brown, and struck up a close friendship with George Eliot. Although there is no record that he ever spoke to Dickens, it is likely that he met him, since he attended three of his public readings and was enthralled by them. Turgenev's English was by now excellent, and he was invited to Edinburgh to give an address in English at the Walter Scott centenary celebrations in August 1871. While there he went grouse-shooting on the Scottish moors, where he met the poet Robert Browning.

Move to Paris

Turgenev followed the Viardots on their return to Paris in October 1871 and, apart from a few brief spells in Russia, he spent four years living as a guest in the various houses occupied by Pauline and her husband. In 1875, he and the Viardots purchased a large country estate at Bougival, near

Saint-Germain-en-Laye, a forty-five-minute ride from Paris. He built himself a Swiss-style chalet on the estate, very close to the manor house where Pauline lived, and it was here at Bougival that he spent the last years of his life. Turgenev now established a very close friendship with Flaubert, and also had frequent contact with George Sand, Zola, Daudet and, some time later, Maupassant.

Virgin Soil, a Prophetic Novel

Turgenev spent his time not only writing original prose, but also translating into Russian from French, German and English: for instance, his was the first version into Russian of Flaubert's *Trois Contes*. His last novel, *Virgin Soil*, a book that he had been planning, writing and revising for six years, was published in the January and February 1877 issues of the *European Herald*. He told the editor of this periodical that, in this last novel, he intended to put everything that he thought and felt about the situation in Russia, both about the reactionary and revolutionary camps. The novel was fiercely attacked in the Russian press, with many commentators claiming that the author had now been so long out of his country he had no longer any knowledge of Russian life. However, just two months after the novel's publication, fifty young people were put on trial for just such activities as Turgenev had described in his book. This created great sympathy for the prisoners both at home and abroad, and *Virgin Soil* became a best-seller in Britain, France and America, with one French critic claiming that Turgenev had shown himself to be a true prophet.

Triumphal Return to Russia

If Turgenev, as a result of the Russian press reaction to his novel, now believed he was despised by the public, including the liberal younger generation, he was mistaken. In January 1879 his brother Nikolai died, and Ivan set off to Russia to oversee the disposal of Nikolai's estate. At a literary gathering, a toast was proposed to him as "the loving instructor of our young people". Turgenev was so staggered at this unexpected reception that he burst into tears. He was invited to meeting after meeting, where he was constantly greeted by thunderous applause, although the authorities still disapproved of him. In Petersburg his hotel was stormed by thousands of people wanting his autograph, or even just a sight of him. He returned to Paris, looking – as friends said – younger and more cheerful. He was now showered with academic honours, including an Honorary Doctorate at Oxford University, for which he travelled to England. The orator at this ceremony declared that his works had led to the emancipation of the Russian serfs.

Illness and Death

Turgenev was by now beginning to feel very unwell. He paid a final brief visit to Russia in February 1880, and spent one further short period in England in October 1881, where he went partridge-shooting at Newmarket, meeting Anthony Trollope, R.D. Blackmore and other writers.

On 3rd May the following year, he wrote to a friend from Bougival that he had been suffering from some kind of angina connected with gout. His shoulders and back ached, and he often had to lie down for long periods. In January 1883 he was operated in Paris for a small tumour in his abdomen. But his condition continued to worsen: he was in intolerable pain and had become very emaciated. His illness was at last diagnosed as incurable cancer of the spine. By now he was bedridden at Bougival, and on 1st September 1883 he slipped into unconsciousness, dying two days later. His body, unaccompanied by Pauline Viardot, was transported to Petersburg. The funeral service was held in the Cathedral of Our Lady of Kazan, and a vast funeral procession followed the coffin to the Volkovo Cemetery in Petersburg, where Turgenev was buried on 9th October.

Ivan Turgenev's Works

Juvenilia

As mentioned before, Turgenev's early works were mainly poems in the high-flown classical style of pre-Pushkin Russian writers. However, he swiftly turned against these models, and strove to achieve for his mature writings a limpid idiom, including dialogue based on the everyday language of the Russian peasant. In sharp distinction to many of the writers of the time, who explicitly tried to put forward a progressive social message in their works, Turgenev aimed to achieve total objectivity and impersonality. Whilst depicting the sufferings of the working people around him, he limited himself to describing their lives without passing judgement and leaving the readers to draw their own conclusions.

Plays

Turgenev wrote nine plays in all, but the only one to have found a permanent place in the repertoire is *A Month in the Country* (1855). Indeed, after 1857 he virtually abandoned the genre.

A Month in the Country

Turgenev wrote the first version of *A Month in the Country* in 1850. It was originally called *The Student*, then *Two Women*. He sent the manuscript to *Sovremennik*, who agreed to publish it, but the censors demanded drastic cuts, as the speeches of the student Belyayev were too inflammatory, and the motif of a married woman in love with another man was morally impermissible. The censors ordered that she be changed into a widow, and Turgenev reluctantly made the relevant cuts. The play was still turned down, and had to be revised even further. This version was published only in 1855, and does not appear to have ever been staged. It was only with the easing of the political climate under Tsar Alexander II that Turgenev's play was published again in 1869, in a version much closer to his original idea. In the revised text, the widow is once again shown as a wife in love with another man. However, even when it was finally staged in Moscow in 1872, under the title *A Month in the Country*, further revisions had to be made because a few of the speeches were still regarded as too incendiary. The play was not a great success, but in 1879 the renowned young actress Marya Savina chose it for a benefit performance in Petersburg, and asked for just a few short cuts to be made on grounds of length. This time it was a triumph, and immediately entered the repertoire.

A Month in the Country predates Chekhov in its depth of characterization and its skilful depiction of the series of barely perceptible changes that take place over a month in the relationships between the characters, leading, by the end, to their lives being totally altered. The play contrasts two social groups, the old and the young, in what was to become a recurring theme in Turgenev's work: the older gentry living fruitless and frustrated lives, with the younger generation full of hope and idealism – and neither of them attaining happiness.

In the play, Natalya is married to the staid and much older Arkady Islayev, while a "friend of the family", Rakitin, also lives in their country house. Natalya and Arkady are clearly based on Pauline Viardot and her husband, and Turgenev explicitly stated in a letter that Rakitin represented how Turgenev felt about his own situation with regard to them. Natalya falls in love with a young, idealistic, socially progressive student, Belyayev, whom she has engaged as tutor to her son. Vera, her seventeen-year-old ward, instantly falls in love with him too, but Natalya, as a result of her own feelings for him, forces her into marrying the much older and boring Bolshintsov. Belyayev cannot cope with the intensity of the two women's passions and flees. Rakitin, badly hurt by Natalya's lack of feeling for him, withdraws from the scene, leaving her alone with her husband, whom she respects, but does not love. They return to their aimless, idle lives after this month of emotional turmoil.

Memoirs of a Hunter

The title which first established Turgenev's reputation in Russia was *Memoirs of a Hunter* (which has also been translated as *Sketches of a Huntsman* and *Notes of a Sportsman*). This collection of tales of Russian rural life was mostly written in France and Germany, where Turgenev lived at the end of the 1840s and beginning of the 1850s. It consists of twenty-four stories of between 3,000 and 12,000 words in length, most of them originally published as they were written in *Sovremennik* between 1847 and 1851. Twenty-one sketches were published in volume form in 1852; a further story was added in 1872, and another two in 1874. The tales were drawn from Turgenev's own observations of the appalling living conditions of the peasants and the cruelty imposed by the upper classes on their serfs, which he had witnessed when he had roamed round the countryside in his childhood and when, as a youth, he had gone hunting in the locality. The style of the stories, set against lyrical descriptions of nature, is totally impersonal. The reactionary Tsar Nicholas I dismissed the censor who had permitted the volume's publication, but when he died in 1855, the new Tsar, the reforming Alexander II, is said to have read the book and resolved to free the serfs – which finally happened in 1861. The book was a great success and was immediately reprinted.

The Diary of a Superfluous Man

The Diary of a Superfluous Man (1850) may be considered Turgenev's first novella. It was with this work that he introduced into the Russian consciousness the concept of the "superfluous man", which had played such a large part in Russian literature before and was to appear in many subsequent literary incarnations. The term denotes either a person who has the education and abilities to work for society and improve social and political conditions, but who through lack of willpower never manages to achieve anything, or someone who strives to achieve change but is totally ignored by society and so gives up in baffled disillusionment. The story is a personal account written by a young, well-educated man who has learnt from his doctor that he may be dying of an unnamed illness. He has drifted through life without any goal, has never managed to make much use of his education, or fulfil any of his ambitions, or set up any permanent relationship with the opposite sex. Now, as he may be approaching an early death, he is left to reflect on his wasted life.

'Mumu' (1854) was based on an incident which had happened at Spasskoye, and the female landowner of the story represents Turgenev's own mother. A hard-working young peasant, being deaf and dumb, has never managed to marry, and the only thing he can find to love is a young puppy that has been abandoned. As he is unable to speak, Mumu is the only name he can give to it. But the landowner complains that the puppy's barking is keeping her awake at night, and the order goes out, via the steward, to kill it. The peasant takes the dog to a river and, uncomplainingly, drowns the only thing ever to have loved him. However, the story ends with him striding away from his owner's control, and readers are left to draw their own conclusions about what his feelings are at this piece of wanton viciousness on her part.

Faust

Faust (1856) consists of nine letters from a character called Pavel to his friend Semyon. Pavel recounts how, a few years after his first meeting with her, he sees again Vera, now a married woman. She had been brought up in a very strict manner, and forbidden by her mother to read any books, especially poetry. Pavel, now he has met her again, visits her frequently at home, and tries to interest her in literature by reading her Goethe's *Faust*. Her feelings are so inflamed by this first exposure to literature that she falls in love with Pavel and arranges a tryst with him; however, on the way to her rendezvous, she sees an apparition of her dead mother – possibly caused by her subconscious guilt – falls seriously ill and dies.

Asya

Asya (1858) is a novella set in a small village on the Rhine and, unusually for Turgenev, it contains no implicit social message. The unnamed narrator, a middle-aged Russian, recalls events of twenty years before, when he was on holiday in Germany and met a Russian painter called Gagin, who introduces him to Asya, a girl he claims is his sister. The narrator suspects she is his mistress, but later Gagin tells him she is his illegitimate half-sister, whom he has been bringing up since the death of her parents. Although loving Gagin with the feelings of a sister, she falls passionately in love with the narrator, who baulks at the idea of marrying her and decides to give the matter some prolonged thought. By the time he decides in favour of the relationship, Gagin and Asya have returned to Russia, and he accepts that he has missed his chance of happiness. She writes to him reproachfully, telling him that one word of encouragement from him would have been enough to persuade her to marry him. However, his feelings prove shallow: he doesn't suffer long, and he never hears of her again.

First Love

First Love (1860) is perhaps the most autobiographical of all Turgenev's works. The author claimed that an identical incident had happened to him in his adolescence at Spasskoye. The hero is a boy who falls in love with the slightly older daughter of a young neighbour. Realizing she does not return his feelings and has a lover, the boy takes a knife to attack his rival. However, on drawing near the girl and her lover, he sees to his dismay that it is his own father. He drops the knife and flees mortified, with bitterness having entered his young soul.

King Lear of the Steppe

In *King Lear of the Steppe* (1870), the narrator is an adult who recalls the time he was an adolescent still living on his mother's estates. The tale's main character is one of her serfs, Kharlov, the "King Lear" of the story. He is a man of gigantic stature and strength, a hard-working peasant farmer who lives in a small house he has built with his own hands. The narrator's mother, Kharlov's owner, had married him off at the age of forty to a seventeen-year-old girl who bore him two daughters but then died. The two girls, out of compassion, were subsequently brought up in the narrator's home, but they became cruel and grasping.

One night Kharlov has a dream he interprets as a premonition of his coming death, and immediately draws up a will dividing his estate between his two daughters. Just a few weeks later he is evicted by them, and is given refuge by the narrator's mother. But, driven mad, he climbs up onto the roof of the house he had built, which has now passed into other hands, and begins to tear chunks from it. He falls from the roof to his death.

Spring Waters

Based on a chance encounter Turgenev had had with a beautiful young girl in Frankfurt in 1841, *Spring Waters* was published in 1872. As he returns home from a party, the fifty-year-old Dmitry Sanin reflects on the futility of life. He recalls a time in the 1840s, when he once stopped off in Frankfurt. A beautiful young girl, Gemma, rushes from a building and asks him to help her brother Emilio, who she thinks is dying but has only fainted. When Sanin revives him, he is welcomed into Gemma's household as Emilio's saviour. Sanin cancels his plans to return to Russia, because he is now in love with Gemma, who is unfortunately engaged to be married to a vile old German shopkeeper. But Gemma returns Sanin's love, breaks off her engagement, and she and Sanin agree to marry. He is about to go back to Russia to sell his lands when he meets an old acquaintance, Polozov, who is married to a wealthy and attractive woman. He convinces Sanin that his wife will buy his lands, but she, simply out of malevolence, seduces him in order to wreck his projected marriage. He becomes totally infatuated with her, and writes Gemma a letter breaking off their liaison. Polozov's wife, having achieved her aim, starts to treat him with cold contempt and then discards him, leaving him desolate and with nothing.

Novels

As well as novellas and short stories, Turgenev wrote six novels. The first four were published in the space of just six years, between 1856 and 1862. Possibly as a consequence of the criticism he had received for these works in the Russian press – especially for the fourth, *Fathers and Children* – his following novel appeared only five years later, and the last one ten years after that.

Rudin

Originally entitled *A Highly Gifted Nature*, Turgenev's first novel, *Rudin* (1856), tells the tale of another "superfluous man". He is a well-educated but impecunious young nobleman, who has been educated at Moscow University, as well as in Heidelberg and

Berlin. The setting is the country estate of a wealthy noblewoman, Darya Lasunskaya, in a provincial backwater. The charismatic Rudin, whom nobody knows, is introduced into their circle and totally disrupts the settled life of the household, especially affecting the peace of mind of young Natalya. When he leaves, things return to their normal state, but some of the characters have subtly changed for ever. The unexpected entry of an outsider into a social circle and the turmoil it causes is a leitmotif in Turgenev's writings: other examples are Lavretsky in *A Nest of the Gentry*, Insarov in *On the Eve*, Bazarov in *Fathers and Children* and Belyayev in *A Month in the Country*. The feckless Rudin now moves into Darya's mansion, sponging off the family, and obviously striking up a liaison with her impressionable young daughter Natalya. This budding romance becomes known to Darya, who strongly disapproves of it. Instead of standing up firmly for their love, however, Rudin declares one must "submit to destiny", leaving Natalya hurt, confused and feeling deceived by him. When Rudin departs from the estate, he sends her a letter confessing that he has always been guilty of such indecision.

The final section of the novel portrays events some two years later. Natalya is now engaged to a staid, worthy local landowner, and Rudin is still drifting around Russia, living at the expense of anybody he can latch on to. There is a very short epilogue which is not entirely convincing, and seems to have been appended as an afterthought: Rudin takes the part of the workers manning the barricades in the Paris Insurrection of 1848, which Turgenev had been witness to. He is shot dead by the soldiers, and even in death his sacrifice appears to have been meaningless, as somebody shouts out: "They've got the Pole!" Perhaps the message of this apparently incongruous ending is that, ironically, the first time this aimless Russian nobleman tries to exert himself to do something useful, he dies, and nobody even realizes that he is Russian, or has any personality of his own. He is still just another "superfluous man".

Although the critics noted the novel's lucid prose style, the press reaction was puzzled; the right-wing journals accused Turgenev of disrespecting the upper classes in his portrayal of them as ineffective drifters and spongers, while the radicals thought that

Rudin was a satirical portrait of one of them – well-educated, full of fine words, but ineffectual, and able to make no lasting impact on anything. As mentioned before, it was even claimed that Rudin was a caricature of the revolutionary Bakunin, who became one of the founders of the Russian anarchist movement, and whom Turgenev had met when they were both students in Berlin.

A Nest of the Gentry

A Nest of the Gentry is Turgenev's second novel. Turgenev had heard, when he was in Rome in 1857, that the Tsarist government was at last considering the question of the emancipation of the serfs, and decided that he should devote himself entirely to depicting the reality of the social situation in Russia in his writings. Accordingly, he started planning *A Nest of the Gentry*, which was completed in 1858 and published in early 1859. Whereas in *Rudin* he had been portraying an aimless member of the educated upper classes, in his next novel he depicted what he most valued in Russian life and tradition and, unusually for him, looked quite critically at some aspects of Western culture.

The setting is the country house of a wealthy family in the town of O— (most probably Oryol, the county town of the region where Turgenev was born). This house, and the family's estate, represent here for Turgenev an oasis of peace and stability amidst the turbulent changes taking place around them. Towards the beginning of the novel, the hero, Lavretsky, comes back to re-establish himself in his real home, his "nest", after years of fruitless strivings away from his roots. We are given a long "pre-history" of the character: his family had used him as an experimental subject for all kinds of advanced educational theories, and so he had fled abroad to escape from them. There he had married a thoroughly vacuous and unscrupulous woman, who soon abandoned what she saw as an uncouth Russian backwoodsman for the greater attractions of the European rakes she encountered. Lavretsky returns to Russia without his wife, embittered but determined to justify his existence by hard work for the social good. He meets again the nineteen-year-old Liza, whom he had known when they were children. They fall in love and, when a false rumour of his wife's death reaches them, they decide to marry. However, they learn that his wife is still alive. Liza is profoundly religious and, believing that she has committed a grave sin in daring to love a married man, she enters a convent to atone. Some years later, Lavretsky visits the convent, although as an outsider he is not allowed to speak to the nuns. Liza passes by just a few feet away from him and, obviously aware of his presence, simply drops her head and clasps her rosary beads tightly to her.

However, Lavretsky, in the epilogue to the novel, seems to have achieved some measure of contentment: he has become a good landowner, and has worked very hard at improving the lot of his peasants. Therefore, he has done something positive with his life, and has to a certain extent re-established contact with his roots and ensconced himself within his Russian family "nest".

The novel was extremely popular in Russia, because it showed the country's traditional values in a positive light. This was acceptable for all sections of Russian society, both the reactionary classes and the progressives who desired political change but believed that the fount of all wisdom was to be found in indigenous rural culture.

On the Eve

The genesis of Turgenev's next novel *On the Eve* (1860) – if we are to believe Turgenev – is very peculiar. While under house arrest at Spasskoye in 1852–53, he was visited by a young local landowner, Vasily Karatayev, an army officer who was shortly due to go abroad with his regiment. Just before he departed, he gave Turgenev a story he had written, based on his own experiences as a student in Moscow, when he'd had an affair with a girl who then left him for a Bulgarian patriot. Karatayev felt he had neither the time nor the talent to work this tale up into a decent artistic work, and asked Turgenev to do so. Turgenev later claimed that Karatayev had died in the Crimean War of 1854–56, and so some years later he had devoted himself to reworking the officer's original sketch.

In the story, Yelena Stakhova, a Russian girl, falls in love with a Bulgarian patriot, Dmitry Insarov, who is an exile in Russia striving to free his country from its Turkish overlords. He and Yelena marry, and leave for Bulgaria together. However, on the way there, he falls seriously ill and dies in Venice. She decides to take on his struggle for Bulgarian freedom and continues to Bulgaria, where she becomes a nurse. After a few letters home, she is never heard of again. There is a brief meditation at the end of the novel on the death of such young, idealistic people. However much Turgenev admired them, he also, with his usual objectivity, seems to have found them slightly naive and perhaps even rather unpleasantly fanatical.

When the work appeared in the *Russian Herald*, the twenty-three-year-old radical critic Nikolai Dobrolyubov issued a long review which, though very warm in praise of the novel's style and Turgenev's sympathy for his characters, took issue with his objectivity and impersonality. He declared that this kind of standpoint was now obsolete and irrelevant, and that writers should take an explicit position as to the necessity of improving the conditions of life around them.

Fathers and Children

Sometimes erroneously translated as *Fathers and Sons*, *Fathers and Children* (1862) is generally considered to be Turgenev's masterpiece. In this novel he attempts to portray the kind of Russian "new man" who has energy and drive, and is actively striving to alter Russian society.

In a letter to an acquaintance, Countess Lambert, Turgenev claimed that he had the first idea of the novel while walking along the beach at Ventnor on the Isle of Wight, but in a later article, 'Concerning *Fathers and Children*', he tells his readers that he thought of it while swimming in the sea off the same town.

Between the writing of *On the Eve* and *Fathers and Children* a vast social change had taken place in Russia: the serfs had at last, in March 1861, been emancipated from their owners. Perhaps buoyed up by this positive trend in Russian social life, Turgenev sat down to write a novel with a central character, Yevgeny Bazarov, who is an idealistic young doctor describing himself as a "nihilist" – a word which, as we have seen before, in this context has a positive connotation, signifying someone who subjects every commonly held viewpoint or belief to profound rational analysis.

The story begins in May 1859. Arkady, a young university student who has just graduated, brings back to his father's estate a university friend, Yevgeny Bazarov, who is a newly qualified doctor and the only son of a family living on a small country estate. Bazarov represents the new young, idealistic, scientific mentality in Russian society. While there, Yevgeny becomes involved in violent arguments both with Arkady's father, who is a well-meaning liberal, and particularly with his uncle who, for all his Western ways, is an inveterate reactionary.

Love interest is provided by the appearance of Anna Odintsova, described as a frivolous woman who spends most of her time reading silly French novels. Bazarov has always scoffed at love as being irrational, but despite that he becomes infatuated with her and has to accept that not everything can be explained scientifically.

After a couple of weeks, Bazarov finally goes back home to his parents. His father is a retired doctor who still occasionally goes out to tend the local peasantry free of charge. Bazarov accompanies his father on some of these missions, and one day, while carrying out an autopsy on a typhus victim without any disinfectant, he accidentally cuts himself and becomes infected with the disease, soon falling ill and dying. His heartbroken parents are depicted as visiting his grave right into their old age, while beautiful but indifferent nature looks on.

The story was met with total incomprehension across the political spectrum, with radical reviewers calling Bazarov a malicious caricature of Dobrolyubov, while the conservative press accused him of prostrating himself to the radicals and grovelling at their feet.

Smoke

Although the idea for his next novel, *Smoke*, may have occurred to Turgenev as early as 1862, shortly after the publication of *Fathers and Children*, he took more than five years to write it, and it was not published until March 1867. He began drafting *Smoke* in Baden-Baden in November 1864, and most of the story takes place there, over less than a fortnight in August 1862, among the large community of wealthy Russians living in the town. The central character, the thirty-year-old Grigory Litvinov, after completing his university education in Western Europe, is awaiting the arrival of his fiancée Tatyana, who is also holidaying in Western Europe, so that they can return to Russia together. However, in Baden-Baden he meets Irina, a woman he had known and been infatuated with some ten years before, now married to another man. Their love affair is rekindled. He breaks off his engagement to Tatyana and begs Irina to run off with him, but she does not have the courage to do so. Litvinov returns to Russia desolate and alone. After several years, he becomes a successful farmer on his estate, meets Tatyana again. She forgives him and they marry.

The title derives from the frequent appearance in the novel of smoke (such as when Litvinov is on the train back to Russia and the smoke from the steam engine is billowing around both sides of his carriage, making the surroundings almost invisible) as a symbol of the confusion and futility of life.

Most of the critics deplored the novel, both for its immorality – a married woman falling in love with an old flame – and for its negative – indeed, almost contemptuous – portrait of the typical Russians who lived abroad.

Virgin Soil

The background of *Virgin Soil* (1877) is the great movement of young idealistic students, most of them from the educated and moneyed classes, who from the late 1860s through to the early 1870s "went to the people". Living among the peasantry and urban working classes, they shared their work and living conditions – and, of course, tried to imbue them with modern democratic ideals. Especially among the reactionary country people these youths were met with anything from amusement to contempt, and in many cases were actually handed over to the police by them as troublemakers, leading to large-scale trials, with many of the radicals being exiled to Siberia and other remote areas of the Russian Empire.

The story, the most complex and ambitious that Turgenev ever attempted, presents many minor characters and subsidiary plots. Mashurina is a follower of the fanatical and charismatic Vasily Nikolayevich. However, not all his adherents are uncritical of him – for example Nezhdanov, with whom Mashurina is in love, who is too objective and sceptical to follow anybody unquestioningly. The illegitimate and impecunious son of a nobleman, he has to earn his living by tutoring the children of wealthy reactionary members of the aristocracy and high government bureaucrats. Nezhdanov, who is in love with Marianna, another naive radical, proves to be a "superfluous man" – unsure both of his revolutionary ideals and of his love for Marianna. He is, more than anything else, an aristocrat who longs to be a peasant, and a poet and dreamer, not a political activist.

Nezhdanov and Marianna run off together, and are given protection by Solomin, a rural factory manager who, although not a revolutionary, is sympathetic to those who want change. He is the novel's real hero, a hard-working modern man: he has studied science and maths, and lived and worked in Britain. He – like Turgenev – believes in slow and patient change. Nezhdanov, trying to become one of the local peasantry, simply succeeds in drinking himself into stupor in the local pubs and having to be carried back home. Solomin persuades Marianna that she can be far more useful to the common people, not by trying to spread revolutionary ideals, but by becoming a nurse or teacher to the local children. Humiliated as a result of his failure to communicate with the local working people, and even more depressed when he realizes that he and Marianna are drifting apart, Nezhdanov writes to Marianna and Solomin telling them to marry each other, then he shoots himself. Marianna and Solomin plan to get married and, although we are never told what happens in the end, they presumably devote themselves to the improvement of society in the ways advocated by Solomin. As mentioned before, barely two months after *Virgin Soil* had been published, as Turgenev was being criticized in Russia as out of touch with the present reality of the country, fifty young people were put on trial – of whom eighteen were women.

Select Bibliography

Biographies:

Magarshack, David, *Turgenev: A Life* (London: Faber and Faber, 1954)

Pritchett, Victor, *The Gentle Barbarian: The Life and Work of Turgenev* (London: Chatto and Windus, 1977)

Schapiro, Leonard, *Turgenev: His Life and Times* (Oxford: OUP, 1978)

Troyat, Henri, *Turgenev*, tr. Nancy Amphoux (London: W.H. Allen, 1989)
Yarmolinsky, Avrahm, *Turgenev: The Man, His Art and His Age* (New York, NY: Orion Press, 1959)

Additional Recommended Background Material:
Costlow, Jane, *Worlds within Worlds: The Novels of Ivan Turgenev* (Princeton, NJ: Princeton University Press, 1990)
Freeborn, Richard, *Turgenev the Novelist's Novelist: A Study* (Oxford: OUP, 1963)
Knowles, A.V., *Ivan Turgenev* (Boston, MA: Twayne, 1988)
Lampert, E., *Sons against Fathers* (Oxford: OUP, 1965)
Lowe, David, ed., *Critical Essays on Ivan Turgenev* (Boston, MA: G.K. Hall and Co., 1989)
Moser, Charles, *Ivan Turgenev* (New York, NY, and London: Columbia University Press, 1972)
Seeley, Frank, *Turgenev: A Reading of his Fiction* (Cambridge: CUP, 1991)
Waddington, Patrick, ed., *Dvoryanskoye gnezdo* (Oxford: Pergamon Press, 1969)
Waddington, Patrick, ed., *Turgenev and Britain* (Oxford: Berg, 1995)
Waddington, Patrick, *Turgenev and England* (London: MacMillan, 1980)
Woodward, James, *Metaphysical Conflict: A Study of the Major Novels of Ivan Turgenev* (Munich: Sagner, 1990)

ALMA CLASSICS

ALMA CLASSICS aims to publish mainstream and lesser-known European classics in an innovative and striking way, while employing the highest editorial and production standards. By way of a unique approach the range offers much more, both visually and textually, than readers have come to expect from contemporary classics publishing.

LATEST TITLES PUBLISHED BY ALMA CLASSICS

286 Stefan Zweig, *A Game of Chess and Other Stories*
287 Antal Szerb, *Journey by Moonlight*
288 Rudyard Kipling, *The Jungle Books*
289 Anna Sewell, *Black Beauty*
290 Louisa May Alcott, *Little Women*
291 Antoine de Saint-Exupéry, *Night Flight*
292 Ivan Turgenev, *A Nest of the Gentry*
293 Cécile Aubry, *Belle and Sébastien: The Child of the Mountains*
294 Saki, *Gabriel-Ernest and Other Stories*
295 E. Nesbit, *The Railway Children*
296 Susan Coolidge, *What Katy Did*
297 William Shakespeare, *Sonnets*
298 Oscar Wilde, *The Canterville Ghost and Other Stories*
299 Arthur Conan Doyle, *The Adventures of Sherlock Holmes*
300 Charles Dickens, *A Christmas Carol and Other Christmas Stories*
301 Jerome K. Jerome, *After-Supper Ghost Stories*
302 Thomas More, *Utopia*
303 H.G. Wells, *The Time Machine*
304 Nikolai Gogol, *Dead Souls*
305 H.G. Wells, *The Invisible Man*
306 Thomas Hardy, *Far from the Madding Crowd*
307 Ivan Turgenev, *On the Eve*
308 Frances Hodgson Burnett, *Little Lord Fauntleroy*
309 E. Nesbit, *Five Children and It*
310 Rudyard Kipling, *Just So Stories*
311 Kenneth Grahame, *The Wind in the Willows*
312 L.M. Montgomery, *Anne of Green Gables*
313 Eleanor H. Porter, *Pollyanna*
314 Fyodor Dostoevsky, *Devils*
315 John Buchan, *The Thirty-Nine Steps*
316 H.G. Wells, *The War of the Worlds*
317 Dante Alighieri, *Paradise*